REDEMPTION

JULIE CHIBBARO

REDEMPTION

SIMON AND SCHUSTER

SIMON AND SCHUSTER

First published in Great Britain by Simon & Schuster UK Ltd, 2005
A Viacom company

First published in 2004 by Atheneum Books for Young Readers,
an imprint of Simon & Schuster Children's Division, New York.

1 3 5 7 9 10 8 6 4 2

Simon & Schuster UK Ltd
Africa House, 64-78 Kingsway
London WC2B 6AH

A CIP catalogue record for this book is available from the British Library

ISBN 0 689 86085 4

Printed and bound in Great Britain by Cox & Wyman, Reading, Berkshire

To J.M.S.S.
and
Myrna Chibbaro
(1932-1992)

ACKNOWLEDGMENTS

I want to thank the children, women, and men of history for enduring all odds and carrying on to bring us into the present. I'm grateful to many people who helped me bring this book to life, especially Jean-Marc Superville Sovak, my love and fiercest supporter, and to the midwives of literary creation, Jill Grinberg and Ginee Seo. Also to Molly Jackson, Clark Blaise, Joy Johannesen, all the folks at Squaw Valley, Concordia University Libraries, Laura Zam, and Audrey Chibbaro, a special thanks for all your support.

PART ONE

ONE

I saw a bird dead once. It looked perfect, just lying on the ground on its side, its little claws curled up, one eye slightly ajar, the inside white. I ran my finger over its fat, puffed wing and tried not to disturb it. It seemed the bird might wake at any time.

I picture my father this way.

We live on a stony track, up a hill, on a small croft father earned singing to the people. Father is choirmaster for the village church, but in the eyes of Frere Lanther, he's a minister.

I haven't seen my father for 8 months, 2 weeks, and 2 days.

The prefect and the beadle pick their way up the track to our cottage with the law in their hands. They want the croft, the cottage, the stable, and the field back, they say, since mother is not the choirmaster. The choirmaster has deserted us, they say; and worse than that, mother took Frere Lanther in, which makes her, in the eyes of the law, a wicked person.

In a low voice, mother says to them, "How many times do I have to tell you, I don't know any Frere Lanther." She shouts, "You take away my husband—now you wish to take the rest?"

The prefect's straight white hair sticks out from under his red cap. "We do not know what happened to your husband," he says, "that is your own business. All we know is you do not deserve to live on the baron's holdings." Crooked lines of sweat run through the white powder on his face. I smell the nervous humors of his body which twitches at mother's every shout like Mistress Knapp's lousey cur. For near this whole September month, these men and others have come by saying the same thing about the baron's holdings and Frere Lanther. Some hit mother; one time they took her into the cottage and locked me outside. I ran to the woodland and stayed there till it got dark.

The beadle unravels the scroll of parchment in his hands and reads:

"'Our Gracious Baron decrees that you'"—he looks up at mother, then brings his shiny face down to me and smiles with his rot-blackened teeth—"'relinquish this property to the use of Our King's proper servants.'"

The beadle is older than the prefect, and has stains where his legs push forth from his purple hose and his gut from his green doublet. He is too tall and spindly to be anything.

Mother draws me to her and stands with her arms crossed over my chest. She has done many things to rid us of these men— slammed the door on them, waved our knife at them—but that only angers them. Screaming is all she'll allow herself now, that and doing what Frere Lanther suggests.

"Without field and shelter, how am I going to care for my girl?" She hugs me closer.

The prefect reaches out and pulls my hair, gently. "I could take her for you," he says to mother.

She urges me round so I'm standing behind her. "No, you will not."

"We could take both of you." They smile at each other.

"If you try, I will cut your tongues out and feed them to the pigs. No, I'll eat them myself, I'll roast them and eat them for breakfast."

Frere Lanther has suggested we curse straight out at the men if they won't go away; he says this will confuse them, as we are believed to be far too pious for the common religious crowd. Mother says it is dangerous to provoke them, that we could easily be disemboweled and quartered for doing so, but it seems to work; the men look like someone has just poked them in their bungholes with a hot iron.

The beadle stands up straight and blows as though he's been holding his breath under water. "You are vile," he says.

Mother puts her hands to her hips.

The prefect says, "We have another offer, since you are such a stubborn woman."

"And what is that?"

"To take passage on the *Adonis* to the New World."

"And die like my husband?"

Yesterday, when Frere Lanther told us about the ship at the port, he asked mother to go, but she said those same words to him, so I know for sure my father is dead. Sleeping with white eyes like a bird.

"We know nothing of your husband."

"Away with you," mother orders them.

"The ship is leaving in one week. We exceedingly urge you to be on it. You will not have this cottage or croft for much longer, Mistress Applegate. We advise you heed this warning."

"You just want to be rid of us! To kill us off in the sea!" Mother is shouting again. The men look at each other with smiles that make their chins double.

"A ship to the New World does not sail every day," the prefect says.

Mother told Frere Lanther that she thinks the evil we know is better than the evil we don't know. She has bad jeevees about it; that is why she does not want to go to the New World.

"And if you don't quit the baron's property soon, he will come himself and remove you. I pledge you," he adds.

"A plague on your house that rots your children's eyes and makes you choke to death on your own swollen throat," mother growls at them.

I look round her and say, "A black plague."

"Go on, chase off. Away with you!" she cries and I echo. We say it as nastily as we can.

The two men's mouths hang open and their faces redden as they stare at mother. "You . . ." The beadle's sentence wisps away. The men back off. They will not kill us and they will not drag us afar. Not yet.

Frere Lanther has hidden his press in our stable, and most times he sleeps there beside it. We have two chickens and Maisy, our cow. We used to have eleven chickens, four goats, two cows, Maisy and Daisy, and a workhorse named Jaspar. Maisy has bluebottle flies that won't leave her alone. We had more animals when father was here.

The press fills a corner of the stable, behind a daubing of manure and mud and straw, where no one can see. Manure covers the smell of ink, Frere Lanther says. He's from the Rhineland and he works with mother to make pamphlets, which they give out to our neighbors who come to Mistress Grey's to hear his word. Father used to read the frere's writings aloud to us, and now Maister Blacksmith does. Frere Lanther sends his pamphlets with messengers to other villages. He's very careful in the stable so no one will catch him. He goes behind the daubing anytime strange men climb the track to our cottage.

Last year, father spent many days by the fire scratching out a letter to the frere on precious paper from Black Mary's prosperous father. When Frere Lanther received the letter, he came from the Rhineland to Myrthyr and made father a minister in his own secret church. Frere Lanther brings us bread and meat and tells us funny stories about the Rhineland. Mother understands German from when she lived in Saxony with grandma, but Frere Lanther speaks mostly English to us. Mother says he's been excommunicated by the Pope of our Holy Roman Empire. That means he can never go back to the church again. Mother says he's still the most pious man she's ever met next to father.

They woke us up one night, the men in dark capes, and took father away. Through a burning fever, I heard the wood-bottoms of their boots on the dirt floor, stomping, heard mother crying, "no, leave him, leave him be." I stumbled from my bed to see men, heads cloaked in hoods, carrying father by the arms, his legs dragging. As they bore father away, one man pushed me back so hard, I felt the imprint of his hand on my chest. I feel it still, as if he had pushed my heart out through me.

I have not felt warm since then.

Mother ran outside after the men fled. She stood clutching her open mouth in the stony track, looking for a long time to see if they would bring father back.

I sleep with mother in her and father's bed now. Every night, she brushes the hair from my forehead and kisses me and holds me close to her. I watch her breath rise and fall in her chest till it is deep and steady. She is safe in fellow Sandman's arms before I let my own eyes close to join her.

When people speak of the New World, I picture a dusty brown ball rolling away from me down a meadow. The boys play ball in the wildflower meadow, the one with the wood fence round it to keep out the cows, but they won't let me play with them, even though I can kick as hard as they. My friend Red Mary says that boys think girls who play ball are secretly witches and would never want to marry such a one, but I don't believe that's true.

Frere Lanther works alone in the stable with the press. I love to watch him print with his large, stained hands, setting the letters, rolling on the ink, pressing down the damp paper and peeling it off, his two fingers holding up a real printed page. But he doesn't much like to be disturbed while he is working, so I must wait for him to bid me.

"Lily," he calls when he hears me talking to Maisy as I brush the flies from her eyelids. I go round the wall to him, and he moves to pick me up under my armpits, but then steps back with a smile and holds up his inky hands. I'm much too big for that anyway, as father would say. I was born in 1512 and I am 12. I have had one birthday, on 24 May 1524, since father left.

I perch on the wooden stall where Frere Lanther lays the pamphlets to dry. He looks seriously into my face as he wipes his fingers clean on a rag, then carefully lays the cloth aside. "Lily, what would you think about going traveling?" he asks me.

"To the New World?"

His head drops like an animal's caught by the scruff, and his words begin again. "Lily, your baron is providing passage for certain people to go to the New World . . ."

"So he can kill us like father?" I ask Frere Lanther. I don't understand. I turn away from him like mother does with the men the baron sends. He holds my shoulders and puts his arms round me. I don't hug him back, and he lets me go.

"I do not think your father is dead, Lily." He makes me look at his wide, solemn face, then steps away and shakes his head. "I say that so often."

"Would you come with us?"

"I have to stay here. I must return soon—"

"But we can all be together."

"There are more people here who need my help than we could possibly take with us, Lily."

"Why do you want me and mother to go, then? Why don't you want us to stay and help? Or go to the Rhineland with you?"

Frere Lanther picks up his rag and studies it. "I want you and your mother to carry the word of God like babies in your bellies that you will give birth to when you arrive," he says slowly.

"Like Maisy and the calf?" I ask.

He begins to wipe off the roller.

"Like Maisy. And I want you to see your father again."

He has gone back to work and is not looking at me anymore. He's put his thinking face on, like when he writes and thinks at the same time.

"My father is dead," I whisper. It rings wrong, like a singing voice out of harmony. I jump down from the stall and run out of the stable. He calls my name, but I ignore him.

Round the croft from the stable, at the front of the cottage, I peek through the kitchen shutter to see if mother is there, or if I have time alone to think. She is standing inside by the fire pit with her arms round her stomach, wearing father's old wool tunic. It hangs on her strangely. My chest swells with a soreness like when father went away. Mother appears smaller, as if she's vanishing. The way she stands frightens me; I want to fly away, to never see her like that.

I run down to the fields and slip beneath the fence into the woodland, under the woven bowers of pine where I have my hidey place. One, two, three, four, five, six, seven, eight; I try to count each needle, each branch, each tree in my woodland. I trace the numbers on my face, the 0's of my eyes and nostrils, the 11's of my brows. I count the breaths I take, the notes to my favorite hymn, the ravens I see.

I pray mother will be better when I return, for today is spinning day.

I think of mother's nimble fingers at the wheel as she twists the threads out long and whole for the weaving. On spinning day, mother tells me of her life in Saxony before grandma and grandpa brought her to Myrthyr. She talks of her sisters and brothers who died in the foreign land from a plague which bloated their tongues in their throats. Mother says she can hardly remember their faces anymore. When she gets to that part, she starts crying.

The stories of her family always lead her round to father.

She clutches me to her when she talks of father and whispers how they met at the village well, and how the chore of carrying water became a joy when she did it with him. "He was so stern," she says, "not like the other boys. He would take the water jug from my hands, leaving his at the well till he'd seen me home." She laughs inside her tears and hugs me. "Oh, Lily, we shall see him again, one day we shall, even if we have to wait till we are in Heaven."

I stay in my woodlands thinking of father and mother, counting needles and trees till God slowly begins to pull the sun back out of the sky.

We sold the calf soon after her birthing. Frere Lanther let me stand near Maisy's head while he pulled the baby from her bum with ropes and pincers. A miracle, the way the smaller animal came from the larger. When father birthed Daisy's calf with Maister Blacksmith, he had me hold the pungent charmed herbs to her shivering forehead so her baby would come out alive.

Maisy's calf was wet and bloody, and Frere Lanther said every birth was a portent. He took me outside when we were done; we knelt down to the dirt, and he scooped up some soil and rubbed it between his fingers. I rubbed a pinch too. Frere Lanther said we hold our breath waiting to see what the young creature will become. He said, "God is everywhere," looking at the dirt in his hand, "He is inside of us, He is a part of us." I asked him what he meant, and he smiled and laced his fingers together as if in prayer. "You and God are like this," he said, "and if you are quiet enough, you can hear Him making His way through your heart."

The sky reddens with evening blushes as I come back from my hidey place in the woodland. I hear voices in the stable: Frere Lanther talking to mother. Often, from behind the wall, I can hear Frere Lanther and mother talking in hard whispers that sound like Angels arguing. Sometimes, I can even hear them from inside the cottage. I don't always understand what they are saying.

"Volunteer, or they will take you away. They are coming for you, I see it. It is not safe for you here, Sarah."

"They can't take me away, they won't take a woman with a child."

"You underestimate them. You know that. They will take you, or they will kill you."

"I don't want to go."

"If you go now, you'll be able to bring some belongings. You'll be able to get a little money from the village church for this croft and the fields."

"I don't want those people to have it!"

"Sell the rights to your own people."

"Pah! They are poor. They are like me. The baron would never give it to them."

"Sarah, think for a moment. Do you want to be dragged off against your will? It's coming to that. How many times do you think they will come here and be turned away? And by a woman!"

"I want to go to the New World, to look for father," I whisper to myself. I step in front of the wall to tell her.

"Lily!" Mother has on her kirtle, and not father's tunic.

"I want to go, mother, I want to go to the New World to look for father. To bring God's words."

Mother looks at Frere Lanther. He returns her gaze. In her pale face, her eyes look like rainclouds. Her long brown hair is tightly bunned; everything else on her looks like it's crumbling apart.

"I want to go, mother."

Her eyes wander down to me. She stares.

"Please, mother."

Her lips curl in tight, her eyes well, she covers her mouth with her hand.

She shakes her head and sits.

Her shaking head becomes a nod.

Every year during the St. Sebastian Day fair, I'd sit atop the wagon of spirits with my straw cherub wings as we wheeled through the village to the old abbey, where people danced the bowhop and the minstrels played the lutes and drums and sang and we drank from the baron's barrels. If we had a chicken to trade at the fair, and some grain or cloth, we'd load Jaspar's panniers and bring them. We ate fried dough and apple slices and blood pudding. I danced with my three friends Mary; we all danced with boys. Father and mother drank from Maister Johansen's hogsheads and danced with all our neighbors.

On the evening after the last St. Sebastian Day fest, we went home and father fetched Frere Lanther from a special place outside our village where he'd been hiding and brought him home for the first time. It was late and they thought I was asleep, but I listened to their talk. From a crack in my eyelids, I looked at the strange blond man who spoke with an accent.

"It is a pagan Bacchus fest, Eric Applegate. It is not what God wants. You are not truly celebrating the saints this way."

I wondered what Bacchus was and how Frere Lanther knew about the festival.

"I agree," father said. "I studied the pamphlet you wrote until it fell apart in my hands. But I must participate to protect my family and our beliefs. The baron would know something was wrong if I did not."

"But have you ever found reason for these activities in the Scriptures?"

"No. I never have. That was why I wrote to you."

"Do you believe they are truly Christian?"

"No, no, I don't. They are merely an excuse for the church to take our earnings. I see that."

"Do you think you should conceal your beliefs?"

"They will find us out otherwise."

"Don't be afraid of that. People will start to change if just one of you joins me to fight against the old ways. Eric Applegate, you can read, and that is rare; you will bring my word to your people. You will be my first minister in Myrthyr."

Father was quiet. I could hear the stool legs moving on the floor as he shifted before the table stump. After a time, father said, "For many months now, I've felt the methods of the church wrong, yet haven't had the strength to fight them. I am honored by your offer, but I don't wish to put my family in danger, Frere Lanther."

"Have faith, Eric. Together we can create a more truthful belief."

Father shifted again upon his stool, turning the pages of the torn and broken Bible which lay on the table.

"Forsake festivals, then," father said quietly.

"I think so, Eric. We must start somewhere."

Each week, as I throw rubbish and dirty water into the ditch in the track and watch it run down toward the village, I listen to the pipes and drums playing to celebrate the holy days or saint's days we have forsaken.

Two

Frere Lanther says Father Leeman's church is pagan Christian and we are true Christian. Mother says we are fighting each other when we should all be fighting the Pope. It's fear, she says, which keeps the village apart; fear of a thing bigger—the wrath of God, she says, or the baron.

But they all make visits to our cottage, neighbors and church members alike, offering what little they have for our journey. They bring us herb medicines: hops for pain; poison ivy to cure ringworm; belladonna to bleed a wound. The Marys come and bring me patches for my quilt. Frere Lanther says not to pack too many clothes. "Fill your sacks with food instead, for you don't know what they'll give you on the sailing ship." He knows because he sailed from the Rhineland to Brighton. He travels far and talks to the captain of the ship for us, gives him our two chickens, cleaned and dressed, so he will treat us well.

"Put what clothes you can on your bodies," Frere Lanther tells us. I think he is worried for mother. He gives me a folded quill knife with a carved wooden handle to keep in my kirtle at all times. "Even when you're sleeping, keep your hand near it, and use it to protect yourself and your mother." Father protected me and mother. Frere Lanther tells me to have faith I will see my father again. Eight months, 3 weeks, and 5 days, he's been gone.

At dawn, Frere Lanther rides us to the port. I've only been to Bysby and Nottingshyre, never very far out of our village. We ride in the back of Maister Johansen's old ale wagon; his bony horse pulls us. As Frere Lanther drives, the sun gets bigger and the world gets lighter. I lie at the bottom of the wagon on our sacks, my head against the small trunk where we have food and our knitting and sewing, our precious Bible, and a stack of Frere Lanther's pamphlets.

I watch the sunlight rising through the leaves of the trees along the road. Cows dot the rusty green hills, horses too, and some pigs and lambs. I wave and shout to the animals, and mother hushes me and tells me it's too early, that I'm disturbing the morning. So I just wave, and some of the animals turn their heads to me as we go by. We ride down a hill that folds into other hills, cottages tucked into their valleys.

At the bottom of a hill, the road turns to mud. Our wheels sink into a deep pit. Frere Lanther tells mother to take the reins as he jumps down and pushes, rocking the wagon with every push. I hold my breath and try to make myself lighter so I won't weigh us down, but he cannot get us out. I jump into the muck after him and help him collect wood to throw under the wheels. My kirtle becomes heavy with dew and mud.

Mother whips at the bony horse. "We will be late," she cries, and we push and shove till we are sweating in the chilly morning. We can't go forward, we can't go back. The wheels are deeply sunk, and will not catch on the slimy wood. We unload the wagon of our sacks and trunk and try again, but it seems to be sinking deeper. We don't know what to do; we should have been there; the ship will leave without us.

"It's a sign," mother says, "it's a sign we're not supposed to go."

"Are you still doubting, Sarah?" Frere Lanther asks her.

"I will doubt till I arrive. Till I get to the New World and step on its soil with my own feet . . ."

"Faith, Sarah, is like a sword that you must use to cut through doubt."

"I don't wish to talk about faith right now. Lily, come up here."

I climb onto the wagon and stand behind her. She is still holding the whip and the reins. Frere Lanther's robes are filthy; he climbs up and sits next to mother. The horse tries to walk again, but he gets nowhere. The wheels will not budge. I feel tired suddenly. Birds sing and bob in the branches—the sparrow, the martin. I feel as though I am somewhere else. I float there for a long time, leaning on mother's shoulders; we are quiet, listening to the birds.

A noise behind us startles us. Two farmers who are very fat stop with a wagon full of wood, their oxen snorting and sneezing. One farmer calls, "'Allo there," and Frere Lanther answers, "Hello, my friends." They cannot get by us, so they help us. They put the heads of the two front oxen to the rear of our wagon and push us forward with one great heave, up and out of the muddy ditch.

I sit backwards in the wagon and watch the men and their oxen clomp behind us till they disappear round a bend.

At the port, more people than I have ever seen together roam upon wide tracks made of smooth, square rocks fitted together like a quilt. Geese and horses and pigs are for sale; pigeons, pheasants, and rabbits, caged and free, honk and snort at the crowd. Baskets of herbs and wild fruits and vegetables sit upon the ground, women behind them hawking as at market. Wooden boxes are piled high against rounded pillars of manors—such a row of grand houses made of long white stones bigger than my whole body. Dogs run about leaving their scent. Men with torn hose shout at each other and spit and scramble round upon the enormous sailing ships tied to metal rings. The ships creak and sway in the water, their poles pointy like spears, like trees growing from their very centers. Dirty, busy people knock into me as Frere Lanther leads us, mother holding tight to my hand, her other hand and her back weighed down with food and clothing and small things. My heavy sack is filled with beets, cabbage, lard, and my arm feels as though it'll break off like a stick. Frere Lanther carries the trunk, the sun is quarter-sky; we are very late, we are running. I am out of breath. We stop far down on the port.

"Your ship," Frere Lanther says. It is shaped like a huge wooden smile. A rot-black smile like the beadle's.

Many people lean over the edges of it, some in the middle and some on the two higher parts where the smile turns up. They lean with their arms out toward the port where we are, looking and looking without words. I think they are like my father, brought to the ship without wanting.

Pennants and squarely knotted rope ladders are tied to the ship. Sailors climb the ropes and shout to each other. Frere Lanther takes us up onto a board leading to the ship. Two sailormen who are so big they make Frere Lanther look tiny stop him. Frere Lanther puts down the trunk.

"Where ye goin', mate?" one of them asks.

"Bringing these two ladies aboard."

"And yerself? Ye got papers?"

"No, not for me—I am only bringing the ladies and then leaving."

"Let's see them papers."

Frere Lanther shows them our parchment marked with the baron's red-wax seal.

"Awright. Cap'n Carta, 'e's up the deck fore. On wid ye."

They let us pass. Sailors run about shoving crates and barrels into holes in the ship's belly. Frere Lanther leaves our trunk by a doorway at one side of the ship. We cross to the other side, pushing past many people, and follow the frere up the stairs to a higher part where a room is built. A man in the small, dark room is bent over a large sheet of paper. The room is crowded with spiky tools. An overstuffed chair is pushed against a wall with scrolls and books stacked about it.

"Captain Carter, here's the woman and girl, Mistress Eric Applegate and her daughter, Lily. Please take care of them," Frere Lanther says to him. The captain looks us over. We look funny in all our shawls on this balmy September day. His face is dark from sun, covered with wrinkles and folds. He wears no cap, but has his hair tied in a long queue. His shirt is made of coarse linen that buttons up his neck. Mother says the merchants' linen is so cheap because it's uncomfortable. She makes a better linen out of her own flax; we did not bring any flax with us, nor do we have a spinning wheel. The captain leans down to me and asks me if I'm a strong girl. He doesn't smile. I tell him of course. He nods at me and mother. "Bunk 13," he says, and goes back to his paper.

The square, dank room with our bunk is downstairs on the other side of the ship from the captain's room. Bunks above and below are fixed against every wall of the airless room, and some stand fastened to the center. The folk on the ship have scattered the beds with their things. Our bed, too, is scattered, but not with our things. People crowd the room we are in, most lying down. I hear Frere Lanther whisper to mother, "These are our people," but I don't see any of our church members.

Our bed is underneath another bed where a man sits, his feet dangling over the side. When he sees us coming, he jumps down. "This your bunk?" he asks mother. She puts her sack on the floor and starts to take off the one from her back. The man's hair is like a beggar's who doesn't wash every Wednesday, and he smells like Mistress Grey's pig stable. He says his name is Peter, and he grabs and kisses mother's hand before she can say hey merry merry. She asks him to remove his things from our bed, which he does with smiles and compliments to her. Frere Lanther says that he doesn't know why they put the women with the men; he slides our little trunk under the bed with angry glances at the man. I put down my sack and look round. There are only four women that I can see in the whole room besides us. I am the youngest one. The men are like bulls lying afield that rise and stare when a person walks past.

Frere Lanther looks at me to say good-bye. He bends and opens his arms, and I throw myself in. I wrap my arms tightly round his neck and squeeze till he laughs. He whispers in my ear that he will see me again. I make him promise. He crosses his heart that it's true.

We hear the sailors shout, "Last call, all board." It's time for Frere Lanther to leave, to go back to our village and care for Maisy. We left her with Maister Blacksmith, a church member who's been leading the service at Mistress Grey's since father left. Maister

Blacksmith also goes to Father Leeman's church since the baron's men watch him so closely. The baron's men let mother give Maister Blacksmith the rights to our cottage, croft, fields, and Maisy for ten crowns and a bottle of dogskin oil when she told them she would sail the *Adonis*. We gave the oil to Mistress Grey for her rheums. Mother passed a crown to Frere Lanther and five to the baron and keeps the rest in a cloth tied to her kirtle. They made Maister Blacksmith the new choirmaster at Father Leeman's church. Maister Blacksmith plays the harpsichord and the virginal. He is letting Frere Lanther use the stable for the press, and to live. Before we left, he told me he would always perform the service at Mistress Grey's. "Don't worry, I will be here when you get back," he said.

I don't wish to be without Frere Lanther. I cannot help crying. Mother, too, is crying. We hear the men moving the boards in front and calling for last people, on or off. Frere Lanther hurries away. We are left alone, with all the people on the beds.

Our bed is straw ticking covered with a rough blanket. Mother arranges our food sacks on the bed near the bottom and hides them with the ticking. Everyone is looking, so I don't know what she hides them for, but I don't say anything. I wish to hide myself in the skirts of her kirtle like I once did, but I've gotten too old and tall for that. I am embarrassed to hide when I told the captain I was strong, so I pretend to be strong.

We watch as the sailormen throw the ropes away, the sails catch on the wind, and the ship parts from the port.

I smell fish and water. I've never been near the sea, only to the stream or the well to fill jugs, and the pond to trap frogs.

People talk about faraway lands in our village; they say men there have dog's heads. I've hated dogs ever since those brown and black strays attacked our chickens right in our croft.

The people and manors get smaller on the port like our village did when I rode backwards in Maister Johansen's wagon. The ship moves rocky like the wagon, only worse, with water smashing into us.

People sit everywhere, on either stairs which lead up to the front and back heights, on the ground which the sailors trample and dirty, and on the rails which go round the whole ship. We push past folk up the stairs to the back of the ship to find a spot in the sunshine. The three big sails fill like two fat bellies front and back, with an even larger belly in the middle. Mother keeps close to me. I find us a place against the rail, where I can lean over to look at the water sparkle as it passes. Mother holds my shoulders so I don't fall over, but she is looking too. We move swiftly.

Peter, the man on the bed above us, shoves his way next to us. Luckily, he is behind us, so the wind does not carry his stink to my nose. "You know, the sea ends in big waterfalls." He glances over to make sure we are listening. We stare at the water; there is nowhere to go; we listen. "We're going to fall right off the earth inside this blasted ship. This bloody waterfalls is going to take us right with it when it goes, and we're not going to have a choice, no one's going to ask us what to do." He spits into the water.

The shush of the sea passes, the flap of sails, then mother asks him, "What happens to us after we fall over the waterfalls?" Many people warned us about this before, but Frere Lanther told us to trust in God. To have faith that something would keep us attached to the world the way it does every day. "Do you think we'll end up in the great fire?" mother asks Peter. That's what some of our neighbors think happened to father—he sailed off the waterfalls and fell into the great fire. Frere Lanther says there's only a great fire down in Hell after you die if you're bad. Some of our neighbors think father is bad for bringing Frere Lanther to Myrthyr in the first place.

"Nay." The man is eating sunflower seeds and spitting the husks. "I'll tell you what's going to happen. We're going to die. Drown like. A watery grave." Bits of husk stay on his mouth, but I don't tell him. Neither does mother.

"Well, I'm glad you're so sure of that," mother says. "At least we won't have to go to the New World, which could be worse. At least it will be over with soon. How long before we fall over the waterfalls?"

"My estimations are a fortnight and a week. Only a fortnight and a week."

"And how do you figure a fortnight and a week?" mother asks. I look up into her face, and I see she is joking with the man. I take her hand from my shoulder and hold it to my cheek. Wisps of her dark hair have come loose from her bun, and in the sunshine, they look bright as copper. Her warm hand on my face gives off the sweet scent of earth and the beets we carry. The smell makes me hungry.

"My brother draws charts. He drew me a chart before they came to get me. He told me it would take a fortnight and a week before we fell over. He got word from other sailors who went and came back. There's a way through it, round the waterfalls, they say. I saw it myself."

Another man is listening. "If Noah could sail the world in his Ark, so can we," he pipes in.

"The Spaniards have been about the world too, look at them, they live on the other side now, where we're going, I heard," another man adds. "We won't fall off."

Peter spits and says Noah didn't sail round the world; he just survived the Flood. The fellows make a bet with him, each a pence, that we won't go over. Peter says he won't bet.

"There's a way, I tell you, and I aim to forewarn the captain and save us all. Anyway, I don't have any coin. It all got taken from me. Only thing they left me with is a bagful of cloth and a handful of nuts."

"They took all of mine too," the Noah man says. His name, he says, is Jed and he's from Brecknook. Our baron is the lord of Brecknook, as well as Myrthyr, our village. Jed's soft, bearded face makes him look like a wee pip; he might be from our church. Maybe all these folks are from our church, and that's why they're here. Frere Lanther says people can be from our church if they believe the same things we do, even if they don't live in our village. Frere Lanther has other churches, here in England and in the Rhineland, too. That was why the Pope didn't want him, because he makes his own churches like the one at Mistress Grey's. And, mother says, because he doesn't think it's right to pay the Pope money to believe in God. Mother hates the Pope as much as she hates King Harry and the baron. I think it's better to give to Frere Lanther whom I know and love than to a Pope I've never seen who lives in a far-off city where I've never been.

"They came and got all my goats. What in the bloody harm were my goats doing, I ask you?" the Spaniard man says. He says his name is Thomas, and the baron owns his land too, in Tydfyl. His skin is very pale.

"Have you seen those folks fore?" the Noah man, Jed, asks. He points to the front of the ship. People crowd the rails between here and there; I cannot see well. "I didn't get a good look, but seems like they're rich folk. A dukedom, looks like. Who knows what they're doing here. I took a gander below, and they have their own rooms, not bunks like us, and their own hearth with good food and—"

"When will we eat?" I ask. The men look down at me. Mother pinches my shoulder lightly. Nobody answers, and I am sorry the question slipped out.

"The captain said . . . ," Jed starts. He stops. The others shrug.

"Well, they can't starve us," mother says. I know she is thinking of our beets and lard and cheese. The food we brought.

"No. . . ." The men look at the water, or into the ship. Thomas walks away.

Mother feels my hot neck with the back of her hand and absently begins to untie my shawls. She takes them off one at a time and hands them to me—my long, heavy top shawl, my itchy brown wool one, my thick linen one, the second itchy one. The wind cools my skin. Water sprays on my face. My stomach gurgles with hunger, but I shall not mention food.

The room where they finally feed us contains a snorting pig which stinks as bad as Mistress Grey's. Wooden bars hold it separate from us. This pig doesn't have the black-and-white skin of a razorback, but rather pink skin like Billy's from our village. Folks always call Billy Piggy Boy because of his reddish pink skin and orange hair, and this pig looks just like that. And it's foul. It's got turds round its bunghole and flies crawl on it.

The room is hot from the soup that cooks on the iron hearth. Me and mother have counted as many folks as we can. We come up to fourteen in our little room and that isn't everybody. I tried to sneak to the other side, to the front of the ship, where the food smells delightful and where the fellow said the rich folks were, dukes he said, but the sailors over there shooed me off. Mother didn't want to go with me. I don't know how that fellow Jed saw anything over on that side of the ship—maybe he gave the sailors a chicken or a crown for a peek.

The soup is of fish and turnip and onion though it's not the time for those vegetables, so I know they're from last year, just like ours. Through winter, we keep our root vegetables in the cold box in Houseman's cave so we have enough through the season when there are none.

We sit on benches to eat, no tables. They pass baskets of bread round; I take as much as I can hold in my lap and pass the basket. Little black beetles wriggle about in the bread. I pinch the insects out and break them between my nails and flick them onto the floor and eat till I'm not hungry. The ship never stops moving.

Several of the fellows talk to mother; they ask her what she did to get onto the ship. Most of them have been forced here, the way Frere Lanther said we would be if we didn't come willingly. Mother answers that we are going to the New World to look for father. It seems that those who speak to mother are church members and have studied Frere Lanther's pamphlets carefully. She does not tell them that Frere Lanther lives in our stable. We have a rule: Don't tell outsiders and ignorant neighbors that Frere Lanther lives in the stable till you are sure they are church members.

But these folks are certainly not outsiders. They are all talking at once about our frere and his ninety-five ideas that he nailed to the door of his church in the Rhineland. They say how the frere has disappeared from his homeland and the cardinals are after him to silence him. Many think the church has burned him at the stake, that he is already dead. Some believe the frere is in hiding. Mother doesn't tell them that he lives with us and makes the pamphlets in our stable. It is important for our church members to know that the frere lives, that we have well guarded all his ideas, and must be strong in our faith in him.

"Frere Lanther is alive and safe," I tell Jed, the bearded man sitting beside me. He doesn't seem to hear. "Frere Lanther lives in our stable. He is well and he makes the pamphlets in our stable," I say to the men across from me. "We have some in our trunk." I look at mother; her eyes are on the men; she shakes her head.

Jed turns to me and snickers. "Sure he does."

Another man laughs. "I think we all have Lanther's pamphlets, lambie," he says. I feel as though with their laughter, the men claim I am a liar. I glance at mother and she shows her teeth to me in an odd smile. I look away, back at the men. A burn sears through my stomach.

"It's true, Frere Lanther is alive. He works in our stable," I say.

"Sure, sure, chicken."

"He does!" Their snickering hurts; I don't see why they don't believe me.

"Yah, and the Pope pisses in my croft," Jed says. I hate him for mocking me with his vulgar words. The other man barks a laugh, he laughs at me. People all round smile.

"Maybe the Pope pisses in your croft," I shout and stand up. My bowl clatters to the floor, "but Frere Lanther lives and works in our stable." Mother pulls at me to sit, and I can feel people looking at me and laughing. These men are too moronic to care if Frere Lanther's alive and his important ideas are safe.

"Sure, and I seen the Virgin Mary cryin' her bleedin' eyes out," somebody says, and the people sneer.

"Righto, darlin'—an' Emperor Charles the Fifth is my best mate!" an ugly, bug-eyed man says. Everyone slaps at their knees and each other with their jokes.

"You're all fools!" I shout.

My mother stands and puts her arm round me. "She's tired," she says.

"I'm not tired. Tell them, mother," I plead. "Frere Lanther lives in our stable, he works with father, it's true." I can hear people talking—saying they see Angels and Devils and making a laughingstock out of me.

Mother pushes me up the stairs and outside. I feel my insides and my cheeks flaming. "Why didn't you tell them, mother, why didn't you tell them?"

"You are never to tell anybody about Frere Lanther till you can trust them."

"But they were all talking about him. And we're not home! Everyone is here because of him. Frere Lanther said so himself!"

"It doesn't matter if they know Frere Lanther lives with us or not, Lily. They wouldn't know him if they saw him. You saw it yourself. They did see him, he was in their very room. Did they even guess who he was?" She shakes her head. The night is warm, and sweat collects under her nose. I feel like giving her a good whack on the thigh for not defending me, but I see she is upset, so I leave her alone.

Our room is nearly empty. All the fools are still at dinner. We don't take off our clothes to sleep as we sometimes do at home when it is hot. Mother and me, we lie on our ticking under our blanket, our legs draped over our food sacks. In the dark, I take her hand. I feel filthy, from the dried mud on my legs, from the people's rude words. I wonder as I drift asleep where we wash ourselves on this dank and foul sailing ship.

THREE

I don't much like people poking fun at me. The mister men used to, the ones who helped father plough the field every season. They teased me for helping father, but never in such a cruel manner.

In spring, right before Mayday, before the May Queen was crowned, and in autumn after the October Hours, they'd gather together and divide up whose land would be ploughed or cropped or reaped and whose left fallow for pasture. Father usually took Jaspar down to meet with the men while I milked the cows with mother, or went to the well, or over to the beehive oven near the old abbey to bake bread. But the year before last, I asked father to take me down with him to the fields. I wanted to see what it was like to plant the seed that made the barley and beans we ate, to watch it grow, to battle the weather and the insects with our neighbor fellows till reaping time. I wanted to work with him the way he did every year, with all the mister men of Myrthyr.

We all worked together in Myrthyr—mother and me had fancies with Mistress Grey, Mistress Knapp, and the Marys where we set the village oven ablaze, or we'd gather with other women to scutch flax or comb wool or sew quilt patches. When Mistress Knapp started making lace for the baron's wife, she'd bring over her bobbins and we'd sew or knit and listen to the tinkling as she wove her thin threads and filled us up with news from the manor, about the baron and his minions, and about our King Harry.

What, I wonder, are my friends doing now?

To push a plough through the earth is not as easy as pushing a needle through cloth, and the first day with the fellows, as I led Jaspar while father guided the ploughshare, they called out fun at us from down the field. "What do you need a son for when you've got Lily, heh, Eric?" said Maister Dulse, the cordwainer who worked at the manor. Father just grinned, the sun beginning to shine behind his damp, blond head. I didn't much like being called a boy.

"Soon she'll be stronger than all of us, hey, Eric?" Old Maister Grey laughed. He was the only one in Myrthyr who lived through the sweating sickness, but it left him with the catarrh, so he couldn't do nearly as much work as the others before his coughs overcame him.

In spite of all their teasing, we pushed on, coaxing Jaspar through the harrows till they were ready for planting. Finally, the fellows let me seed a whole harrow by myself, patting my head and telling me they were merely jesting with me.

How I waited for the barley to rise and bloom its way toward the sun. I ran to the fields every morning and laid my head so close to the earth, I could hear the worms that crawled through it.

When I think of the taunts of the old rotters on this ship, my belly boils. Already, I miss the smells of the earth, the feel of its warmth between my fingers and the friendliness of those so close to me.

In the middle of the night, I have to make water. The piss bucket sits behind the curtain next to the door. I go in and lift my kirtle. I can hear the sound of my water hitting water in the wooden bucket; the last person to use it didn't empty it, and I can smell their stink. When I finish, I take the bucket outside and throw the stinking water over. Everyone sleeps, even the wind. Puffs fill and empty the sails like my mother's breath in her sleeping chest. I let the bucket down into the black sea by its rope and swish it to clean it. When it's clean, I fill it and pull it up. I dip my hands in and throw the water on my face. The cold, salty water and the chilly night raise my flesh like a goose's, but it feels good, better than the room. Many of the men snore and break wind in their sleep, and the air down there smells bad. Worse than sleeping in a stable of animals.

I splash water on my face again and it runs into my hair and onto my collar, wetting it. The moon is just a faint sliver, and tiny stars light the sky; some fall from their places, some glint on and off, some sit in shapes. I begin to count them.

Father told me about the stars when I was little. He used to sit with me in the woodland and tell me, "Lilykin, look." We'd sit under the pines and he'd point up. "There's the father dipper." He'd always point to the big one, and I'd point to the small one, like the big one was him and the small me. "And there's the daughter dipper," I'd say, and he'd smile and pull me into that warm place between his arm and his chest. He would tell me about the old Greek people from far away, how they discovered the signs we were each born under. My sign is Gemini, for the twin stars Castor and Pollux; his is Cancer, for the crab. It makes me sore inside to think of him, so I turn from the sky.

The salty seawater stings my tongue. I sit on the ground and look down the ship to the front. I see shadows like ghosts lurking at that end. The ship's wood creaks, ropes dangle, and metal clanks and sways, making flickerings like people walking. I feel as though some-one is looking at me, watching me from someplace I can't see. It's not like when I feel spirits gazing; it's closer, like heat from a candle. Maybe it is father, watching me from wherever he is. I wish I could see him. I close my eyes tight and hold my breath till sparkles explode under my lids, but still, I don't see him.

"Father," I whisper. "Come to me. I miss you. Visit me." His spirit has never visited me, though I have begged him.

I hear the crack of knees and open my eyes, but it is not father. A person is there, kneeling down to me. "What are you doing?" he asks quietly. I cannot see him very well in the dark, but I know his voice is not familiar. I can think of no reason to answer him. I'm angry, a little bit, that he heard me. -

"Praying," I answer.

The person stares at me, his face and body in shadow. He is a boy a little older than me, I think. I haven't seen anyone on the ship before who is my age. An orange light from behind him begins to glimmer like a spirit's. Suddenly, I feel touched, as though father came and patted me.

"You are a protester, aren't you?" he asks. His voice is gentle, like a friend's. I think he is a protester too.

I look at the orange glow behind the boy. "Yes, I'm of the church of Frere Lanther. He lives in our stable."

"Frere Lanther lives in your stable?"

I don't know if he heard me telling the others, or if he believes me. I don't remember him with the fools who poked fun at me.

"Yes. Father wrote Frere Lanther a letter after the Pope made the frere leave the church. Then they came and took father away."

"For writing Frere Lanther a letter?"

"No," I say. I stop. I'm not sure why they took father away. Many reasons have been spoken, but I'm not certain which is the right one. "It is because he doesn't like the Indulgences."

As the boy sits back on his heels, a slip of blue starlight catches his nose and mouth in a way that is pleasing. The look on his face is one of surprise. "How is that possible?" he asks.

"I don't know." I try to remember father's ministrations. "He does not believe it is right to pay for God's forgiveness." The boy, I now see in the blue light, is wearing velvet sleeping clothes. "You look rich," I say with a smile.

He grins. "My father is the baron of the Highlands, so I guess that makes me rich."

"The baron!" I say loudly. The boy stands and steps back in alarm and hushes me. I scramble to my feet. I can't believe he is the son of the baron. And I told him of Frere Lanther! "Is the baron on this ship?"

"Well, of course. If I am here, he is here."

"I don't understand," I say. "I thought the baron was trying to get rid of us. To kill us like he did with father by sending him to the New World."

"Talk quietly," the boy urges. He shakes his head. "We are going because of the discovery of gold and silver that the Spaniards have made in Hispanola. Father thinks we can find gold for the King. He and his men are on the ship. He's taking freemen with him to work. I guess you are one of them. The protesters, he calls you. That's what I heard."

"To work! Then what—what happened to my father?"

"Father is going north to find mountains of gold and make us even richer. He told me that." He shakes his head. "I don't know what happened to your father."

I am horrified to think that the baron is this boy's father. The boy seems so kind. "I'm going back to bed," I say. I don't know what else to say. I pray to the great Almighty the boy does not remember my foolish words about Frere Lanther. I dump the bucket of water over the side of the ship and walk away from him, but glance back when I reach the stairs to see where he's gone. He is still standing in the shadows.

I go down to mother and slip into bed beside her. My blood races inside me as if I've run through the fields to the woodland. My heart beats loud in my ears in the quiet night.

"Mother." I awaken her with a jab in the side and a whisper. "Mother, wake up." When she turns to me, I tell her the baron is on the ship. She grunts and throws her arm across my chest and falls back to sleep. I cannot wake her again.

In the night in our cottage in Myrthyr, when father was with us, I'd often wake and stare into the pitch darkness, unsure if my eyes were open. I'd listen for the sound of father's and mother's breath across the room, a sound that was like the rush of wind through trees. Sometimes, the sound would get louder and louder till I felt myself lost in a stormy wilderness, unable to escape.

I'd get up then, and feel my way over to father's side of the bed. I couldn't see him, but I felt him, and waited for him to feel me near his eyelids.

"Lilypie," he'd whisper upon waking, "can't sleep again?"

"No."

He'd pick me up and put me into my own bed and slide his leg and back next to me. It felt like he was a blanket filled with sleeping powders. He'd put his head by mine and sing in my ear:

"Once there was a child,
who couldn't sleep.
Her name was Lily,
she never made a peep.
She woke her father,
but didn't complain.
Oh, fellow Sandman,
fill her eyes again."

I'd stay awake as long as I could just to hear his voice.

I cannot sleep now, with mother's heavy arm over me. The hasty words I spoke to the boy repeat in my head. The whistling and snoring of so many breaths keep my eyes open wide. I think of the stories about men with dog's heads in faraway lands, but I cannot imagine seeing them for real. I fear dogs almost as much as I fear the Devil or the plague.

Starlight pours down the steps, into our door. I sing the words of father's song to myself in my head like a psalm, and I can almost smell his sweat from working in the fields. His smell, of sunlight and happiness.

I tell her again in the morning about the baron. Mother knows I would not lie, but she says it is hard to believe. "Where did you see him? Tell me, Lily," she asks. I did not see him, I say, I saw his son in the night on top of the ship. I say nothing of my careless words to the boy. Mother sits on the edge of the bed staring into the air in front of her, her face dark.

"What are you thinking, mother?" I ask her over and over, but she will not answer me.

Breakfast is a thin and watery pease porridge which smells like

Sunday porridge before church, except we used to have it thick, with milk. I am thinking a lot about Frere Lanther and father this morning. I clearly see father's hands—not his face so much, but his hands that I used to study, his work-roughened palms, the blond hair adorning his fingers, his square nails with their half-moons at the base. I can see Frere Lanther's face, his moles and his eyelashes and the look in his eyes as though he's always pondering deep within himself.

Mother lets me go upstairs alone into the sunshine after breakfast; I go close to the rich side to see if the boy is nearby. A few rich ladies sit on the higher part of the ship by the captain's room wearing three-cornered caps and long keercheefs. They upturn their cheeks to the sun like daisies. As I walk toward their side, a sailor swoops from nowhere and puts his hand out to my chest and stops me. "Where ye goin'?" he asks.

"I don't know," I say.

"This ain't where ye belong, is it?"

"I don't know."

"Ye don't know nothin', eh, girlie?"

I start to turn away when I hear someone cry out, "Wait." I look up and see it is the boy standing by the captain's room. In the light, I see he has dark hair, and his bright, smiling face gladdens me. He waves to me from a little perch he is standing on. I think, despite his wealth, that he wishes to be my friend, and I hope he has not told his father of our words. I can still feel the sailor's hand on my chest. Though I want to speak to the boy, to find out why he's called to me, I don't move toward him.

He jumps down from his perch and heads for the stairs. Behind him, I hear a woman's voice cry, "Ethan. Ethan, come," and he stops walking. I cannot see the woman.

"Ethan," I say in a low voice to myself.

"Later?" He mouths the word several times without sound till I understand. I nod, wishing to know what thoughts he holds behind his friendly eyes.

"Night?"

I nod before he disappears behind the captain's room to where the women sit.

I go to the very rear of the ship and stare at the froth which follows us. Several people are washing themselves with buckets of salty water. I know from washing my face that the water does not clean.

Mother finds me. "Lily, I must talk to you," she says urgently. She pulls me to a spot empty of people and bends and whispers to me. I can feel her breath on my cheek. "Lily, you said you saw the baron's son last night. Are you sure it was the baron's son, the son of the baron of Myrthyr?" she asks.

"That's what he said, mother."

"I don't see . . ." She pauses, shaking her head. "What would the baron be doing on the ship? What did he say?"

"They are looking for gold. That's why they're going to the New World."

"Gold?"

"Like the Spaniards found in Spanola, the boy said."

"What else did he say?"

"That—that he is bringing us protesters to work for him."

"To work?"

"Yes."

"What else? Tell me, Lily."

Mother stares at my face, but I can't meet her look. I don't want to tell her that I slipped about Frere Lanther, and that I know the boy's name, and am meeting him later. She straightens up and looks out over the vast and endless water. Sweat shines on her forehead; her cheek has drained of color. Her green eyes go far away and don't bring me with them. Maybe she is thinking about father, about seeing him soon. I lift her arm and put it round my shoulder, and she pulls me to her. She hugs me for a minute, and then leaves me standing alone.

I wait till I hear mother's soft breathing and the snores of the men before I go outside. Brown clouds cover the sky, making the night dark and starless. I can see very little. No people run about; the ship feels empty. I pull my shawl closer round my shoulders to fight the night air. I think of myself under the bowers of my pine, alone with God. I don't dare speak out loud to Him now, in case someone should hear, but in my mind, I ask Him to watch me and get me somewhere nice, where it is warm and cozy as the evenings by the fire. I think of the times we spent—mother, father, and me—reading the Bible at the hearth. God has written so many stories for us. The stories make me think of the thousands of people who've lived before me. It seems to me now, on this big, constant water, that the stories have ended with me.

I sit on a wooden step on the invisible line that divides the ship, poor side from rich. Divide means to separate things in groups. Father taught me math and mother taught me the letters she learned from father so I can read the Bible too. I wish I could see where we're going. I do not know what time the boy will come. Night, he said, but he is not here.

I don't know many boys. There is Billy, and Simon, and Ralph McGee, who runs like a horse. They have strange breath, strange smells. Mother says I will one day soon understand them, the way she did with father. A picture comes to me of the boy, Ethan, of him and me standing together, our faces very close, nearly touching. There is an orange glow about us. I don't know what it means, but I savor the picture like a happy memory, one that makes me feel warm inside.

I see a shadow at the front end of the ship, and slide down to a dark pocket of the stairs to watch. I can tell from the striped pants they all wear that it is a sailor. He walks slowly, looking down into the water on the opposite side, his hands tucked in his jacket. He's humming softly, but I don't recognize the song. The sailor frightens me; I think to make a dash for our entry, but I cannot reach it without him seeing me. I must wait for him to pass to the back end. He takes his time.

I see the boy coming. I look at the sailor; his back is to the boy. I don't want trouble, but I do wish to talk to the boy. I can see him looking for me, but I think if I get up, the sailor will see me. When the boy comes closer, the sailor hears his footsteps and turns. He goes to the boy, and I hear them talking.

"Where ye headed out this time of night, sir?" the sailor asks.

"I couldn't sleep. I'm out for a breath of air."

"Ah. It's dangerous to be out this time of night. Some flyin' fish could get ye, or a protester."

The boy laughs. "I hardly think they're dangerous."

"What's that, the fish or the protesters?"

"Neither."

"Well, methinks ye should be down with yer people, sir."

"I think I know what's right for myself, sailor," the boy says.

"Surely ye do. But if somethin' happens to ye, yer father 'ud never forgive me, sir."

"My father knows I'm out here," Ethan says indignantly.

"Oh, does he?" the sailor says. "So ye don't mind if I just go check with 'em then, do ye?"

"He'd be very upset if you bothered him, I'm sure."

"But yer his precious cargo, my boy. We 'ave to take good care of ye."

I hope that the boy will make the sailor go away. He stands there with his hands on his waist, staring at the man. The sailor folds his arms in front of his chest. They don't say anything. I wonder what I should do.

"I find you quite a pestilence," the boy says.

"And yer quite a sweetmeat," the sailor says.

"Fine. I'm going back inside now. But I won't forget this!"

"I'll walk ye back," the sailor says, following the boy to the front of the ship. I take off my shoes and run to the opening of our side. I slip down the stairs and climb into bed next to mother.

FOUR

When I smell pigflesh as I do now, it reminds me of October. In the Book of Hours, October is the month of Slaughtering the Pigs, and every year, father and many of our neighbors would gather at Mistress Grey's and slaughter her pigs for her. Two days after hanging the killed pigs, when the heat had left their bodies, we'd roast and eat one of them, and the rest would go to the smokehouse.

To roast the pig, father and the men would first gut it, then skewer it from snout to bum, put it on the spit, and turn it over the fire all day. The fatty fragrance of cooking pigflesh pulled at my nose from morning till night, till the moment I put the dripping meat into my mouth, and the joy I'd imagined of the salted, roasted flesh finally became real. My mouth drools at the thought, and the empty well of my stomach echoes. It's been days since I had a good meal.

The October before last, Maister Grey died. We visited the Greys often, and were very sad when God took Maister Grey back into His arms. Father offered to make the Office of the Dead for him, and Mistress Grey let him. Father lit spirit scents and sang beautiful songs over poor Maister Grey, carrying his soul past Purgatory and up into Heaven with the Angels and God. Afterwards, Mistress Grey said he did much better than Father Leeman ever could, she was sure.

We had our church gatherings at our cottage then, in the one room where we slept, cooked, read, sang, ate, and bathed. There were only five church members, plus me and mother, but other neighbors were starting to ask about Frere Lanther's word.

After the Office, Mistress Grey told father she wanted to give him her stable, which was bigger than ours, and separate from her house. "For your services," she said.

"Do you understand what this means? It could be very dangerous for you," father said.

She nodded her old head slowly. "It's time something changed round here. Maybe it's because I've just lost Daniel, but I think the world is going straight to the Devil. The young people today, with their wildness at the pageants, and the priest always asking for a coin, it's not Godly anymore. What you're doing is right, Eric. I'd like to help."

As I listened to her, I thought about the stink of the pigs, and how awful it would be to sit through church with that smell. But at our first meeting, she'd cleaned the dung and put away the animals. The wide floor was spread with fresh, sweet-smelling hay. Though we could hear an occasional animal snort through father's sermon, his words carried us high above the pigs, straight to the heart of God.

In the first week after we moved the church into Mistress Grey's stable, seventeen people joined us. Maybe they came for the blood pudding Mistress Grey passed out after the service like the Marys said, but I don't think so. I think it was to hear father read from our Bible the true stories of how God created the Earth and how He tested His people to separate the wheat from the chaff. They came to hear about Jesus and how He made miracles happen. They came to hear father sing the hymns in his clear and tender voice.

But most of all, I believe they came to listen to the pious words of a true Christian, written by our Frere Lanther.

Day after day, people mock me and call me Miss Lanther and I send a plague on their houses, a black plague with bloat and death, which makes them laugh and laugh. I don't know how to stop their teasing except to ignore it. Jed comes to me while I sit with my back to the sun and join with needle and thread the small squares I brought. I'm making a butterfly quilt for father.

Jed has nothing to occupy his hands. Those who got taken from their homes don't have much with them, but I don't feel sorry for him. He's nasty; he squeezes at the boils on his arms, and I always catch him watching me too closely. I see him when I look up from my stitching. The movement of the ship makes me sick if I stare down too long at my hands.

This afternoon, Jed sits himself in front of me so when I look up, I look at him. He stares into my face, which makes me feel sicker. I get up and move a few times, but he has stuck himself to me, it seems. Finally, I ask him what he wants.

"I've been thinking on what you said for quite some time and I want to know. Does Lanther really live in your stable?" he asks.

"No."

"That's what you said."

"It wasn't true."

"Changing your story, hey?"

I pay attention to my stitching so I won't stick myself.

"Does he talk to you?" Jed asks.

I clear my throat.

"What does he say when he talks to you?"

I look at the man's doltish face. His small eyes shift above his narrow nose. I do not want to tell him about Frere Lanther.

"Why should I tell you? You'll only jeer," I say finally.

"Ah, I did that because we were in front of folks. I didn't want them to think I believed you," he says.

There are people sitting all round us in the sun, and I am sure they can hear. I look at them and look at him.

"So, it took me some time. Now I believe you," he says. He glances round at the people, who shrug their shoulders or pick their teeth. He says, "It's just like if you said Jesus Christ lived in your stable, you know? That's just a little hard to believe."

"No, it's not. Jesus Christ lived fifteen hundred and twenty-four years ago. Frere Lanther is alive today!" I can hear people titter. "Fine thing!" I cry. I don't want to have them laugh at me again, so I look down at my square. They smell like rats, like pigs, all of them. Every one of them is a dullard.

"I do believe he lives with you, pet," Jed says. He's not laughing at me. "Really, I do." He gets up and walks away. I add a green square to the blue. It reminds me of the sea. I wish I could jump in and swim away.

The middle sail flaps above my head as I crouch in the center of the ship watching the sky. Two sailors grab hold of the sail and start to roll it up. They are always rolling the sails up or down and tying them or moving them side to side and making everyone get out of the way.

My nightmares have been filled with mountainous waterfalls and two-headed monsters, and I wonder if the captain truly knows where we're going. The sailors must know, since they've sailed before.

"Excuse me, but how do you know where we're going?" I call out to one of them. He ignores me.

"Do you know about the great waterfalls?" I cry out over the shriek of the rope wheels and the men's grunting and the water hitting against the ship. Neither of the sailors answer. I go as close to them as I can, and call out my question again. "Excuse me? How do you know where we're going?"

"Chart," one calls back. He's winding a rope round itself on the ground.

"Where did you get the chart?" I cry. Peter said his brother made a chart for him, a chart that said we would go down the falls in a fortnight. Though we have not been on the ship quite so long, still, I worry.

"Chart maker," the sailor says, tying the ends of the rope together very quickly. With the same water everywhere, it doesn't seem like anyone would truly know where they are going.

"How does the chart maker know what's ahead of us? How can he tell where we're going?"

"Hang on there—" He wraps another rope round and round itself. He's sweating in the sun. He doesn't answer.

We could be riding in one great circle. "How do we know what's ahead of us?" I repeat.

"Fella's been there before."

"But we never have. How do we know?"

The sailors don't answer right away. One says, "Forgit it, girlie."

"This man said we would sail right into a waterfall and off the Earth," I say.

"Balderdash."

"Hooey," says the other fellow, who hasn't said a peep.

"He says there's a way round it," I say.

"That's bloody rot."

"Horseshit. People been there and back lots of times with hulls o' loot. No waterfalls. Don't need no way round it."

The sailors start up the stairs toward the back of the ship. I think of Black Mary's monster, which has haunted my dreams. I want to ask them about the illumination I saw of the monsters that go after sailing ships—the picture of how ships that sail in the sea get eaten by huge serpents with two heads, one front and one back, that eat a person twice, going in and coming out. I run after the sailors, but they are already climbing a rope ladder at the very back of the ship. I call out to them, "What about the monsters?" and run directly into another sailor who's working there.

"Hah," he cries. "What the Hell ye doin'?"

"I'm sorry."

"Watch where'n the Hell ye goin'," he growls. He talks with an accent the way Frere Lanther does, only his is different. Gray prickles grow from his dark face.

"I'm very sorry," I tell him. He goes back to work; I stay and watch him. He's wiping something on a piece of leather. "Do you know? Are there monsters in the sea?" I ask.

He grunts what sounds like yes and doesn't look up from his work.

"With two heads?"

"Could be. I only ever saw 'em with one," he says. He's making the leather shine like iron.

"Did you ever see them eat someone?"

"Surely."

"Truly?"

"Truly. They like to eat young girls specially," he growls. "I seen 'em eat a dozen girls just like you with one bite. Swalla'ed 'em whole, without chewin'. Those monsters're too lazy to chew. They just gulp. Gulp, gulp." He's studying the piece of leather; he dips his rag into some yellowy slime and rubs it on the leather.

"How did the monster get to the girls?" I ask, just to see if he knows.

"Cap'n threw 'em overboard 'cause they were makin' too much noise. All screamin'. And they weren't helpin' out none, so he chucked 'em over the side, one by one. They didn't learn their lesson neither, 'cause they all screamed when they went over too."

I look at the sailor closely. He is smiling a little to himself.

"That's right," the sailor says. "And the monster just floated there with his mouth open, waiting for the cap'n to pop the next one in." When he's rubbed all the slime into the leather, he cuts two big swatches of it with his dagger.

Though I feel the sailor is jesting with me, the sea suddenly seems even more enormous than before. I cannot touch with my mind how enormous it must be, and how small I am compared. "Do you think the captain would throw anybody off this ship?" I ask with a little laugh.

"Surely," the sailor says.

"You do?"

He finally looks up at me. He's from somewhere different, I can tell, but I don't know where. His face and skin are darker than mine or mother's, like he's been very burnt by the sun. His grayish hair is curly, and it sticks together. "The cap'n's a short-tempered man, so short-tempered, he sometimes eats you urchins himself. That's all I'm gonna tell ye," he barks. He pulls a trapdoor out of its hole and nails half the leather swatch to the side of the door, and then half of it to the side where the door fits in. He lets me watch him work the way father used to and doesn't chase me away.

"One question more?" I ask after a time.

"Only one."

"Do you think the monsters would come onto the ship to eat anybody?"

"I never seen that," he says.

At church a week after they took father away was when I first saw the picture of the sea monster eating the ship.

That week, Maister Blacksmith led the service in father's place. When the service finished, Black Mary held the picture of an enormous sea monster up to me as I sat with the girls in the hay. I know three Marys: Black, Red, and Blond. I see them on Sundays and holy days when they come to the pig stable, and other days when we sew or bake together. At Mistress Grey's, we sit back in the sweet hay after services, eating sausages and talking.

"This is where your da went, Lil. Down this fellow's throat," Black Mary laughed, shaking the picture at me.

"Where'd you get that illumination?" Blond Mary asked. "You're going to catch terrible trouble if you stole another from your father's book."

Black Mary's father was the baron's scribe. He was wealthy and kind and had lent us paper and writing quills before. Black Mary was a wicked girl and often stole from him.

"Father doesn't care. He's got three grand books full of pictures just like these."

"Mary, that's awful," Red Mary said. "You went through all the trouble of thieving that picture just to upset Lily?"

"It's a jest. I'm simply ribbing her." That was Black Mary's way. I stared at the picture she'd stolen from her father's book, its ripped edge.

"Why do you want to upset poor Lily like that?" Red Mary asked. She was older than me and boys were all starting to ask for her hand in marriage.

"She's not upsetting me. I know she's just teasing," I said.

"There's all sorts of monsters in the world, Lil. They come in all shapes and sizes," Black Mary went on, "but any way you look at them, they're just one creature . . . the Devil." Because all the Marys were older than me, they acted like my mother sometimes. But they told me things mother wouldn't tell me. "He gets in you or he swallows you, and that's it, you're part of his evil world." She waved her finger at me and her black hair fell over her face. "The Devil takes different shapes, and you just have to know what shape he's in and fight him," she said.

"And how do you know it's the Devil?" I asked.

"Oh, you always know."

"What if he's in a good shape, and you can't tell it's the Devil?" I'd heard of that happening before.

"You have to feel him. Me, I can feel him on the back of my neck. Everyone has a special place where they can feel the Devil. Some people feel him in their heart, or their throat."

"How do you fight him when you feel him?" I asked her.

"Sing to God! You have to sing loud to God for Him to truly hear you over the Devil and protect you. That's why your da sings hymns, so God can hear us over the Devil." Red and Blond Mary agreed with her.

"The Devil has to hear that you have God inside you," Blond Mary told me. "That's why he doesn't come to church, because he can hear God there."

"If you're too quiet and your thoughts are too dark, he can slip inside your quiets and take you over. Like mud," Red Mary said.

"Yes, he slips inside you like mud," Black Mary said. "He takes you over if you're not careful."

After, Black Mary gave me the picture to hold because she didn't want her father to catch her with it if he found it missing.

At home I put the picture under my ticking and tried to see where the Devil was in me, but I couldn't feel him. Maybe the girls were only teasing me, or maybe I didn't feel him because my father's choirmaster, and a minister too, so I am protected by God all the time. That's what I feel in my heart when I am quiet. God. Not the mud of the Devil.

Black Mary's father noticed the missing page the very next day. He knew it was Mary who'd taken it. All over Myrthyr, we heard her repentance to God, hymns her father made her sing to get the Devil out of her.

Dinner this night is soup and bread. The pig still snorts in our eating room, though we often smell meat cooking from the rich side of the ship. Salted pork stew, someone says.

The bread they give us is black and hard. The soup tastes like bathwater with a few lentils sunk at the bottom. They pass round baskets of bruised green apples. Apples are fall fruits. They must store them with the beets and turnips in the cold cellar. I see a woman across from me take five apples and put them in her kirtle. I've never seen a person eat five apples in a row, though once I ate four and it gave me such a stomachache, I thought I would surely die.

I tell mother what the sailor told me about the monsters. Though I don't quite believe what he said, I do think there is some truth to his tale. "The sailor says they don't even chew," I say.

She's seen the picture also. "He's just telling you stories, Lily, same as the girls used to," she says.

"But he said they don't have two heads, only one. That must mean he's seen them, don't you think?" I tell her about the captain, and about him not liking girls.

"I heard that monster story too," says the man next to mother. He slurps his soup loudly. "One head."

"They swim round the water eating everything in sight, even sailing ships, I heard," another fellow says.

"You mean, they could eat us?" the lady with the apples asks, her eyes wide in her skinny face.

A man down our row sucks his teeth impatiently. "It's called a whale. Don't you folks know anything?" I look; it's Jed. "The story in the Bible of Jonah and the whale? Where he disobeys God and gets swallowed by the whale?"

"He was talking about a whale?" the slurping man asks.

"That's it, just a stinking whale. I'm sure of it."

Of course, that was what the sailor meant. People hunt whales and kill them and we trade for their tallow at market. I smile at the thought of the sailor's joke with me.

"See, Lily. It's just a whale, a creature of God." Mother laughs and squeezes me.

I've never seen a whale, and now I hope to. Even if he does swallow people whole, it's possible to live inside of him for three days at least before one safely got passed out the other end the way Jonah did.

We finish the last of our soup and bread and apples and get up to go outside. As we push past the people, I hear a sailor say, "Where ye going with them?" and I turn, but it is not to me that he is speaking. He says it to the woman with the five apples in her kirtle.

Her cheeks pinken. "What do you mean?" she asks.

"Them apples."

"I . . . I'm taking them for later, for when I get hungry at night."

"No hoardin'," the sailor says.

"I'm not hoarding."

"Taking any food outter the mess is hoardin'. No hoardin'." The sailor goes to the woman and roughly sticks his hands into the pockets of her kirtle. I put my hand in my own kirtle and feel the knife that Frere Lanther gave me. I would poke it into the sailorman if he touched me or mother that way.

"Give 'er a chance," a fellow says.

"Yeh, let 'er give 'em back." A couple of the men stand up.

"No one told us—" the woman cries out.

The sailor lets her go and holds out his hands for the apples. He grabs them back from her and shouts at us, "No hoardin' on this ship! We have a long ride and we need all the food for everbody. No fukkin' hoardin', ye hear?" Then he stomps out of the room. Nobody says anything or moves.

Mother turns and walks up the stairs. I follow her.

Outside, a fellow is sitting on the rail and playing a pipe. The music sounds sweet in the evening. Me and mother stand by him and listen. Soon, other people come up from the meal, out into the air, and listen to the fellow playing. He plays a hymn, one of father's favorites, and mother begins to sing the words:

> *"When God made Heaven, He made it for us.*
> *His glory is truly to be seen.*
> *When God made Earth, He made it for us.*
> *Let His beauty always be seen."*

Thomas joins mother in her singing. His voice is deep and rich like Maister Blacksmith's, and I wonder if he can play the harpsichord too. Other people begin to sing, the apple lady and some of the men, and together, they sound like the choir, bumping along in the water, the sea taking their beautiful voices out into itself like a starved whale.

I look over the edge at the jumping fish, at the fins and tails flickering through crests of waves. Water animals, God's creatures filling the sea. How deep does it go? I can only see the rippling skin of it, ever moving like the skin of a mighty beast. And the peace of it, still as the dead.

"Hallo, little chick."

I turn to the voice beside me. It is the apple lady, with sad eyes in her thin, pocked face.

"Hallo, mistress."

"Margaret. You're a friend, little one, and I want you to call me Margaret."

"I'm Lily."

She nods. Her eyes are so downcast, I turn away, back to the sea.

"I got three girls at home awaiting me," she starts. Her voice gets higher, which tells me she's going to cry. I look over my shoulder, into the ship. Folks are sitting on the wooden floors, napping or playing pickage with pebbles. Mother lies below with a bad belly. Sailors climb the rope ladders above like monkeys, or whittle their sticks like old men.

"They took my Philip, they did. They are dreadful men, the baron and his kind."

I glance at her and nod. She touches my shoulder. I feel like holding her hand and patting it, but I look away again.

"I have a son too, about your age. He's took over the croft, poor thing. The girls help him, and their grandma, but I don't see how he's going to do it all himself."

Her tears fall heavy as rain. I cannot help her, though I wish I could. I let her hold on to my shoulder, feeling the heat gather behind my eyes.

Fins, like wings, break through the skin of the sea.

FIVE

There are more things living on this ship than people. Fleas, for instance. They have gotten into our things, and mother has the itches. She doesn't scratch, but I can see that she wants to. We had fleas in our cottage once. Mistress Grey came in and set fire to a pile of damp oak leaves in an old pot by the door and smoked them to death. We have no oak leaves on this ship. The fleas haven't taken a liking to me yet, but mother has small red bumps up and down her arms. That time we had fleas, I scratched my bitten ankles till they bled.

I see rats, too. Sailors catch them and throw them overboard. Round our stable, cats eat the rats. I do not know how these living things came here. Perhaps someone brought them along.

I've heard the sailors talking of the New World, of fruits that smell like perfume and gold pieces the size of a man. They talk of a captain of a sailing vessel who steals gold and silver from the Spaniards when they go across the water. Other vessels or ships do not exist here, I think. We have only seen water and waves, fins and swimming creatures. When the sailors talk of the captain who steals other people's gold, they make him sound like a great man.

Father says it's wrong to steal, it says so in the Holy Book. Once I stole a warm and very delicious little peach cobbler from Mistress Knapp's window and ate it all up in the woodland and threw the crockery into the stream. I blamed the theft on her cur. But father found out. It was almost as if God had seen me through His omnipresence, and had whispered my bad deed to father. Father reminded me of the Ten Commandments received by Moses on Mount Sinai. He made me tell Mistress Knapp the truth, that it was me who stole the cobbler, and he made me bake her another. Mistress Knapp's shack smells terribly of people dung, and he made me stay in there with her and make her a cobbler like the one I stole. I never stole after that.

Mother has emptied her stomach into the water three times today and twice yesterday. She has eaten the last of the hard cheese we brought to settle her stomach. She has tried the medicines from our neighbors, but none have worked. I tell her not to look down at her knitting, that looking down makes a body sick, but that does not seem to help. We tried a bit of beet and prayed to St. Anne to settle her vapors, but nothing will stay in her stomach.

A sailor comes to mother this evening, just as darkness is falling. I rub her back while she loses her dinner over the side of the ship. The sailor leans over and says to mother, "Is ye Sarah Applegate?"

Mother retches.

I answer, "That's her."

Mother croaks into the water, "Yes, what is it?"

"The baron of the Highlands wants ta see ye."

"What for?" mother asks.

"Damn if I know. He don't tell me things. Just orders. Says he's got somethin' for ye."

Mother wipes her mouth on her rag and stands up straight and looks at the sailor. Her eyes water and she smells of vomit. "I am indisposed at the moment."

"Bad luck, miss. The baron must see ye, so ye must go." The sailor's voice is sharp and crude. Mother looks pale and clutches at her stomach and sighs. I think of jabbing my knife into the sailor-man's leg.

"Very well. Come with me, Lily."

The sailor shakes his head. "Ye alone, mistress. Leave the kitten here."

I feel cold and scared suddenly and wish to make sure nothing happens to her.

"Come on, come on, I hain't got all evenin'."

Mother wipes her face again and tells me she'll be right back. I am worried for her; I follow them as far as I can, till the sailor stops me. The baron said he wanted to give mother something, and I wonder what it could be. Nothing the baron gives could be good. He always takes half of everything we have.

I wait as close to the rich side as I can for mother to return. I look up and down for the boy, hoping he might tell me what his father wants with my mother, but there are not many people outside tonight. I wonder if the boy got into trouble for trying to meet me. I have gone out ten different nights to see if he would come, but he never does.

None of the rich people are on the top deck, as the sailors call it. First deck, second deck, swab the deck, they say. The deck is so empty.

I lean over the side, staring into the moving water, waiting and waiting.

I begin to think of the dead bird I saw. I cannot imagine father lying on the ground, his hands still like the bird's wings. "Mother," I whisper. I cannot imagine being on this ship alone without her. Men came to the cottage and took father. Men hit mother, hurt her, they took father and hurt mother.

I say her name louder. "Mother?" But there's no answer, so I begin to squeeze my knife in my pocket and shout, "Mother, mother!" but she does not answer. So I shout louder. "Mother! Mother! Mother!" Someone comes running from the back of the ship, a sailor who grabs me by the shoulders and shakes me.

"Shut the Hell up, ye brat," he yells.

I holler, "Where is my mother, what have you done with her?" into his ugly face. I pull my knife from my pocket, but I can't get it open. He snatches it away from me. I scream and he slaps me across the cheek.

"Give it back," I shout. My cheek stings. "Give it! Frere Lanther gave it to me, so give it back!" I scream at him. He gives me a shove and tells me to shut up. "Where is my mother?" I shout and kick him as hard as I can in the knee. He calls out in pain from my kick and grabs me round the throat; he is choking me. But I can still scream. "Mother! Mother! Mother!"

Mother doesn't come, but I see Thomas standing before me, pulling the sailor off of me. They start a row like the drunkens in our village, cursing and yelling and punching till more men come and shout at them to stop. They try to pull them apart. The captain comes too, and other sailors and people from our side. Some of the rich people too, I can see, are standing on the deck. All except mother. The captain bellows at the men, and they stop fighting. He tells everyone to clear out. Behind him, I can see Mother, running from the rich people's side toward me.

Night has come completely, and her face looks hollow in the bright moonlight. She runs strangely and has dark red blotches on her cheek and neck like she too has been hit. She comes to me and pulls me by the arm without a word, across the ship and down to our room. I ask her twice what the baron wanted from her, but all she can do is shake her head. When we get to our room, she slides the trunk from under the bed and begins digging frantically through the herbs, the pamphlets, the knitting and sewing there. I ask her what she's looking for, but she just shakes her head. I tell her about the fight, about the sailor who took my knife, and she stops.

"He took your knife away?" she asks.

"Yes, and he struck me," I tell her. "He hit me, mother."

Her head drops and she stares into the dark trunk. I feel, suddenly, that the ship is getting smaller and smaller, that the sailors and the rich and the captain are moving closer, and that there is no way to breathe, nowhere to run.

The wet earth smells of mushroom and loam. I race through the trees. Branches reach for my eyes and tangle my hair. My kirtle rips, but I still run, faster through the woodland, escaping the murderous men who chase behind me with vicious, barking dogs. The men are my enemies and the woodland is my friend. I climb a tree to its tip, to where the branches thin, and I see the dead bird there. Only its mouth is open and it is singing with the voice of my father. I touch the bird, and it flies away.

I wake. For once, the quiet sea is a relief.

In the morning, her bruises are as purple as a cock's comb. "Mother," I say, "your cheek, and your neck!"

She puts her fingers to her cheek and winces.

"You're all bruised. The sailor . . . was it—"

She shakes her head, but will not tell me what happened.

Peter notices as he comes down from his bed.

"Got caught in the ruckus, did you?" he asks her, but she does not answer him.

At breakfast, Thomas too is covered in cuts and bruises. I wonder if any have appeared on me. He sits next to mother and asks her softly why her face is bruised. She shakes her head; she doesn't eat her porridge. He asks her where she was last night, and why I was calling for her. I can see Peter and the other fellows leaning in to hear.

"The baron," she whispers, looking up at the sailor who lurks at the edge of the room.

"The baron? What baron?"

"The baron of the Highlands, our baron. He is on this ship."

Everyone begins whispering loudly at once, asking mother what the baron is doing on the ship. Mother cringes at their insistent questions. Thomas shushes them and tells mother to explain.

"He called me to him. He . . . he threatened me. He heard about Frere Lanther, about him living in my stable, and he said if I didn't . . . if I didn't"—she shakes her head—"he would send the shallop back to England and have Frere Lanther killed."

"If you didn't—?"

"If you didn't what?"

All the fellows are asking her:

"What's that, Sarah?"

"If you didn't what?"

"If you didn't bed down with him?" Jed asks in a nasty voice.

Mother gasps and starts to cry.

"Her child is sitting right there," Margaret says. "Watch your manners."

"You needn't be so vulgar, Jed," Thomas says.

"Guess he'd be hankering after a beauty like you," Jed mutters.

The men look at each other, and then at mother, then at me. I thought 'bed down' meant making babies, but now I see by mother's sorrow that I was wrong, that it is something awful.

One man whispers, "How'd the baron find out about Lanther?"

"Maybe from the sailors talking . . ."

"They don't know who the Hell Lanther is," Thomas says.

I feel the men looking at me as though I told the baron myself.

"They can't send the shallop back, we're too long at sea! It'd never make it," Thomas says.

"You ought to teach your girl to keep her mouth buttoned," Jed says to mother. I want to tell him to shut himself up, but I know he's right, and it's true. I should have kept my mouth buttoned, I shouldn't have told everyone, not till I could trust them. I look at the men, and they angrily look back at me.

"It's not her fault," mother says. "She thought we were all together in this, in our faith."

I examine their faces, and Ethan's comes into my mind. Ethan, the boy. The baron's son. He is the one who told. I should never have spoken to him.

"Do you think he'll do it? Do you think he'll send the shallop back?" Thomas asks.

Mother shakes her head.

"You did it then," Peter says.

Mother says nothing.

I feel as if she has struck me. I feel as if she has died from something I did to her. From the Bible, I remember 'bed down,' but not as a terrible thing. Now I'm not sure exactly what it is. Mother's bruises show me that it is horrible. I begin to cry into my pease porridge and put it on the floor. "I'm sorry."

"You're a bad girl," Peter says to me.

"Leave her alone," mother cries.

"I'm so sorry, mother."

"What the Hell is the baron doing here, that's what I'd like to know," Thomas says.

I dare not mention the boy. I cannot believe I ever told him or anyone about Frere Lanther. Why did I break the rules?

Mother shakes her head and wipes off her tears. "He says he has his spies. That he knows everything that happens on the ship and not to do anything rash."

Everyone who is listening stops eating. They're like chickens in a coop who sense a dog nearby.

"Let's not be divided by this," mother says. "He is only trying to make us suspicious of each other. I spent much of last night thinking about it. Believe me, I have seen it before, and that is what he's trying to do."

They're quiet, not looking at each other.

Thomas breaks the silence. "What about you, Sarah? Is he going to come for you again?" he asks.

"I . . . I don't know."

"We'll try to do everything to stop him if he does, right?" Thomas says, looking at the other folks, who seem to have lost their spirits. Their words stick somewhere in their mouths. They frighten me with their silence. Slowly, I get up and leave the eating room. Mother does not ask me where I am going.

* * *

Numbers keep everything in order. When I know how many, how long, how much, I feel there is peace in the world.

At home, I counted forward—days till a feast, till harvest, till I saw the Marys again. Forward was a good place to count.

I counted things planted, growing, finished—harrows of flax, rows of wheat, millet blossoms, woven shirts. I counted animals—chickens, goats, cows—as they went from stable to pasture and back. I counted needles on my pines and branches and cones. I counted things getting more and things getting less—beets stored, cabbages eaten, tubs of butter used. I counted how many we had and how many we needed before we went to market.

I have nothing to count now. Nothing to keep in order. I don't know how many more days at sea, how long we'll be here, when we'll reach land, or if I will see my father again.

I can only count backwards the days since I left home and counting backwards makes me feel like everything I love has gone away, that time has stopped, that I am not living in God's world.

I no longer see the use in counting.

The fleas punish me. After a few days of being haunted by the words 'bed down,' I go to our room to get the Bible from our trunk to find out why it is so terrible. The fleas have taken over the trunk, and they attack my wrists with pinching bites. I see that mice have finished off our lard. The box is nibbled and there are turds next to it. I dig farther down, past the sewing and the knitting, to the bottom of the trunk where we last laid our Bible, but it is not there. I find, instead, at the very bottom, a knife.

It is like the one Frere Lanther gave me, but not as small. Frere

Lanther used the knife he gave me to sharpen his quill pens, but this knife is much too large for that. I don't remember this knife, but I do know the Bible was in the trunk. I glance round the room. It is empty. Everyone is outside. I look to the bottom of the trunk again, puzzled by this change of Bible for knife.

I reach in and lift the knife. In the palm of my hand, the weight feels heavy and solid. I open its blade; it snaps up the way mine did. The sharp metal cuts easily through a piece of straw from our ticking—it could skin a rabbit, carve a tree branch. Carefully, I fold the blade and slip it into my pocket. I tuck everything gently back into its place except a few patches of my quilt, and return the trunk under the bed.

When I stand, I can feel the knife against my leg through my pocket. I will not tell anybody I have it. I will keep my big mouth shut.

The morning has clouded over, making the sky small and dark. At the back of the ship, Thomas and Peter and Jed stand round mother like a protective fence. I sit nearby, but not in her view, and stare at her now-greenish bruises. She holds her stomach, the nausea upon her again. The baron bed down with my mother because of me. Bed down, or beat down? Maybe I misheard. No, Thomas said it, bed down. Because of me. Because I told the baron's son, and he told the baron about Frere Lanther—

The baron's son, the boy, Ethan. It is his fault that mother is hurt. If he hadn't told his father about Frere Lanther, the baron would not have hurt mother. I see clearly what the knife is to be used for. It must be used on the baron's son as punishment.

I take out my sewing and thread my needle in and out of the squares, joining them together. Every now and then, I glance up at mother's bruises and wish that I could soothe them with my thoughts.

Sailors climb above me, sticking their feet into the rope ladders and pulling themselves up and down. The clouds tighten into gray and black sheets. The sailors scramble faster round me, tying boxes down, winding ropes, talking of a storm. They sense it coming, they shout to each other. One cries that he can feel it in his fingerbones like fire. From the front of the ship, I hear a man begin to sing. A sailor. As though a choirmaster were conducting them, the other sailors join in with refrains of the same song. I have not heard them sing all together like this before. Without the harmony of father's choir, the sailors sing different words in a similar tune. Some sing:

"Git me ta 'ospital,
Git me ta 'ospital,
I feel ill. . . ."

And others sing:

"It tickles, don't do it.
We'll make a baby fast."

"Git me ta 'ospital,
I feel ill.
Ya cun rub me belly.
Ya cun rub me all over. . . ."

"It tickles, don't do it.
We'll make a baby fast.
Oh, nursemaid, don't do it,
We'll make a baby fast."

The song fills the ship, the sailors working to its rhythm, laughing at some lines. I see the old dark sailor who told me about the monsters. He is twisting a rope, working alone as he matches his voice to the other sailors'. I ask him to teach me the song. He doesn't look at me, but wrinkles his brow and stops singing. I tell him I know how to sing, and sing some of the words to encourage him.

"Shut ye trap," he says.

I stop. "Why?"

"It hain't a song for girls." He won't look at me, but I can tell he's upset.

"Why not?"

"It's nasty, that's why not."

"Nasty how?"

"It's about ruttin'."

"What's ruttin'?"

"Ruttin', ya know."

"No, I don't know, please tell me."

He sighs and shakes his head. "Ruttin', ruttin', ya know, beddin' down an' makin' dirty."

"Bedding down? Please tell me more. I mean, I've heard the words, but what is it, actually?"

He snorts. "Ya ever seen a animal climbin' on another?"

"Like Maisy and the bull?"

"What's 'at?"

"My cow and her bull."

"Yah. Cows and bulls, hens and roosters, mans and womans. That's ruttin'."

"Making babies?"

"'At's it!"

"Is it bad? Does it hurt?"

He bursts out into laughter and won't answer any more of my questions.

Black Mary said a baby came out of a girl's bunghole like with the animals, but Red Mary said no, no, no, it came out of her weehole, that they come out of everyone's weehole, even the animals', she'd seen it herself a dozen times. Blond Mary agreed with Red Mary.

"A baby comes from the bunghole, I swear on the Holy Mother," Black Mary said.

"Blasphemy will not prove your point," Red Mary said.

"Of course that's not true, Mary, and you know it. It comes straight from the weehole," Blond Mary said.

"Does not," Black Mary cried. "Lily, don't listen to them, it doesn't."

"What would Lily know, she's never seen it. She's got no sisters, and her mother stopped having babies after she came along," Blond Mary said.

"One look at Lily and anyone would stop," Black Mary said.

"I'm surprised your mother survived your birth, Mary," Red Mary said.

Our baby animals came out from between our big animals' legs, from their bottoms. I looked at my own holes, but they did not seem big enough to fit a baby. Midwife Samuelson only let mothers, sisters, and girl cousins into the room where a girl was birthing, so I don't truly know how it happens.

Black Mary said they put you in the grass and let you roll round and scream while the baby tore your bunghole apart and made his way out like with the horses, the cows, and the sheep. Red Mary said how fool-headed she sounded, that she didn't know what she was talking about. Red and Blond Mary had seen it; a baby came out of the weehole with lots of screams and blood. It was blue and covered with snot.

"But, Mary," I asked, "isn't a person's weehole too small?"

"The weehole grows when your belly grows, that's what happens," Blond Mary said.

"If it grows when your belly grows, why doesn't the baby fall out while you walk?" Black Mary asked her.

"You have to keep your legs closed and not walk round too much, or it'll fall out," Red Mary said. "Lots of girls stay in bed so that doesn't happen."

"I've seen different," said Black Mary. "A baby comes tearing its way from a bunghole with its little hands and feet. That's why some mothers die."

"When did you see that, the bunghole birth?" Red Mary asked her, smiling like Black Mary was too silly for words.

"I did, I saw it when my mother had Mathias and Ann."

"You were at my house when your mother had Mathias and Ann because you hate seeing blood!" Blond Mary cried.

Black Mary laughed and poked me for no reason. Red Mary said one of us would have a baby soon enough, and then all of us would know for sure.

The days run into each other with a sameness that is wearing. The same sun going round the Earth, its heat burning through the chilly dawn and shining all day. The same stories from people's mouths.

Since the baron called for my mother, she has not slept and has eaten very little. The fellows stand round her morning and night, protecting her should he call again.

With less and less food and clean water, many of the fellows have gotten sick and weary. A stomach without nourishment makes a person very tired, even if he does not work.

Most days we sit in a heap at the end of the ship, mother and me, Peter and Margaret, Thomas and Jed, one or another of us rising to vomit over the side, talking little. The baron seems to have forgotten about mother. At night, I lay with my head close to hers, listening to her breathing.

I did not know how much time had passed on this ship till last night, when Peter started running back and forth on the deck with his hands to his hair, pulling it out in clumps like weeds from the dirt, screaming, "Stop it, stop the ship, I want to get off. Over a month, more than a month, a month too long. When will it end? When will it end? I can't see. Stop the ship. Throw me over, I'll end it myself, throw me over. Forty fukking days, oh, help me, forty nights, oh God!" The sailors caught him and wrapped him in blankets. His head bled. They brought him below and I could hear his muffled screams and cries throughout the night.

The sun rose again this morning, burning off the chilly dawn. At the back of the ship this afternoon, Peter, his head bound in dirty cloth, asked me to go below deck so he could talk with mother and the fellows in private. After, mother would not tell me what he said, so I sit alone on the deck, ignoring her, hiding my face in my raised knees from the never-ending pounding of sun.

Clouds, and the flickering of lightning come first, then the faraway warning of thunder. The captain calls out orders to the sailors to use the wind, of which we've felt so little. In this storm, the only things we have to hold on to in order to steady ourselves also move with the ship.

The sun's been shining so long, I've almost forgotten the way the clouds turn black and pink in a storm, the way God's sky roils, fat with water. I am ever so grateful to Him for the change.

Father says movement is caused by the elements air and fire, which reach upwards, and earth and water, which press downwards. On this ship, the elements are not acting properly. The water jumps up and throws us; the air blows every which way. There is no earth.

Sailors hold on to the bucking ropes of the middle sail, the only one that is up. Others push and pull at a long rod while the captain shouts directions that sound like "Tackonnamains'lstarboard, boys, tack, tack 'ard." The rain has not yet begun.

I do not get as sick sitting outside in this weather, though mother and most folks prefer lying abed. Despite the cold, the wind makes it easier for me to breathe, and watching the sailors makes me not think so much. Curled beside the middle stairwell, I stay out of the sailors' way.

How long, I wonder, does it take to get to the New World? We have been on this ship forever. Will there be anybody there to greet us? I think of the dream I've dreamt many times, of the bird with father's voice who flies off when I touch him, and I think this means father is not dead. That he will be there when we arrive, arms open the way they used to be. I feel the lightning and the thunder crack inside of me as though I had swallowed them whole.

The rain begins to pour from the sky.

I am folded into the stairwell when he comes to me. He is dressed in a cloak with a hood and he stumbles through the wind, past the sailors, and throws himself to the ground next to me. He frightens me, since I don't realize it's him till he glances at me from under his hood. In my surprise, I forget my distant plan to stab him. I've been holding on to the knife so long, it's become part of me.

"Ethan," I say.

"Lily."

"You know my name—"

"I must talk to you."

His light, quick voice that is very close to my ear sounds panicked, troubled.

"What happened?" I ask him.

"My father. Your mother."

"You told your father about Frere Lanther—"

"I didn't. I did not, I swear, Lily. I don't know how he found out. One of your people is telling him everything." I wait to hear more. "I overheard my father talking about what he was going to do with your mother, and he discovered me. I tried to get to you, to tell you, but he stopped me. He's been keeping me in the kitchen, locked in. He doesn't want me near you people. He knows I am on your side!"

"How did you get out?"

"The storm. The sailors are too busy to watch me. Grandmama came to give me some food, and I pushed past her to find you. I heard everything, Lily. I heard everything Father did to your mother. It was—dreadful. I hate him. It was terrible." The rain comes down heavily; I can see into his hood, his face, covered with wet. Rain, or— tears. I have never seen a boy cry. "And he told me what he did with your father. You were right, he sent him off—that is why he keeps me away from you. He thinks I will help you to fight him! A mutiny!"

"Ethan—"

"Father has bad intentions for your mother and for all you people—"

His tears frighten me, make to want me run away.

"What's he going to do?"

"Lily, you have to tell your mother, he knows everything. Your men, tell them not to go through with their plan. He knows it already!"

"What plan?"

The rain is drenching me through to the bone quickly. It gives me chills. I shiver and shiver. As the ship rocks in the storm, Ethan is thrown into my lap, or I his.

"Lily, he has firearms. Tell them not to do it!"

"To do what, Ethan? What plan?"

When he is thrown into my lap, he puts his mouth to mine and it feels warm and wet. "Be careful, Lily," he whispers. He puts some cold metal in my palm, then jumps up and scurries between the sailors, back to his side and down, away, where I can no longer see him.

I sit in the rain, listening to its pelting, the thunder, the shouts of the sailors and their captain.

SIX

I once before stayed outside a whole night through a rainstorm in my weave of pine bowers. That night, anything seemed better than going back to the cottage, where father and mother were having a row. It was the night before they took father away, and I became fevered the next night from the rain. I thought the men in cloaks who came for father were a howling red dream.

Father and mother together. They are, in my mind, like an illumination in a book done by someone who knows them very well. Neither of them smile in my picture, but they are both soft with a warm light about their heads and chests.

That night they were fighting, father didn't believe mother. I don't know what he didn't believe, but that's what he kept saying: "I simply don't believe you, Sarah. I can't believe you."

And she kept shouting, "Well, that's what they said, so you'd better believe. Do something, Eric!"

"I can't believe you, Sarah. I simply don't."

"For Christ, Eric, why would they say it if it weren't true?"

The row had started before Mistress Grey took me home, so all I knew was there was no supper on the fire pit, so father and mother must have been quarreling for hours. Father was very angry with mother, even though he wouldn't shout at her.

I ran to the woodland. I curled into my hidey place and wondered why father and mother were so upset. It was not the first time I'd heard their voices angry at each other in that way.

It took a long time for the rain to come down through the trees enough for me to feel it as I sat on the ground. The cold wetness crept through my kirtle to my skin like a giant spider. The shivers set in, but by then, I was too sleepy to go back. I thought I heard father calling me. He didn't know about my hidey place. I was too deep in fellow Sandman's arms to heed.

Just before morning light, when my eyes usually flew open and I ran out to the cows for milking, I woke stiff as a pit stone, not sure where I was. I went home and met father in the stable, where he stood with lamplight, looking at the wall he had finished for Frere Lanther. He grabbed me by the ear when he saw me, not hurtfully, but with a firm grip, and pulled me to him.

"Don't ever disappear like that again, Lily, do you hear?"

"I'm sorry, it was just that you and mother, fighting—"

"Your mother," he said. "Ah, forgive me, Lily."

"What . . . why were you quarreling, father?"

"Gossip and rumors, my child, that is all. I'd be a fool to believe other people's words."

He brought me into the cottage, where mother was heating water for porridge. She, too, cuffed me when she saw me. She looked like she'd been crying awhile.

That night, the men woke us. They were holding candles and wearing dark cloaks that shielded their faces. They came and left so quickly, we hadn't time to know the men who took father.

I've seen folks with their hands and feet locked in wooden stocks, but I have never seen this happen to a noble, so I can hardly believe Ethan's words, that he is a prisoner. The baron's son being punished like us.

The rain comes down all night.

The boy did not tell his father. The men have plans. When I go to mother to tell her, I see she is lying down in the early-morning dark of the room, her arms swollen with bug bites, her hands to her eyes, covering them from nausea, and I do not wish to disturb her. I don't believe she is strong enough to have any kind of harmful plan.

The wet of the rain brings out the smell of piss and dung in the room, of people rotting in their stew. None of us have bathed or changed clothes since we began this journey. I stand beside our bed. Everyone in the room is still sleeping, some quietly, some with loud snores. Most scratch themselves in their sleep; we've all got the itches.

I open my hand. In it are the crowns Ethan gave me, mother's gold. I close my fingers round them.

I think to rid myself of the knife. I have been carrying it far too long. The room is full of sleeping folk, and someone may wake and notice, but I do not wish to carry it any longer. I want to lift its weight from me like the weight of my bad feelings. I feel it is dangerous to carry the knife as a sailor may take it away and use it on me or mother. Carefully, I wrap and tie it tightly in my quilt squares and pull out the trunk as quietly as I can.

There was no dinner last night because of the storm, and there will be no breakfast, I'm sure. As I push past the things in the trunk, I smell the cheese that is no longer there, and feel my hunger like a cold rock in my stomach. Some days, Frere Lanther does not eat, and this, he says, lights his brain and brings him clear words from God. I put the knife deep at the bottom, underneath the pile of Frere Lanther's pamphlets. I slide the trunk under the bed and sit on the floor next to it. Perhaps, if I do not eat, God will give me some light and clear words. I wait for them, wishing I had the Bible to hold to my heart, to fill it.

I think of the words Ethan told me. "Lily," he had said. He used my name. How did he know it? But they know all. "I heard everything Father did to your mother . . . he told me what he did with your father . . . he knows everything . . ."

My father. What does he know about my father?

And the men. I don't know about a plan. I think to wake mother and tell her, but it seems that every time we open our mouths, somehow the words fly back to the baron. I do not wish to let out any more secrets that may hurt mother. I scratch at my flea-bitten wrists, pulling off the scabs to draw just enough blood to ease the itch. I watch mother sleep till my own eyes droop.

In my half dreams, I can still feel the boy's mouth on mine.

The urge for land is upon us desperately. Our skin is beginning to crawl away like maggot-filled hides that weren't cured properly. A few days ago, the morning after the storm, a sailor spotted a floating log.

"Land, land ho, land, land ho!" he cried. "Lookee, Cap'n, barnacles." His shouts brought us all. Even some rich folk ran to our side, for it was from the back of the ship that he called. Excitedly, the sailor pointed out the wood. But the cry was false.

"Yer wrong, 'ats from the storm, sailor. 'Ats only evidence o' land, it hain't the real thing," the captain said, squinting into the sun at the water all round him. "Git back to yer places, men."

That cry of 'land' gave us a taste for it, like being starving and smelling peach cobbler and wanting a piece bad enough to steal it. A far worse wanting yet.

It's been eerily quiet. I feel like parts of me are coming off, big huge flakes. Mother's teeth too, she says, hurt. Lots of the fellows are sick and skinny, vomiting and running to the bucket every minute.

I have not seen Ethan since the storm.

I am very angry at mother. She pulled me to the deck when the rain finally stopped and people were beginning to rise from their damp beds. She whispered in my ear, "Lily, what have you done with the knife that was in our trunk?" and I worried for her. I had not believed him, but I knew then that what Ethan had said was true. Mother had a plan with the men. I was grateful she had not found the knife that I hid in the quilt squares.

Sailors were passing, and Thomas and the others milling. I didn't know what to say, how to stop her without alerting all.

"I don't know, mother. Maybe it fell, when I was looking for the Bible." She stood up straight when I mentioned the Bible. "Where is the Bible, mother? It's long been missing."

She looked at me darkly and folded her arms. "Do not think about it, Lily," she said.

"Why, mother?"

"I threw it over," she said.

"You what?"

"I threw it over the side, Lily." She shook her head and pointed at me. "Do not ask me any more about it." Her angry eyes made her look ugly to me, like a serpent.

"But . . . what about me, mother? I loved that Bible."

She spat at me with fierce whispers, "It's not real, Lily. It's all false, all lies. It is not the true word."

"I can't believe—"

"Lily, it's over, it's gone."

My mother has thrown over the Bible? A soldier in Frere Lanther's army, faithful to the Good Book, to the Holy Scriptures written by the ancient scribes, throwing over the only book that I've ever read, the book of stories and rules that tell us how to live and why everything exists?

"Mother?" The beautiful stories of God and Jesus, of Moses, of Mary and Joseph, the horrible stories of war and famine and locusts and plagues . . . "Mother?" I felt like she'd thrown my life over to be eaten by the whales.

"Stop saying that!" she cried.

"What?"

"That. 'Mother.' Stop it." She put her hands to her ears and shook her head.

"But you are my—" Pain caught in my throat, tightened it, and I began to cry.

She grabbed me by the arm and bent over me. "Where is that knife, Lily?" she asked harshly in my ear.

I would not tell her, no matter how much she punished me.

"Don't do it, moth—" I didn't know what to call her.

"What did you do with the knife?"

"What do you want it for?" I was afraid she had plans to use it on the baron, that he already knew, and would take it from her the way the sailor took mine.

"I'm going to cut my own throat!" she shouted, making me cry harder. She held her hands to her forehead and sat on the wet ground, rocking, it seemed, to the rhythm of my tears and the ship. "What do you think I want it for, Lily?" I could see she was crying too. People were starting to come nearer, to stare at us like animals in a pen, so I grabbed her head and whispered in her ear what the boy had told me in the storm. I returned her coins to her as proof.

She stood quickly and walked over to Thomas, who was settling on the back deck with Peter and Jed and Margaret. I watched their gestures and saw them deflate like pig's bladders as she spoke to them. They did have a plan, the baron was right. Somehow, he does know everything.

I am still angry at mother. I haven't seen the boy in forever, it seems. Maybe he is dead. There is no way for me to know. Like with father, I just have to have faith that he is not.

It is not the first time mother harmed the Bible. I do not like to remember it, but she did it before.

I was sitting in our cottage with father. He was making music for a hymn and I was helping with the melody. We had just come from church and confession, after which Father Leeman had asked father for money. Father Leeman pulled father aside and spoke with him, leaving me and mother standing in the pews long after the other church members had left. I saw father pay him finally, and we went home. I listened as father and mother talked on the way up our hill.

"You cannot confess such things, Sarah, not to him, not to Father Leeman. You know that, we have spoken about it. It always costs me dearly."

"Forgive me, I am not perfect, Eric, and I never will be."

"I am doing everything I can, but you must be patient. And you mustn't talk to Father Leeman. He doesn't believe what we believe."

"I don't know what I believe anymore."

"Sarah, now is not the time for a crisis of faith."

"Tell that to my heart—it believes what it wants. I cannot control it!"

"Go back to the beginning, Sarah. Do you believe that God made this beautiful Earth?"

"Of course I do, but—"

"Stay there, hold on to that."

"That is too . . . too simple, Eric. The church, the church is so much more complicated than that. It has become like . . . like a market! And I cannot always be a modest wife, a silent wife; I am not always . . . charming and accepting."

"You're a good wife. That's enough. And I am doing the best I can to battle—"

"Sometimes, I wish I were a man. Then I would have my say! I would fight—"

"Sarah . . ." I felt father's hand tighten on mine. Mother hushed after that.

And as we were sitting in our cottage singing, mother was making supper over the fire pit. After a time, she stopped chopping, but we were singing and hardly noticed the smell of burning paper till it reached our noses. Father stood and went to her and saw that she was ripping pages from our precious Bible and throwing them under our cooking supper. I thought he would rage at her for it, but he just held her two hands in his one, and took the Good Book away from her.

I wish I could see the sea closing behind us and moving us toward father, but it's as if the entire world were water. Anywhere one looks, water. I stare at it, becoming blind with its sameness.

It is a long time before the baron sends a sailor for mother again. She is ill, curled into herself on the back deck, sitting with Thomas and Peter and Jed. The fellows try to stand, to stop the sailor from taking her, but before they can even rise, he whistles, and other brutes come running. There is no fight, and mother goes with the sailors. I wait for her as close as possible to the rich people's side where the sailors have taken her. I sit on the deck by the middle stairwell, watching like a falcon. A falcon can kill another bird in the air; I have seen it.

With my piercing eye, I try to look through the walls of the ship. I can see through the opening in the captain's room; he is up there, his head bent over his desk. Below his room are rooms like ours, I think. If the ship is equally shaped on both sides, then the rich folk have a sleeping room, and a storage room with a metal hearth that is also used as an eating room, though I know there are not as many of them who crowd together like pigs to eat and sleep. I have never seen the baron on the decks, so some of the rich folk hide away, perhaps behind the captain's room, and below. The sailors sleep in the middle of the ship, underneath the trapdoor just in front of me. I know all of them down to the pimples on their ugly noses.

If the ship is shaped the same front and rear, where does the baron sleep? Does he harm mother in front of everyone? The thought makes my stomach sour. No, I think, the baron must have a private room; and so the ship is not equally shaped. Where is his room, then? To the left of the stairs, or to the right? And where is Ethan? The ship is not very wide after all—I can cross the middle with a few giant steps—so the rooms can't be far from each other. That is why Ethan can hear everything. I wonder if there is some other way from the middle of the ship to get to their rooms, underneath perhaps. Or up, over, and then down, on the many rope ladders that lace the upper part of the ship like spiderwebs.

I follow each rope with my eyes, those that hang from the sails and the nets of ladders. Most of the ladders join from the top of the center pole to the outside railings of the ship. I have climbed ladders of tied ropes into apple trees before, and I wonder if it's the same thing. But sailors scrabble all over them like nut rats. It would be impossible to climb them in daylight without getting caught.

I try to hear past the shouts of the people and the whistles of the sailors and the sound of the sea for a note of mother's voice. I wish to know if he is harming her, if he makes her cry out. When I asked her about bedding down, she just looked at me in horror and would not answer. Her look repeats in my head as I wait for her, and I can almost feel her pain inside me. My eyes burn with tears at the thought of mother hurting.

The fellows come to me as I wait for her and they settle round me like bees on a rind. Margaret, too, comes—she's been hanging round me often; she misses her girls, she says. Like us, she came to look for her husband, Philip, but she left her four children, three girls and a boy, at home with their grandma. Both my grandmas died. Father Leeman did an extreme unction for each of them as they died, so their souls are safe in Heaven. I could not bear the thought of mother leaving me anywhere.

I see mother coming, a sailor at her side. He gives her a little shove toward me. "Git on wid ye, ye whore," he says, and she turns and growls and holds her fists up at him. He laughs and walks away from her, and my stomach jumps like a bonfire.

I run to her and hug her. Her hair falls down round her shoulders in sloppy waves; she is thinner than ever. When I grip her, she winces. I check her face and neck for bruises—there are none. The fellows don't look at her, but stare at the ground waiting for her to come to them. I breathe in her sweaty smell and kiss her hands. She holds me by the shoulders and looks into my eyes.

"Come, Lily," she says, and walks away from the fellows.

"But Thomas and Jed—"

"Leave them." She walks me to the back of the ship where other folks sit, the ones who have formed friendships separate from us— the women and the other men on the ship. "Lily," mother says, "we must stick together, you and I."

"We are together, mother."

"I mean always, always, stay together. Never leave my side."

"Never, of course, never."

"The baron is talking to one of the men, that is certain, but I don't know which one. He came very close to telling me who it is. He knows things I have told them. Certain private things. I cannot trust them. I can only trust you."

The men have been surrounding mother, to protect her, they say, but easily she was taken from them. I do not blame her for not believing in their help. "I will stay with you forever, mother."

"We can speak to them, but not about anything important—the

way we used to do with our neighbors about Frere Lanther. Yes, Lily?"

"Yes, of course, mother." At her mention of Frere Lanther, I feel the ache of all the pain I caused mother by talking about him. My fault, my fault. It is impossible to keep one's mouth shut on such a small ship. But I will try.

Like Hessian flies on grains of wheat, the neighbors started to pass by our cottage when we began to miss fairs and festivals after Frere Lanther came.

I was surprised to see Maister McGee the elder at our door. We always ate his fried sweet dough at festival. He was cook for the baron's estate, and never much came our way, except to sit in Father Leeman's church of a Sunday with Ralph the younger and listen to mass.

Maister McGee the elder looked stout in our little cottage as he held his cap and talked to mother. "You didn't come for the sweets as usual, mistress. I thought maybe there was a death in the family."

"Ah, Maister McGee, yes, Lily was very sick, and we didn't want her to catch her death."

"She recovers fast, eh?" he said, glancing at me. "The young folks, they've their strength." His eyes were moving all round our cottage, as though he were looking for something special.

"Yes, it's a blessing straight from Our Lord," mother said, trying to still his eyes, I think, with hers. "Would you like a sip of barley water, Maister McGee?"

"Why, I'd like that, mistress. Thank you."

As mother began scooping up the water, another knock came on our door. I ran to it; it was Mistress Cupperton, the baron's seamstress, who traded mother's good linen on market days for wool. Her mouth opened and closed like a fish's when she saw Maister McGee the elder, and then she smiled at him and mother.

"Fancy I should see you here, Ralph."

"Martha."

To mother, she said, "We was worried about you, Sarah, not being there to celebrate the Corpus Christi. We guessed it was something bad, and we'd come have a look at you."

"I'm fine, Mistress Cupperton. Lily was rather sick, was all. Would you like to stay for barley water?"

"Surely I will, thank you."

As mother was pulling our wood scoops from the shelf, another knock sounded at the door. "We might as well leave it open," mother said as she answered it. It was Maister Season, the fellow who bartered our goat cheese and eggs for the baron's kitchen.

"Sarah! You're alive!" He was tall with thin black hair through which I could see his shiny scalp when he bent down over our goods at market. "Ho ho, Ralph, and Mistress Cupperton, 'magine you bein' here!"

Mother told him about me being sick, and asked him to stay for water. I had no sense that these folks were so friendly with mother. None of them had ever stepped into our cottage before. I looked up at mother, and could see the kind of smile on her face that she wore for people she didn't much like. She kept glancing out of the shutter, too, and I thought maybe she was looking for father.

I excused myself and ran round the back of the cottage to the stable, where father was working with Frere Lanther over papers and books. I told him what was happening inside.

Father stood quickly. "As I feared, Frere Lanther," he whispered.

"They are just curious. They will go off again," Frere Lanther said.

Father moved toward the door, but not enough to be heard from the cottage. "Strange how they are the baron's people."

"Aren't you all?"

"Not so directly as these."

"And you think they have come from the baron?"

"Well, yes. I do."

"Lily, what did your mother tell them, as reason your family hasn't been at festivals?"

"She said I was sick. She didn't want me to catch my death."

Frere Lanther turned to father. "Your wife is very capable." Father nodded. "Let's be patient and stay here. We have a long way to go, Eric. This is not the last time this will happen, you know. Come, sit beside me once again, and let us work." Father did not move toward him, but listened at the door. "Come, Eric, your wife is very capable. Trust her," Frere Lanther said gently. Slowly, father returned to the table.

When I got back to the cottage, more folks had gathered, sitting and standing, all talking and laughing as though they'd brought an Easter fest to mother. She stood in the middle, conducting the activity as if she herself were choirmaster.

SEVEN

The rich are down to the last of the pig, salted or live. We have eaten the dregs, the bones and rind in our soup, but the rest has gone to the rich and the sailors. I do not know what they will eat when no pig flesh is left.

We have only a beet, and it has grown stringy roots in the dark.

A steady, chill wind mixes with the sun, a wintery autumn feel comes to the air, rains come and go. Equinox has long passed. I have seen the humps and backs and heads of many large swimming animals, but I've not seen a whale.

The baron's men have come for mother every day for several days. She goes from me to the baron and back to me. When she returns, she is confused; she doesn't know what to think of all he tells her, she says.

He talks about God, she says. He shows her paintings, of the Virgin Mary, and of Christ.

"They are the most glorious images, Lily, with gold round their edges, and the Virgin so beautiful, Christ suffering so. They are this big," she says, holding out her arms to show me.

It sounds as if she is speaking with admiration for the baron.

"He talks about the Pope, and about the bishops and cardinals. He too doesn't believe in Indulgences, he says. They make him pay dearly." Mother shakes her head. "He knows Frere Lanther's work. He has read the pamphlets. He says he does not wish to befriend us, but that he also believes that the church has gone to the Devil's Hell."

I feel I am just a faraway listener, like mother is talking to herself. I cannot tell what she thinks of the baron, but the hatred has disappeared from her voice.

She covers her face with her hands. "Oh, I don't know what to think, Lily. I don't see why he is telling me all this."

"He is a bad man, mother. He took away father. He wanted to take our land, don't you remember?"

"Why, yes, of course, Lily! He is hateful. He says he did not want to take the land, but he wanted us on the ship, and he thought that would be a way—oh!" She begins to cry, tired weeping sounds. We are on our bed, lying on our backs, looking at the ceiling. I roll over to her and hold her head as she cries. "I don't know what he wants with me, Lily. I don't know! When I ask a question, he tells me to shut my trap."

"Mother, mother, shhh. I will help you, I know how. I'll find his son, and he'll tell us what to do. He'll help us, I know it."

"His son—his son is locked in the cooking room—he keeps him there for safety, he says. Oh, this man, he is a lunatic, a fiend, a horrid monster!"

She cries and cries, no longer trying to hide her tears or words from the worn-out folks in the room.

I work on my butterfly quilt and listen to talk.

"How long they expect us to live like this?"

I have one wing done, all colors of the prism, each color folded into the other so one can't tell beginning or end.

"How long's it been, anyway? Two months? Three?"

I have finished the head and the thin, oval body.

"'Cordin' to my calculings, it's been two months and 'bout a week."

Today, I start on the last wing. Butterflies see the world through their feelers, but this one has no feelers. It is a blind butterfly.

I smell him, feel him before I see him. A change in the day like clouds covering the sun. I'm sitting on the middle stairs between Margaret and Jed, working on my quilt, when I sense him. The baron. He stands beside the captain's room, looking over at our side. The sailors and the other folk, rich and poor, stand fixed when they see him suddenly there. They watch him.

He is a very tall man, a Goliath, it seems, with enormous shoulders. His face is striking, with deep circles round his huge black eyes. He wears a beard but no hat over his black hair. I cannot stop staring at him. I have never seen him up close.

He seems to move very slowly, like a dark animal hunting in the shadows with its eyes only. I know that he is looking for mother, and that she is sleeping below. I cannot imagine speaking to this man, this beast that silences all my thoughts. I see him looking over at me, and I freeze. Then I notice it is not at me that he is looking, but at Jed. Maybe I am mistaken, but I feel something pass between them.

The baron strides across to our side and down into our rooms. He comes out with mother, holding her by her arm. She has been sleeping, and her hair is all fallen about her shoulders. It is lank and greasy. Because of his size, he seems to carry her by the arm, though

I see he is barely touching her elbow. He disappears with her down into his side.

I stare at the place where they were. I feel as though he has just eaten her alive.

She does not come back to me this time. I sit waiting on the freezing deck in all my shawls, my knees tucked into my chest, my arms clutched round them, holding on to myself. There is no breakfast, no lunch, no dinner. No mother. Rats run about the ship and sailors run after them. I cannot rouse myself from the ground.

Night comes; the sailors do not bother to chase me downstairs as they retire to bed. For all my exhaustion, a restlessness comes upon me, raising up my head. I find myself following the rope ladders with my eyes, to discover a way to climb over to the rich side without being noticed by the sailors who roam the ship at night. I need to save mother from the baron. I stand and stretch out my stiff body. I check to make sure no one is looking as I step to a rope ladder, and begin to climb it.

On the net of it, I wobble back and forth as I pull myself up slowly. The water seems entirely too near, the ground gone. The higher I go, the stronger the wind whips into me. My feet slip on the cold ropes and I cling for my life. Bobbing back and forth, I creep over toward the rich side. I can hear snoring—of a sailor asleep in the bird's nest way at the top of the ship. I am freezing so high up in the blowing wind, freezing and frightened I will fall and smash my skull and never see the New World or father again. I wonder what I am doing; it feels like I am following myself.

When I am high enough, I look down and can see their side, down their stairs even, but there is no way for me to reach the stairwell from the ladder. I must climb down and get there another way. But I cannot move. That is when I see Ethan.

He sneaks up from the stairs in his cloak and creeps close to the wall, moving quickly toward our side. I know he is coming to look for me. I make a hissing sound, to alert him without waking the sleeping sailor above me. He stops. I hiss again, and he looks up and sees me. I hold on ridiculously to the rocking ladder. I will fall backwards into the sea and drown. Ethan stares at me for a moment, then begins to climb the ladder toward me.

He reaches me and stands beside me. My teeth are chattering.

"Lily, what are you doing here?"

"La, la, la," but I cannot get real words out.

He crawls over and puts his arm round me. I cannot ask him what he's doing, with the ladder bouncing all round in the wind, with our weight; I cannot speak, so I hope he hurries.

"All right, Lily, take a step down. Good, and another." With his words, he guides me down the ladder. When we reach the bottom, he takes off his cloak and puts it over my shoulders.

"You were looking for me," he says.

I nod. "Nnn mmmy mmmy . . ."

"I finally broke the lock free, Lily, I waited till all were asleep—"

"Mmmy mmmm . . ."

"You are freezing," he says. "Come with me. It's warm in my room." He grabs my hand and pulls me toward the door to his side. My curiosity about their side has been sinful, but now that I am to discover what it looks like, I'm terribly frightened. I hesitate, but he pulls me along. At any moment, I expect to be stopped, by a sailor, or his father—

The steps are the same as those on our side. They lead down to a quiet hall with doors at the end. We walk slowly. I hear a bump inside one of the rooms. We stop and listen. Someone breathes behind a door, sleep breath, it sounds like. Ethan silently opens a door on the left. Light pours out, and for a moment I cannot see. He pushes me in quickly and closes the door after us.

Entering his kitchen corner is like walking into church. Lamps are lit about. I have been used to living in darkness. He is not the kind of prisoner I imagined. On the wall hangs a glorious painting of the Adoration of the Magi the way it is in Black Mary's book. It looks like it was painted with real gold. On another wall is the Death of the Virgin, with unicorns and huge flowers dancing about its edges. I have never seen real paintings. I stare at them till Ethan pulls me to the couch, a red velvet one with a white pillow and blanket upon it. I touch the velvet. It feels like rabbit fur, so soft. He hands me the blanket to put over the cloak I wear of his, but I still shiver.

"Now," he starts in a whisper. He sits in a chair in front of me. I look at his face, his gentle face. "Now that you are here, I don't know what to say." When I look at him, I have the sense of warm water filling me.

"My mother, where is she?" I whisper.

He shakes his head. "Father has her. Father, I don't know what's happened to him. I think . . . I think he's in love with her. It's horrible!"

I cannot imagine love with a rich baron. Only father and mother—

"He's keeping her in his room. I can't understand why he is doing this."

"But he hurts her. How can he love her?"

"He's changed so much, he's so cruel now. He was never so cruel when Mother was here." Ethan gets up and listens at the door. "I don't trust him—he will have his spies here, his ship rats, if I'm not careful. He's horrible—"

"Ethan, tell me where my mother is so we can help her."

"My mother made him good. And now, now, he's dangerous." Ethan's voice is becoming louder, and I am afraid the baron and his beastly sailors will come any minute if he is not quiet. "He's a liar. I hear him speaking to your mother, talking about Lanther and your people's beliefs—it's all rot! The only reason he thinks your people are right is because he doesn't want the Pope to take all his money."

"Mother told me of that."

"Your poor mother. Father's room is right next door, and I can hear them together and he grunts with pleasure while she makes no sound."

It makes me sick to hear such a thing.

"I hear her crying after, and he comforts her, the lout, even though he's the one making her cry! And my own mother, not even a year . . . We have to stop him—" Ethan yells.

An earsplitting crack of wood fills the room and an enormous crash throws me from the couch to the floor. The lamps blow out. I scramble to rise, and am thrown over again. I hear shouts and feel the boy pull me to my feet and out of the room, up the stairs and outside, where people are beginning to run in the dark. We hear shouting from above. "Land! Land! Land ho!" The sailor in the bird's nest is shouting over and over as he clambers down the ropes. Everyone pours from the insides of the ship onto its falling decks in a mad race.

We have crashed into the New World.

PART TWO

EIGHT

The ship breaks against the rocks, falling sideways into the waves, a murdered bird, monstrous plumes of water crashing it, pulling it apart board by board, water in my mouth, nose, salt sea down my throat, drowning, choking me. "Help!" Waves roiling, dark, the night swallowing us, the sea taking mother away, away. "Help!"

Wood under my hands, a piece of ship.

"Mother, where are you?"

Sailors shove me from the water, throwing me and others and barrels and boxes, one to another up a line that reaches to the shore.

"Over 'ere, goddamn rot."

"Pass it, pass it, pass it—"

"Fukkin' horseshit, who was the blasted—"

"Help, help me! Mother, help me!"

I am thrown wet in the dark onto the hard, cold rocks. I scramble round and fall between them, slipping on the slime that catches the wood bottoms of my shoes.

"Roger, what's wrong with you?"

"My God, I'm down, my leg is broken."

"Drowning, I'm drowning."

My kirtle is heavy, soaked, my ears full of the shouts of sailors, the screams of women, the sounds of people vomiting against the waves of the outraged sea.

I am without my mother. I wail for her.

She was with the baron on the ship before we crashed. I was with the boy. "Ethan!" Where is he?

A tall man stands in the sea, hollering and waving his arms at sailors who fish out people and goods from the rough waters. The tall man is the baron, but I do not see mother. Did the sea suck her in with its long tail? Did she fall between two rocks, down, to the other end of the Earth? Will I never see her again?

In great and awful heaves, I spit up salt water.

I kick off my shoes in the cold night and crawl over bodies upon the slimy rocks with my hands and knees, rough pebbles digging into my flesh. Away from the loud sea, I reach tall leaves like grasses and stand exhausted amongst them. Shadows move on the rocks, up to the grasses in the night. I feel creatures creeping behind me and fear a dog's-head man will snuffle up and eat me. They say dog's-head people live in the New World. New World.

I am a bedraggled butterfly caught, wings too heavy with sea to move. I collapse onto the grasses, and hear the thumps of bodies falling down all round me.

Dog's-head men come with their knives and fire to burn and eat me. They run all about, howling like madmen, like monsters. The New World is filled with monsters and they're going to boil and eat me, monsters, eating my legs, eating. I feel them, they've got me, they're clutching me and covering my face with their hot breath and they know my name, they are calling me, and I am too frightened to open my eyes, to see their sharp, white teeth. I cry out and hit them as hard as I can, hit and kick them, to get them away from me before they kill and eat me—

"Lily! Lily, stop it!"

A woman heads the pack; she grabs me tight with her knife-claws and I cannot get loose. I hear her, her voice familiar, her voice—

I open my eyes and do not see a dog's head, but mother's above me, holding my arms tight, a light gray sky behind her.

"Lily, it's me," she says gently. She pulls me to her and I bury my face in her neck, smelling the sea salt and her sweat. "Lily, I thought, oh, I thought the sea—I found your shoes amongst the rocks in the night, and I thought the sea had taken you."

"And I thought you'd fallen to the other side of the Earth, mother." I hug her as hard as I can, feeling the wet shawl that covers her thin shoulders. She takes my arms and pushes me back to look into my face; I stare at her dark green eyes, brown eyebrows, sickly cheeks, blue lips. With one finger, she cleans the sleep from the corners of my eyes. To look at her, I feel as though I am drinking the fresh water my mouth aches for.

"You are saved, Lily."

"The ship?"

"Gone," she says.

I look into her sad eyes. Though I have hated it, I cannot imagine the ship gone. I struggle to sit; mother helps me to stand. As if the sea has drained, down at the shore are many more rocks than I remember from the night before, and wet, foresty weeds, shells of sea animals, white and gray birds. Up on the dry rocks, and in the grasses all round me, folks sleep curled up into themselves, moaning, or they watch the land drink the sea. Broken chairs and hogsheads and trunks clutter the rocks. No ship. Nothing to take us back to Myrthyr, no place to go if the dog's-head people come to eat us. I shiver in the chilly morning and move closer to mother, drawing her arm about me.

The sailormen become industrious. Cutting with knives and swords through the tough grasses, they try to make a path to the flaming red trees which fringe the dense wood beyond. I have never seen such a frightening forest before, dark and towering, wide and endless.

Several sailors make fires in the rocks on the shore. They light one for us, and we stay by it, mother and me and Thomas and all the sick, poor folk from the ship who are still alive. We feed the fire with the smooth wood we find in the dry rocks nearby, barkless, washed-clean wood. The rich folk have their fire in the rocks just past us. Gathered before it, some of the people retch with empty bellies, some lie in the grasses, just like our sick folk, while others tend to them.

A few sailors bury a small heap of purplish dead folk in the tall grasses, while one of our fellows gives last rites, words of God to pass them through to His Kingdom. Maister Grey was purplish white when he died, as were my grandmas and all the other dead folks I've seen. I shiver in the cold air and turn away.

Everything we had was eaten by the hungry sea. Our pamphlets that Frere Lanther printed by hand, our trunk with mother's knitting, my quilt that I was making for father. Only the baron saved some things, which are scattered about the shore or in a pile near the rich folks. Ethan, I think, is afraid to move, for he sits beside his shivery grandmother on a stone by their fire. The baron has begun storming about, hollering at the captain and the few sailors who are on the ground, looking at the crinkled, torn charts they rescued from the ship.

"You're going to find a way, goddamnit, if it's the last bloody thing you do. This is all your fault!" the baron shouts at the captain in his deep, furious voice. His shouts hang in the air like animal bellows.

The captain replies with something I cannot hear.

The baron stands over him. "You're the fukking mariner responsible for all this and you will pay! I want you to build me another ship and speed me away from here. This trip has already taken far too long and I am sick of it! Bring me to the gold as you promised!"

The sailors sit on their heels and fold their arms. The captain stands slowly and points a finger at the baron, saying, "I promised ye nothing, sir, if ye remember correctly. I brought ye where ye wanted to go. The responsibility of this ship lies with no one but ye, sir. And I have no capabilities of building another ship. With what pitch, sir, what tools, nails, planks . . . ?"

"Where in the pissing bloody Hell is the fukking gold, the fukking savages, the fukking first shipload of protesters? You said you would take me to them. What am I going to tell—" The baron stops shouting suddenly and looks round at us. He pushes back his hair. He looks at the captain. "Goddamnit all to Hell!" he roars, and I hear the echo of that curse against the shore and in the grasses, as though the baron wishes to shake up God and the New World with his bitterness. Along the rocks and in his pile lie shattered paintings, trunks, a broken-legged couch, hogsheads, a chair. The baron storms away from the captain and climbs amongst his things, touching them and moaning and shouting and stamping like a wild bull.

"He's bedeviled," Thomas says.

"We're all bedeviled," Peter says.

I see mother looking at them—and at the baron. "He was going to leave us here like he did with Eric. Now he must stay," she says.

The day wears slowly, and inside me I still feel the movement of the ship in my legs, the back-and-forth of it. I walk away from the fire where we have roasted and eaten several stringy white birds and some fish that the fellows caught. I listen to the New World. Spirits and saints, Angels and the Lord hide silent under every odd stone, inside every strange shell. I must remind myself that God made this land as He made all others, as He made man himself. It is unfamiliar, but it is His. I say this to myself with words, yet I do not believe it with my heart. With the air full of piercing bird cries, savage animal howls, fantasic trees, and the slapping sea, it is very difficult to believe. My head is too thick with stories of the Devil and exotic lands and all the man-eating monsters who walk the Earth to keep God so close to my heart, as close as Frere Lanther says I need Him. Frere Lanther—I cannot hear his words so clearly now.

I shut my eyes and think about our journey, how I had not known where we would arrive, nor what it would look like, nor who would be here. And now I am here, and I know the overgrowth of smelly dark green waterweeds and the dry, gray rocks with white lines in them and the tall grasses that swish in the cold breeze like horses' tails. I know the emptiness of no one but beasts to welcome us.

In the mighty wall of trees just behind me, I feel, lies another

New World, vast as the very sea itself. A world completely unknown and full of evil mystery that twists like the thick vines up the huge round trunks of trees whose names I do not know. They are nothing like the pines in my woodland, nor the simple, small-leafed oaks, nor the gentle walnuts. They are too grand and fearsome, fed by some horrible power. In the darkness of their branches and leaves, they hold too much unknown.

I open my eyes quickly and look to the gray expanse from whence we came, wishing I could see Myrthyr, if just for a moment. Folks huddle in clusters along the shore. Mother sits with her hands warming at the fire, and Thomas breaks pieces of wood. Farther along, past the gatherings of folks, a lump of rocks curves out and back into the sea like a long nose. As I follow its shape with my eyes, I see something on it start to move. I try to tell myself that it is one of God's creatures, but that does not make me fear it less. It crawls about on four legs, this small monster, and then on two, two like a man—and then I see it is the boy. He is crawling about looking for something very intently.

I walk along the edge of the grasses round the people, past mother and our folks, past the rich and the captain and the men working till I reach the land that curves out into the sea where the boy is catching and throwing what look like giant spidery things into a cloth. I go down to the water, then crawl toward him along the rocks, slipping and sliding on the wetness.

"What have you found?" I cry out.

He looks up and smiles and waves. A filthy blanket is tied about his shoulders to keep him warm, and his clothes are as stained and torn as my own. He catches another spidery thing and tosses it in. Others try to escape when he opens the cloth.

"Father has ordered me to make myself useful. I'm catching crabs," he says.

"Like the ones in the sky?" I have never seen creatures so ugly as these. They do not look like the Cancer crab I imagined, the one father showed me in the stars.

"Crabs, crabs. For eating. They are quite good. Haven't you ever eaten them?" He holds one up. Its pointy, hard legs wave at me, and I think it looks too foul to eat, though I am always hungry and will eat nearly anything. He shows me how to catch the deep blue creatures with their many legs scuttling about. How to grab them from behind and throw them into the cloth quickly, before their sharp grips pinch a finger.

"Aren't they too hard to eat?" I ask.

"That is only their outside. Their inside is soft, like eating a nut. I don't know how to cook them, but I will give them to the cook and he will know. We used to eat these when we went seaside every summer."

I look at him as he speaks, at the slight bit of hair growing above his lip, at the black fringe of lash on his eyes, at his bony hands. It is the first time I have really looked at him, in daylight, without fear. He is a bit taller than me and breathes and speaks like me. I do not know if it is true that boys are so different from girls.

When the cloth is full, he picks it up and carries it in front of himself as we clamber along the rocks, back to the shore. "The sailors, you know, and the captain, they are as thick as thieves, the lot of them," he turns and says, smiling. It is not a smile of joy. "I do not think they will help Father find his gold."

I don't know what to say because the baron's plans with his minions are a secret to us. And though we are no longer on the ship, I don't feel that any of us are free of him.

Ethan laughs harshly. "Father thought it would be easy. But he has lost more than he has gained."

"You don't believe your father will force his men to make a ship?"

"How, Lily? The captain's right. He hasn't the tools, the way to make a ship."

Without a ship, we are trapped on this world, so far from anyone or anything we know. I feel suddenly that I cannot breathe.

"What will we do with no means to travel away from here, Ethan?"

"I think the only choice is to go inland." He raises his arm like King Harry's fighting men. "To explore!"

I begin to sweat in the chilly air. I stop walking to catch my breath. Go into the strange and wild forest with no way to escape if the savages who live on this land come to eat us? We could be killed before we found father!

"But the savages—the men with dog's heads—the wild beasts with long teeth that tear out your throat?"

Ethan calls as he scrambles ahead: "What are you talking about, Lily?"

"You know, the stories . . ." I slip over the rocks toward him.

"Widows' talk and rubbish. I don't believe you believe that rot." We reach the shore, and he stops. I catch up, breathing hard. "Lily, just think. At least we won't be on a ship. We'll be able to walk round and find new things. Maybe we'll even find gold from the savages, and maybe you'll get some and you can go back to England and buy fifty cows—"

"How will we get back to England with no ship?"

"When you have gold, you can pay people to do anything," he says excitedly. "Look at all these trees. You could pay the savages to build you a ship from them. That's what the Spaniards did in Spaniola, they used savages!"

I look round to see the savages that would build me a ship so I could go back to England and buy fifty cows with their gold. It hardly seems possible. But for a moment, I dream with Ethan. I dream of all the milk from the cows to make curdled cheese and butter to melt on my fresh baked—oh, the pain in my stomach! And the fear.

"Let's not talk of it, Ethan."

He laughs and turns. We walk up along the grasses to his folks. "I will come and get you when the crabs are cooked," he says. I look round at the rich folk as he speaks and they do not look so rich suddenly. The ladies' kirtles are dirty and torn, the mens' doublets and hose ripped; their faces pale, hair knotted.

Hungry as I feel, I do not think I can bring myself to eat crabs amongst these people.

Mother is not well, so I sit by her side. We sit with our feet toward the fire, and I hold her cold hand. I think about what Ethan said, about the dog's-head people being widows' talk. Widows' talk is always filled with rumor, but I feel the stories are true.

"Mother, what do you think of the stories of men with dog's heads? You know, the ones Mistress Knapp and the folks in Myrthyr used to tell us?"

"Men with dog's heads, Lily?"

"Remember? When we were leaving, they came and told us all the stories about Sir Mandeville, how he said there were men with dog's heads in the New World. Do you believe it, mother?"

"No, Lily, I don't," she says. She rubs a finger along her teeth and gums; they have been bleeding and hurting her badly. The pink part is no longer pink, but dark red, almost black. Some of Peter's teeth fell out in the night, and she is afraid of this happening to her. I am also afraid. With no teeth, she will not be able to eat, and will waste to death like some of the other men and women. "That's just people talking, Lily. Trying to make you scared because they are scared."

"But I do feel scared, don't you, mother?" It is not just the rumors which frighten me. The vicious hunting birds which circle above, the enormous sea below the heavy sky, the wild animals which infest the land, and the very earth itself do not truly seem to be God's creations. I think perhaps the Devil has created this place.

Mother looks at my hand, strokes it. She pushes her fingers between mine and locks our hands together. "Of course I am afraid, Lily. But not of folks with dog's heads."

"Ethan says the stories are widows' talk. He says they're rubbish." If only I had a moment of that talk, sitting safe in Mistress Grey's kitchen, eating cobbler with her and the Marys.

"Well, Ethan is right," mother says.

We watch the fire crackle. I breathe on her hand to warm it. "What do you think will happen to us now, mother?"

She shakes her head slowly. "I cannot see the future, Lily." She squeezes her hand tighter round mine. I know that our thought is the same—that we will find father somewhere in this world and that he will save us and take us back to Myrthyr. Neither of us dare to speak this, but it is our only hope that there was sense to this pitiful journey.

"All right, grab an end, grab a sack, grab a chair leg, take what you can. We're moving out!" the captain hollers.

We've been eating fish and crabs and birds and grass. It is cold and gray; the sun does not shine in the New World, it seems. Some of the sailors prod us with heavy sticks till we struggle to our feet.

Along the cut path, the strongest men carry trunks and hogsheads. The weaker take wet and reeking sacks. Me and mother take either end of a broken wooden painting that shows the calm face of the Virgin Mary, which has remained whole. She looks upon baby Jesus, whose legs are splintered in half along with her arms. Mary's lips are frozen in a tiny smile. We walk in the middle of the great struggle of people through the shortened grasses into the dark and savage forest.

I stare at baby Jesus in the frail light as we walk. He started out as a little baby, then grew and became a man, the Son of God. He seems to burst from the painting as we pass under dark branches, under the unfamiliar trees that tower over me. As I watch He grows from a small baby into a child, then into a boy like Ethan. Before me, He becomes a real man with long curly hair and a beard. Wise, clear words fill His mind and leap from His tongue. He speaks to me. He speaks to me! "Once," He whispers, "once I was just like you. I could not lift my head to the world, could not look into my Father's branches and see the patterns of leaves there. Look round you, Lily. Everything you need and want is here. Just open your heart."

I gasp and look up from the painting, wondering if anyone heard. I feel more frightened than ever as I hear the caw of birds and the rustle of movement in the fallen leaves. A ball rises in my throat and I swallow it. "Did you hear Him, mother?" I whisper, but she does not turn.

"Oh, my God! It's them." A shout rises through the forest. One of the men at the front of the line, then others shout, "Mother o' God," and "Lord help us," and I hear the belches of retching. The line stops moving. The folks round us drop their things. We put the painting down and look at each other. Them? What do they mean?

Mother is the first to understand.

"Eric?" she says, her face puzzled. "Eric!" she screams. She runs forward, to where the men shout, with father's name on her lips. I run after her.

In the bed of leaves on the floor of the forest are the rotted bodies of human beings without heads.

I am sick to the bottom of my stomach.

The sailors lean over the bodies, talking.

"Them's the folks from the last sailin'. Lookit thar clothes."

"Lookee 'ere. How come thar's missin' thar 'ands an' feet, too?"

Their words make me sicker. I hear mother crying, and Margaret. Through the burning in my eyes, I cannot see if any of the bodies are father.

"Thar's been cut apart."

"Some animuls gotten to 'em."

"What a stink!"

"Shut your traps, all of you!" mother screams. She runs at the baron, who stands with his arms folded into himself. "You bloody bastard!" she screams at him. "You took Eric! You killed him! How many others did you take?" She begins to pound and scream at him. Birds fly low in the branches, screeching. The baron grabs mother and turns her round, putting his hand over her mouth and holding her head against his chest, her hands behind her back. I run to him, to protect her, to hurt him for what he did to father. I scream and kick him in the leg. He kicks me back, knocking me over.

"Get this fukking little peasant shitter out of my way," he roars at a sailor.

He holds mother while the sailor drags me by the throat to the back of the line. With my fingernails, I try to tear his hands off me. I kick at his legs and hit at him. I scream, "I'll kill you, I'll kill you," till he knocks me in the face. Everything goes very bright, like the white light of God pulling me up to Heaven.

NINE

Someone is pouring broth down my throat and it spills into my hair. I feel its heat on my scalp like mother's fingers soothing me at night. I open my eyes to see her, but it is Thomas who leans over me, a shell of hot liquid in his hand.

"Drink this, Lily," he says. "Wake and drink it." I open my mouth wider and feel the soreness in my gums. Thomas shakes his head. With my tongue, I touch the gap where one tooth is missing in the front. "Where you fell," Thomas says. Hot tears well in my chest, rise to my eyes. I feel like someone has stolen something from me. "Drink," he says.

"Is mother near?" I whisper, afraid to hear the answer. I am frightened the crazed baron has done something with her. Perhaps he has cut off her hands and feet. I begin to sob. Thomas pulls me to him awkwardly and holds me. His stench penetrates my nose, quieting me. I feel safer with his arms about me. "Where is everybody?" My heart is as sore as my mouth.

"Shhh, Lily. Mother's right over there." He wipes off my tears and points. I do not know if it is day or night, the forest is so dark. The trees are fat and close, but I see we are in a small clearing, with fires lit to make warmth. To the side of one tree ahead, I see mother. She is with the rich folk. The baron sits beside her and everyone is eating. Mother's face looks orange in the firelight. She is so thin, I am afraid she will disappear. She does not look up at the talking people, does not laugh when they do.

"He will not let her go?" I ask Thomas. His skin has become so wan, I can see the blue lines inside his head running from his ears into his eyes as he shakes his head no.

I drift as my head heals from its blow. I wake to see figures walking about, to eat from Thomas's shell, to make water and dung. Then I return to sleep.

When I begin to feel better, I see Ethan staring at me from behind a tree. It seems as though he has been watching me for a while, because his face brightens when he sees me looking at him. He comes and kneels beside me. He smells of fish rot and stink weed.

He touches my leg fleetingly. Looking at him, my insides fill with warmth. "Your face, it looks better today," he says.

I put my hand to my mouth where I lost my tooth. "What did it look like?"

He holds his fingers out far in front of his own face. "Big. Purple." I wish I could hide for looking so big and purple. "Like a ripe fruit." He laughs. I smile though I feel my mouth has grown large and ugly.

"They have found a river, Lily," he says. "It is wide and fresh, with huge fish the size of your arm."

A river. I have never seen a river. "Where?"

"A short way into the forest, not far. Would you like to go?"

I think about going into the forest and I think of the dead bodies. Our people. They lay rotting, headless, handless, footless. Without faces, we do not know who they are. Is father among them? I hope to our dear Lord he is not.

"Ethan, those men in the forest, the dead ones. Do you think father . . . my father was among them?"

Ethan's mouth opens and closes. His eyebrows furrow, he shakes his head. "I don't know, Lily. The protesters buried their fellows a day ago."

"What?" I push myself to sit up. "They buried them! Without me? Was mother there?"

He shakes his head no, and looks down. "Father will not let her out of his sight."

"Plague!" I cry out. I force myself to stand. Ethan gets to his feet with me. "How could they do that! My father—now I won't know!" I feel flushed as if with a sudden brain-fever. Ethan looks at me dully. They all knew I was searching for my father. Why did the fellows not wait? How can I live not knowing if my father is alive or dead? "I don't understand. How could you let them do that? How will I ever know?"

"I'm sorry, Lily."

I burst into tears and Ethan walks away quickly.

I ask Thomas and Peter and Jed what the bodies looked like. Were they tall, with long arms, with a patch of hair at their necks? Was it father, was it father? But they are vague and no one can answer. I go as near to mother as I can and shout at her.

"Mother, do you know? Did they bury father, was it father they buried?"

She is so weak and sad, she can barely raise her head.

"They buried them without us, mother. Do you know that?" I cannot bear the thought alone. I need her. I must rouse her to help me.

"Go'an, git otta 'ere!" a sailor shouts at me.

I see mother's eyes catch on me. "Is that true, Lily?" she cries. No one has told her. How can they be so cruel, to bury father without his family?

"Ye gonna lose anudder toot if'n ye don' git otta 'ere," the sailor growls.

"What should I do, mother?" We've journeyed so long and so far, and become so sick, only to have lost him. Or worse, to never know his Fate.

The sailor rises from his task.

"Ask the fellows, Lily. Do it now!"

The sailor comes close to me. I run away, back to where the fellows are sitting round the fire, sharpening sticks. They heard me.

"No, Lily, we're not digging them up," Jed says. "Makes no sense."

"Don't need to keep on worrying about them," Thomas says.

The burn in my stomach is almost as painful as my mouth. "Please! We have come so far. I beg of you, please!"

"They were gone near to the bone. You couldn't tell what was who, anyway," Jed says.

"Go ask Margaret," Peter says. "She was there watching, looking for her own man."

"Even she couldn't tell one man from the next," Jed says.

They cluck their tongues and shake their heads.

I feel that I would know my father by his bones, by the length of his arms and legs. "Where is Margaret?" I ask.

The men look round the trees; they shrug.

"Everyone wanders off. They come back when they get hungry enough," Thomas says.

I run away from them, my insides breaking like a crashing ship. They will not help me and I cannot wait for Margaret. I run, fast as I can, into the forest, alone.

I do not know exactly where the bodies are, since I do not remember coming to our camp. But I try, in the suddenly silent forest, to feel their spirits in the Earth, to let them draw me the way the spirits drew Mistress Fink to the edge of our village every Hallows' Eve.

As I try to follow paths made by our folk, pictures of the bodies come into my head. The flesh was mostly eaten off under the worn-out tunics. Nothing but bone left. And the smell of death.

Things often die: animals, birds, children, men, women, fields of grain. God calls back His every creation, and that always seemed natural to me. But now that it is father, it does not seem natural anymore. It seems a harsh God who would take such a kind person, my person, back into His arms.

In all the months father's been gone, I never really believed till I saw those bodies that God could take him away for good.

Father was mine. He is mine.

I walk slowly through the dark trees, trying to push out my spirit, which I imagine is blue as a clear sky, to push it out with all my heart in the direction of father, to meet him. If he is but a spirit, he would certainly look for me. I put my arms out to help his spirit come to mine more easily. I call to him softly, to help him hear me.

As I walk farther, deeper into the enormous forest, I try to listen among the quiet rattles in the leaves for father's call.

With all my spirit, I push to see his there.

I ask the Lord to help me see, to give me a hint, a show, a wisp of father's hair, the sound of his laughter, a touch of his finger—to lead me to him and let me see him just one more moment, just a moment, so I can ask him what to do, so I can tell him, "I love you, father."

But there is nothing.

I feel no spirit; I do not sense him at all.

Over and over, I kick a tree, kick and hit it, to hurt it as much as I can. I curse and insult this living thing of God, punching at it till my knuckles scrape red.

Sitting down, I lean my back against the trunk, fists and foot sore. I bury my head in my arms to shut out all of God's creations. I do not want to see anything He's made. It will only be taken from me.

Margaret does not come back to camp that night, nor the next day. The men who have gone looking for her return alone. I worry for her and cannot ask her about the bodies.

The baron skulks round mother like a drooling pig.

The sailors' hands are idle and they grumble. Our fellows too have little to occupy them. We listen to the captain and the baron shout at each other all morning. The captain threatens to take his men and leave us. The baron screams with his mighty lungs retributions enough to scare even the bravest of captains. The air in our camp feels thick—hard to breathe and dense.

Folks have made weavings of broken, leafy branches above the fires to keep off the rain. I stand under one and pull some meat from an animal that is drying by the flames. The flesh is chewy and smoky like pig jerk. A fellow snaps at me, "That ain't yer meat, now is it?"

Several men clean the skin of a large deer by tying its empty arms and legs to two trees. Mother naps on her side in a bed of leaves; women sit by her. The baron comes to look at her, touch her, and goes off hollering again.

I do not wish to talk with anyone. I nibble at the bitter nuts everyone is eating. Ethan climbs in the trees above me like a nut rat; I feel his eyes upon me, watching. He thinks I do not know he is there.

I cannot ignore the trees for very long. I walk about the forest near camp and examine those that grow in the New World. Some are tall and fat with yellowing leaves that are long, with wavy edges. From these trees, the bitter nuts like acorns come. Smaller trees with smooth bark and oval leaves are turning orange; trees with star-shaped leaves curl up their red edges. Among these trees are stands of fir, birch, pine. I am glad to see the familiar pines, so thick among their fellows.

I walk deeper into the forest to escape the harsh shouts of the men. Dreary daylight pushes through the heavy autumn flora. Ethan plays in the trees, climbing up and down them, hiding and following me. His presence comforts me, but finally I tire of his game. I look up the tree where he is and ask him to come down. He slides down a trunk noisily and lands, covered with dirty scratches.

"I would not make a good spy, I suppose," he says.

"Your grace does not exactly equal that of a cat."

"Are you still angry?"

I shrug. I do not know what I am. I am a floaty being, I have no spirit, no soul. I am just a body. "No, not at you."

We continue to walk in the forest. He shows me nicked marks in the trees. "To guide us to the river. I made them with my knife," he says, pulling it from his sleeve and holding it up. The carved wood handle catches my eye. It is my quill knife, the one Frere Lanther gave me when we started this awful journey.

"Ethan! Where did you get that?"

"From Executioner, the sailor—"

"He stole it from me!"

"Do you want it back?" Ethan asks, disappointed.

The knife sits in his palm like a piece of home. I wish to just grasp it, to feel the moment the frere gave it to me. His promise that we would see each other again seems so far away. I feel that I am going to cry, but I do not wish to do so in front of Ethan. "Can I just hold it for a moment?" I ask. He hands it to me; it fits so comfortably in my palm, but it's too much of all the things that I want and miss— home, father, God. I return it to Ethan. "You keep it," I say.

He ties it into his sleeve and we walk on, following his marked trail. "Lily, did you—did you find your father yesterday?"

The day is so cold, I can see our breath as we walk. I feel mine, caught in my chest. "It was dreadful, Ethan."

"I'm sorry," he says.

I shake my head and tell him about trying to send out my spirit, about wanting to meet my spirit with my father's, and how nothing happened. It is a relief to talk.

"You mean, you did not feel your father's spirit at all?" Ethan asks.

"No."

"Not even a little flicker, the edge of a halo?"

I feel impatient at his question. "No, Ethan. Nothing. Nothing at all."

"Well, that's a good sign, Lily," he says.

"Good! How can it be good?"

"Well, perhaps his spirit is not free from his body."

I stop walking. That had occurred to me, but not so clearly.

"It is so hard to know," I say. "Sometimes, back in Myrthyr, when father was far afield, I could tell him in my mind that I missed him and he would come home early as though he'd heard me. Now my mind is cloudy with doubts, and I feel I cannot even hear myself."

"God has placed us on this New World for a reason, Lily. This is our destiny. Maybe it would be best if you had faith that you will see your father again."

"Frere Lanther says to be wary of false hopes."

"If you did not hear from your father's spirit yesterday, I don't believe he was amongst the dead."

Ethan's faith feels like a strong hand guiding me, pushing me past my doubt. The idea that father is presently using his spirit for the purpose of living and not to contact me is a joyful one. But like a night-brown sky threatening morning rain, my doubts hang constant over me.

"Do you think—truly think it could be so?" I ask.

"I do, Lily."

With an uneasy heart, I ask forgiveness of God for doubting Him. Ethan's words echo those of Frere Lanther: "Faith is the sword you must use to conquer doubt." The possibility of seeing father again makes the dull leaves which surround us glow bright red in the gray light of the day.

The river runs quickly over flat boulders which make it bubble and sing with white splashes. My blood begins to rush, to match the water's rapid time. "Where's the river going that it must run so fast?" I ask Ethan, laughing. I've never seen such a wide body of fresh water, though I've imagined the river Jordan and all the rivers from the Bible.

"I have followed it far, and it flows deep into the forest! Taste it, Lily. It's so delicious!" He kneels at the edge and scoops up a handful. It drips off his fingers into his mouth. I follow, scooping up the water in my hands and putting my lips to it. The water is freezing and sweet. I swish it over my tongue, over my sore mouth. It is like drinking laughter. I swallow as much as I can and throw some on my face. So cold and fresh and delightful.

"I've bathed in it," Ethan says. "The cold makes your head hurt. But after, you feel light as a leaf."

"I cannot imagine going in that water with my whole body, Ethan. How did you do it?" He grins. "I wish I could wash, but we do not have a bucket."

"I'll help you," he says. "I'll wash your back. Just take off your clothes and jump in!"

"I cannot take off my clothes in front of you!"

"Why not? They do it at the festivals. I have seen lots of naked people. There is no harm in it," he says.

It is true that people often took off their clothing at festivals, but that mostly happened late in the night, when they were in their cups and I'd already gone to bed. We have since forsaken festivals for such sinful, pagan behavior.

Yet I long to be clean. And cleanliness will bring me closer to God.

"But I will freeze to death," I say.

"You will not. Here, I'll wash too. We can help each other." He begins to untie his blanket. I have not seen many naked people, and do not remember seeing a whole naked boy before. I've never seen father naked, though I have seen mother and other girls. But girls are not the same as boys.

He has the blanket off and is removing his doublet, and I have not moved. I begin to unwrap one of my many shawls. As I remove them one by one, I feel colder and colder, but I ache to get clean. The more clothing Ethan takes off, the more curious I become about what he may look like underneath. He is not watching me undress, but is struggling with his buttons. I go slowly, so that I may see his nakedness first. I am not sure I wish myself revealed so.

In summer, men work in the fields in the hot sun with their upper bodies bared. Ethan's chest is smaller and much whiter than I remember theirs to be. I can see his every rib. His teats are brown, and so is his belly button. He sees me staring at him and folds his arms. "Come on, Lily, hurry up."

I unwrap more quickly, till I reach my kirtle, which is all of a piece. I cannot remember the last time I removed my kirtle. The smell of me is horrid. I do not look at him as I unwrap and peel the kirtle from myself like an old skin. I stand in my bloomers and look at the empty kirtle. I hear a splash, and see that Ethan has not waited for me.

"Ahhhh," he cries at the cold on his feet, "it's freezing." His bum is white as a rabbit's.

His cry does not make me want to go in, but I run to the edge in my bare feet and bloomers. Ethan hops the flat stones to the middle of the water and jumps in. His head disappears, then comes up. "AHHHHH!" he cries again. "Lily, come in, it's wondrous." He splashes about like a startled frog in the stream. "You just have to keep moving."

I run across the flat stones, feeling the splashes of water on my feet, freezing as balls of ice in a hailstorm.

"Don't dip!" Ethan shouts. "It's not deep. Just jump!"

And I do. I jump into the clear green water with my best scream, feeling all my skin rise. I find the bottom with my feet and hold on to the rocks. My hair is soaked, my bloomers stick to my body, and I shiver uncontrollably.

"Move!" Ethan shouts. "Keep moving!"

I jump up and down and feel his cold hands on my back. He has some tiny pebbles in his hand, and rubs my skin with them. It feels as though it is coming off in flakes like bark. I rub my body and hair all over with my hands; Ethan dunks down into the water, getting handfuls of the pebbles from the bottom of the river, which he uses to scrub me. The river pushes past us, carrying away pieces of my skin. We lean against the slimy, flat boulders to keep steady. He is laughing; I am laughing, freezing, laughing, clean again, finally.

At the water's edge, I wet and scrub at my filthy kirtle. Ethan helps me to wash it. I can see his privy. It looks similar to that of animals, only with less fur. "Stop looking at me," he says.

"I'm sorry, it's just . . . I've never really seen . . ." I laugh. I am shivering and laughing so badly, he laughs too.

"Well, I'm sure yours looks"—he shakes his head and smiles—"looks like a girl's."

"Right."

We twist and twist my kirtle to dry it; the water tumbles out; we hang it on a branch. He pulls on his hose and doublet. I put my shawls on and stand in my bloomers. Ethan throws his blanket round his shoulders and asks me if I would like to come under with him, "to keep warm," he says. I look at his skinny body and think no warmth could come from him.

"I'm fine here," I say.

"You're freezing. Here, come under," he says. He holds up an arm like a wing, and I move under it. We stand, watching the river hurry by to its destiny.

When we return to camp, it is quite empty. Everyone is out hunting, maybe, or—I look to the place where mother was, by the tree near their fire. She is not there. Ethan's father is surrounded by thin, sickly rich folk; they stand in a circle, listening to him talk. I do not see the captain, nor a single one of the striped-pants sailors. Looking round, I see that very few of our folks sit on our side of the camp. I do not see Thomas, nor Peter. Jed is standing in the circle with the baron, listening to his words. The baron is talking very angrily, with big waves of his arms, talking so quickly, I cannot understand what he is saying. Suddenly, I feel a flush of cold inside me.

"Where is everyone?" I ask Ethan, who stands by my side, seeing what I'm seeing.

"I don't know," he says. "I will ask—" he approaches a nearby man who is sitting at our fire, a man to whom I have never spoken. I follow. "Sir, where has everyone gone?" he asks the man, whose rheumy eyes and purplish lips indicate he does not have much life in him.

"They up and left us," the fellow says weakly. He points at me. "They took yer mother with 'em, girlie."

My heart seizes and falls.

"Couldn't wait fe you, couldn't wait fe me . . . ," the man trails on.

"What do you mean, they took my mother? Who took her, where

did they take her?" I ask him carefully, pushing away the feeling in my stomach like I'm tumbling to a very low place. Why did they take her without me? Falling, everything is falling and I must hold on.

"Who is 'they,' sir? Who has gone, exactly?" Ethan asks the man.

"The captain and the sailors and most of our fellas. Them sailors done took all the firearms, held 'em at the baron's head as they took yer mother, carryin' her, and marched off. Marched right out of here, they did. Only ones left is them richers and fellas like me, fellas can't walk."

"Marched which way? Where?" Ethan asks.

The man mumbles, "Which way? Which way? What way—we have no way here . . ."

"That way? That way?" Ethan turns and points, looking for the man to nod or shake his head, but the man has fallen into a kind of stupor, and won't say more. I feel the same as him—I can't, I can't imagine mother gone, same as father. They have taken everyone, everyone who is mine they have taken from me and there is nothing I can do and everything is falling and I am tired, so tired. My stomach churns and bitters rise in my throat. The Earth reels before me as I shiver and sweat through a sudden chill. I shouldn't have left her alone, should never have left her, should have watched her all day and not left her for a moment—

"Ethan," I croak, "help me."

"Wait here. Let me ask Father. Just wait!" he cries, sitting me down by the fire with the sick man.

I watch the flames dance up toward the sky like the Devil's tail and horns. There is evil in this place, it is all evil and no good. I feel only a coldness here, a cold, empty pit like a well, like the well behind Ralph McGee's cottage that his little sister fell into and never came out of. I feel the darkness of the Devil's well and I know I'll never get out of this evil place with its bad spirits. I wish Frere Lanther would come and give me his sound guidance. I wish I had the Bible to read, words to follow, stories to help me understand where mother went and why I was left behind. But there is no one now, no father, no mother, no Frere Lanther, no saints or Angels to protect me. I cannot hear God like Moses could in the wilderness, like Jesus in the desert. . . .

My eyes become heavy and I feel sleepy, like father is singing to me, singing me to sleep, old Sandman coming for me. I put my thumb into my mouth, right in the hole where my tooth was, and feel the warmth of my mouth spreading over my cold thumb, warming me as I sleep. I can smell the peach cobblers, all the cobblers in the world made by all the best cooks, made specially for me. . . .

"Lily, it's true, the captain has taken his men and your fellows. They went against Father, they put firearms to his head. They used them like bludgeons. I cannot believe it. What—Lily, are you all right?" He shakes me, and I start to feel the cold on my wet hair, hair clean and wet from the pretty river, pretty river. "Lily, come now, wake up, are you all right? Lily?"

"All right." He is so insistent. I didn't know he was so insistent or I wouldn't be his friend.

He grabs me by the hand and pulls me to my feet. "Father says they went that way, through the trees." He points in a direction I have never gone. "He says they have all the weapons. They've been stealing powder from the sealed hogshead since we arrived! They used their heavy sticks to smash open the trunk that held the firearm stores. One brute hit Grandmama across her back! They are very dangerous!"

He holds me so tightly by the arms that he hurts me, but I cannot say anything. I try to find words, biblical answers printed on my insides like illuminations, like pamphlets of knowledge.

"Your mother is with them. The captain took her from Father. Father is very upset. But he brought it upon himself!"

At the mention of mother, I know, suddenly, what to do. "We must go."

Ethan sets me loose and pushes his hair back from his forehead, grabbing it in such frantic clumps, I want to cry. "I—I cannot go, Lily. How can I leave them?"

I watch his eyes turn toward his family, then back to me. "I must find her," I say.

"You can't go alone. Stay with us. Father will help you." He glances at his father angrily. "No, I will help you. But I cannot leave him."

"I must go," I say, looking about me for something to take with me, something to eat or to protect me, a stick of fire, a sharp rock. I left her alone, now I am the one who must find her.

"Lily—"

I grab a torch from the flames and begin to run in the direction Ethan pointed out, away from the river, into the threatening branches. I hear him behind me, calling my name. I run deeper and deeper into the forest, following the trail of branches broken by the footsteps of the captain and the sailors and our fellows who carry mother. I run till I don't hear Ethan's pitiful cries anymore.

TEN

My kirtle is still wet from the river and the torch I hold sputters and flickers as I hurry through the thick trees. Cold and fear speed my feet as I try to close the time between when mother left and when I discovered her gone. On the path as I run, branches loom suddenly before my face. They pull at my hair and shawls. Roots rise up to trip me. Falling leaves hit my cheeks.

At every turn, I hear footsteps and wings flapping. I hear the breathing of fiery dragons with too-large wings flying close over the trees. The snickers of long-clawed satyrs and wrong-headed nymphs shudder through me. I think I see dog's-head men and the Devil slither through the far trees. They are red as embers, with pointy teeth and evil smiles that could take me over and make me one of them. They have the evil power to steal my good spirit through my breath, to disease me with their badness. He is an angry Devil, Lucifer, the Archangel who fell from God's good graces, tumbling straight down from Heaven into His black pit of Hell. I do not know how to fight such evil. Why did I not speak of this to Frere Lanther? The Marys never said what to do if I saw the Devil in the forest. Devils and imps and hellions and demons. I hurry faster.

Large animals run near.

I lower my eyelids so I do not see so much. I cannot remember why I left mother alone. If I had just stayed with her, we would still be together. Frere Lanther told me to protect her, and I did not. I didn't protect her on the ship when the baron took her, I didn't protect her from the cruel sailors. I pray no one has hurt her. Is this my punishment? To be left alone in this horrible, dark forest with the threat of evil at every turn? I should never have left her, I should never have left her, I am being punished for leaving my mother in the hands of bad men. This is God's sure retribution.

Must keep moving, must keep following the path of broken branches and chewed bones that lead the way to her.

I saw Jesus in the forest and He told me not to be afraid, to lift my head to the world, but I cannot do so without seeing the Prince of Darkness. Is that what Jesus intends me to see? Does He mean for me to have such a fright? I wish to call out for mother, to holler her name past all the dark spirits that live in this forest, but I daren't, for fear I will get the Devil's attention. Animals crawl and creep and skitter in every shadow, startling me.

I wish to run all day, but a stitch in my side halts me. I cannot catch my breath; sweat pours from my forehead. My feet are torn in my shoes and they ache. Must keep going.

I pray and think good thoughts as I walk quickly. Mother and the folks are ahead of me somewhere, yes, of course, I can imagine it. They are waiting just ahead. They are making a path through the New World, through God's green Earth that He made. Yes, yes, they are just ahead of me, look at them there, I can almost see them. I know they are there, I can smell them. They are just past me, leading the way, taking us away from the baron and toward father. They know the way to father, yes, they are old and wise, they know the way. The captain is leading them, taking them to a warm place where I will find them with food and drink. Mother has found father and we are together. We will go back to Myrthyr with lots of gold and buy fifty cows and be happy in the bright sunshine that warms the flowers so they smell good. I see her, I see him, there they are, I can almost touch them. We will go where the forests are small and the meadows are big and I can run in the grass freely.

I feel as though I've seen this patch of forest before, so many times before. These paths, these branches. I am moving my legs but getting nowhere. I begin to cry. Why didn't I stay by mother, why didn't I watch her all the time, every moment of the day and night? Why didn't she wait for me? Where was I? Off, away, playing in the river with Ethan. Ethan, who has also left me.

The air gets colder as the forest darkens. I hold one hand and then the other near the torch to warm them as I walk, but I cannot warm my cold toes.

My legs ache with exhaustion. I wish to stop, but I cannot. Mother is just ahead, waiting for me. I must make it up to her, I must keep going and make sure she is not hurt. I need to know that the sailors have not touched her wrong. Frere Lanther would never forgive me. God would be forever angry with me. Father would be very upset if I let anything happen to her. Oh, father, why did they take you away? I am without you, so alone, so tired and hungry and alone.

The misery in my tight belly makes me shake. I do not remember the last time I ate. I search the ground for food, with only my torch to cast light. As I walk, I pick up bones I find. Perhaps mother may have eaten from them. I put them in my mouth and suck the last marrow from their insides. If a whole pig appeared before me, I could eat every last morsel of him myself.

An evil red glows against trunks, movement catches in the corners of my eyes—a person? a two-headed monster?—but it is only an animal, a bird.

The trees look alike, trunks, branches, turning leaves, trunks, branches. I think I am going in a circle. Maybe I am going backwards and if I keep going, I will end up right back in the camp with Ethan.

Maybe I should never have left him.

Maybe I should turn round and go back to the camp where there is food and water and fire and blankets and people. And firearms with explosions that surprise. I wish I had a firearm to shoot and kill an animal to eat. I have never killed an animal myself. Father doesn't have a firearm. I do not know anyone who does.

At this moment in this forest in this New World, I do not know anyone at all.

With shaking hands, I stuff my mouth full of yellow leaves till I feel less pain in my stomach. Mother has always told me I should take care to not eat nature's poisons, but I do not have that care inside me now. I know I must rest or I will not live. I collect wood for a fire. On a dry patch under a tree, I throw twigs and sticks and light them with my torch and feed the fire till it is high. I take off my shoes and drop down next to the heat, putting my feet and hands as close to the flames as possible. The fire reminds me of baking bread and boiling soups. It reminds me of fancies with the women of Myrthyr. It reminds me of all the good things I left at home and feel I will never see again, all because I said I wanted to come to the New World. It was my idea to come, and now everyone is gone. Why have they all left me? Why did God take mother and father away? Why?

My wrists and ankles and bloody toes ache with pain. When the fire dies down and I am warm, I lift out a torch of thick wood, and start into the forest again.

A nut rat skitters about the trunk of a tree, his fluffy tail flickering back and forth as he chatters. He seems to be watching me as he climbs up and spirals down, watching me rest against a great stone. The men hunted such rats. They used sticks rubbed against the ground to make a pointed tip.

I quietly choose a stick from the underbrush and begin to scrape it against the rock, keeping my eyes upon the animal. His face is familiar, his eyes black and soft. I have eaten pigs, cows, rabbits, but none that I have killed myself. To plunge the pointed stick into this animal's little breast—I stop sharpening. My hunger squeezes me like a giant hand from within.

The nut rat sits on his haunches at the base of the tree, rubbing his little black paws together, scratching at his ears. I look up, high into the crowns of the trees, to try to see past them to the sky, deep into the sky where God's stars live. My torch does not shine so brightly.

When I look down, the nut rat is gone. I throw the stick away and move on.

I stumble through profound darkness and thin daylight till my face feels as though it has heavy weights hung upon it, pulling down my head, my neck, my whole body, pulling me down till I am lying upon the ground with wood for a pillow and my kirtle and shawls for a cover. Thirst and hunger make my mouth ache. My body feels flat as rolled-out dough.

In sleep, demons and monsters come out of the forest to take over a person's body, and the dog's-head people to snuffle in one's ears. I must stay awake, to keep watch. I close my eyes to rest them, but I do not sleep. I cannot help thinking about the dog's-head people who must be very bad to live in this dark place. Every shadow of the forest is filled with an evil that I must fight. I cannot sleep or the Devil would come inside me. I am so tired I cannot see. The forest seems to move before me, filled with creatures and horrible, wicked beings.

I feel like wailing for mother, but I hold my cries silent.

Questions repeat in my head as they have with every step of my search. Why has mother left me? Why did she not protest? Why didn't they leave me a sign? Why did they not wait for me in the forest? Hot tears of anger burn in my eyes. Why did they take father in the first place? Why didn't father fight them? Why didn't father listen to mother?

Suddenly, I sit up.

That was their argument that night, the night I spent alone in the woodlands in Myrthyr before they took father away. Mother knew that the baron's men were coming to take father, and she was trying to warn him, to make him hide and save his life.

A new question arises: Why didn't he listen?

I cover my face with my hands and sob. I do not see. I do not see how it all works, it does not make sense to me, the world. God does not make sense to me. Why would He take mother and father away from me this way? Why would He leave me alone in the forest to die, never to find food or comfort? Why is He punishing me so harshly? Yes, I left mother alone, but why was father taken from me in the first place? Why didn't he listen to mother when she warned him? I wish for God to speak to me, the way He did with Saul and Samuel, to tell me His plan so I do not think Him so cruel.

But it was cruel of Him to take father and mother, it is cruel, and I do not understand His cruelty. Frere Lanther has never explained this part of God to me. I remember from the Bible that God commanded His chosen ones to destroy whole villages. He told Abraham to kill his own son. How could He? I do not understand His violent ways.

"God," I cry out, and my own voice frightens me.

Mother burned pages of the Bible. She threw the Holy Scriptures into the sea. God punished many for forsaking Him.

Is He punishing mother? Or father? Or all of us?

I lay back down on the ground and grab a stick and hold it close to me. So much punishment and violence and horror. I cannot bear to see this part of God, to have Him hurt me this way.

I cannot tell the difference between my fear of the Devil and my fear of God's punishment.

I do not know who frightens me more.

The sun lights the forest floor in rays like broom heads, long and yellow and twigged. I have not seen sun in this world before. The pungent smell of woods, with its layers of leaves, rises. It's morning.

I must have fallen asleep.

The fire has gone out. I dig in the pit for a coal, a hot spark even, but only white ashes fly up into my face. Too weak to be angry—I am already cold—I crawl over into the precious sunshine. Its rays are warm, its light on my face gladdens me. I push away the thought of a dark night without fire.

The sun shows me things I have not seen before. Against the far tree grow mushrooms. I get up and pick one, smelling deeply its fungusy scent. It looks like the dull brown sodomite heads I used to pick with mother and the women every October in Myrthyr, right after fall harvest, when the heavy rains came. The women used to laugh at the name, called so because their flavor was so sinfully good. Mother used to warn me of the poisonous caesarheads, which looked like their delicious cousins and also grew in late October. I wonder if the New World has an October.

I gather handfuls of the mushrooms and hold them in the skirt of my kirtle. The caesarheads have a pink fringe round their bottoms that these mushrooms don't have. Eagerly, I brush the crumbly dirt from the body of one, bite off its head, and chew it slowly. It tastes as rich and sweet as the good mushrooms. I clean and stuff as many as I can into my mouth, filling myself with the nourishing food.

When I have eaten all I have in my skirt and feel my stomach swell, I continue walking on my sore feet, picking the abundant mushrooms and putting them into my pockets as I go.

The sunlight changes the dark trees; it takes away the spirits, and the forest becomes, simply, woods. Cones appear on pines, and sap and spiderwebs on other trees. Birds fly from branch to branch, and the wind blows lightly in the dead upper leaves, rustling them.

Then another sound underneath these comes, a sound like a faraway breath. Like footsteps. Like me. An echo of me from inside the labyrinth of trees.

I stop moving and listen. Yes, it is the sound of another body walking, breathing, but I do not know from which direction it is coming. I creep off the path and stand by a big tree with rough bark, stepping round it to listen, using the tree as a shield. The footsteps are one pair; they are bringing their person closer. I can feel my heart beating faster, high up in my ears. I think I should run away, but I do not know where away is, so I stay where I am and wait.

The person is behind me, coming closer. If I do not move, I think he won't see me, and I can see who it is. Maybe it is mother behind me in the forest. Yet the footsteps are heavy, and I feel that it's not mother, but a man. Sun shines down; I am alive and wish to stay that way. I pray that the man will keep walking, will walk right past me—

Unless he could help me find mother. Unless he could give me food and shelter and the company of people somewhere.

But what if it is a dog's-head man, ready to eat me with his dripping teeth?

His footsteps are so close, just by the tree I hide behind. He crunches along the path. I hear his breath, the leaves under his feet. I don't breathe. I stay still. He is past, he is round the tree. I look to see who it is.

His back, his thin shoulders, and black hair, I know them. I feel like laughing, like rushing after him and laughing, but I do not wish to frighten him. I step out onto the path. He hears my footsteps in the leaves and turns quickly. We stare at each other. He smiles and breathes. "Lily! My God!"

Smiling and shaking my head, I am so relieved, I cannot talk. A strange giggle rises up from within me.

"I'm so glad to see you're all right," he says.

I feel the warmth of him spread in my heart as I laugh and stare at his face.

"You are all right, aren't you?" he asks.

The sun lights his pale skin, shines in his teeth and eyes. He is carrying an animal—a huge hare—and blankets, a pot.

"Ethan, I—I'm so glad it is you!" I cry, finally finding my tongue.

"Lily—" He drops the pot and the rabbit and opens his arms to me, and I rush to him and hug him and hug him as though I could stuff him inside me like a whole roasted leg of lamb.

"Where—where have you come from? What are you doing here?" I say into his hard chest, his buttons pressing into my cheek. I cannot breathe for the surprise he's given me.

"I've been looking for you for days! I've come for you, Lily," he says.

I look up into his face, so grateful he has come. "But what—what—your father—what happened?"

His eyes and mouth twist into a scowl as he lets me go. "My father is a royal rotten bastard who deserves all he's gotten. He hit me and insulted you after you left. He doesn't need me. I'd rather be alone—I'd rather be with you in the forest than with that old bloody scab!"

My arms and legs feel light, as if a great weight has been taken from me. He is filling me with his words. "I'm eternally glad you've come, Ethan, very much so."

He looks at me and smiles and the shadows pass from him. "I had to come, Lily. I kept thinking about you, all alone here—and that I let you go alone. I don't know what I was thinking. It was so wrong of me, please forgive me. You shouldn't have to look for your mother alone."

I shake my head.

"Lily, you've not found a sign of her?" he asks me gently.

I stare at the pale shape of his face. Tears fill my eyes, and I cannot stop them. Ethan puts his arms about my head, burying me in the flat land of his chest.

"We will try to find her together," he says.

As he walks ahead of me, I stare at his heels and hardly look into the forest. I listen to his breath and try to match mine to it. I imagine myself the dagger in his belt, the wineskin over his shoulder, riding with his every footstep, without thought. He carries us over hectares. I feel the wool of the blanket he has placed about my shoulders warming me.

We walk for hours along a rough and rocky path, up hills and down, near caves, past streams where we collect water in the wineskin he has brought. I watch his shoulders as he moves, and they seem to widen as we continue on. Redheaded woodpeckers, birds with blue and yellow feathers, and brown bears and deer weave through the trees. Rainbow-colored threads bind me to Ethan; wherever he goes, I go.

"Let's stop," he says, turning and waiting for me. The sun has begun to fade. "You must be as tired as I am. We need to find cover for the night, Lily, don't you agree?"

"Oh, let me see, a tidy cottage or a stable with fresh hay will do," I say with a laugh.

He smiles. "I was thinking of branches, the way they had them at camp, you know," he crosses his arms, "thatched."

"That's how father made the roof to our cottage."

"So you can help me," Ethan says, setting down his dead hare and pot and breaking a branch from a tree. I break a branch; he climbs the tree, and I hand them up to him. He lays the branches into crooks and begins to wind them together. On top, he tucks in still-green leaves, creating cover.

When we are done, he climbs down, and we stand beneath and look up at our work. "The palace," I say.

"We are the king and queen," he says with a smile.

We gather twigs and leaves and branches for a fire. Ethan kneels to the pile and pulls a small box from his waist. "And now for a bit of magic," he says. He sprinkles some powder from the box onto the twig pile, and strikes together flint and steel. A spark shoots up and catches on a dried leaf. It lights the twigs round it. "A bit of fire-powder from the dregs of the good baron's sealed hogshead." He grins.

The fire burns full and hot. Ethan pulls the dagger from his belt and shows it to me. The blade glints silver in the light, its handle encrusted with shimmering red and green jewels. On the blade is engraved: TO SIR BRYAN OF MYRTHYR, FROM LORD ALFREDSON.

"This is from the good baron's hoard. It comes from my uncle," Ethan says.

He cuts the hare from bunghole to throat and throws its insides into the trees. Watching him, I do not feel hungry, but sick to my stomach. With quick cuts of his dagger, he skins the limp rabbit, then pushes the body onto a branch and holds it over the fire. I think of the nut rat I could not kill.

"How did you kill this animal, Ethan?" I ask him.

"With this." He holds up his dagger. "It was resting. I think it had a beggar leg and could not run from me. One stab," he says, mimicking his deadly thrust.

"But I mean, how—how did you feel when you killed it?" I ask him.

"What do you mean, how did I feel? Why are you asking me that, Lily?"

"I . . . I don't know. I'm thinking . . . Since my father and mother left me alone, since I've been searching for them, I've been thinking about, well, death and killing." I shake my head. "Did you hear or feel God telling you to do it?"

"What on Earth are you talking about, Lily? Of course not. I heard my growling stomach!"

"I don't know, Ethan. I have been wondering about God. Do you ever wonder?"

"What about God?"

"Well, what about Him? What do you think of Him? Of the way He works, with so much violence? So much retribution?"

He looks over at me unwaveringly. "That's rather blasphemous, Lily, questioning God that way. You could get into a lot of trouble," he says quietly.

"I'm sorry," I say.

He shakes his head. "You needn't apologize to me."

His rabbit cooks.

"Does your Frere Lanther teach you things like that?" he asks.

My insides cringe at the thought of Frere Lanther hearing me speak this way. "Ethan, no! Please don't think that. Frere Lanther says that God is everywhere." As I say it, I try to feel God everywhere, but I can only stare at the rabbit's carcass. A piercing frost fills my belly.

Ethan turns back to the hare, and we watch it cook. The rich scent of it fills my nostrils. All day, we've been eating cold mushrooms, dried berries, and hard nuts.

When the rabbit is ready, Ethan offers me a steaming, fragrant leg, and I cannot refuse him.

* * *

We gather up leaves and throw them into a pile to make a soft bed. "Nearest the fire is the best spot," Ethan says, gesturing for me to lie there. I do, on my side; he settles down behind me and covers us with the blankets against the cold night. I can feel his warmth.

"Lily, is it hard to be a poor person?" I hear him ask behind me.

"That's an odd question, Ethan." I think about it for a moment. "Being poor is all I know. Yes, it is very hard. We never have enough to eat or wear, never enough."

"I think I will be a poor person now," he says.

"Why do you think that?"

"Without my father, I will not have any gold."

"I do not think your father has much gold right now either."

"I wish to be poor."

I turn onto my back so I can look at him. "Why do you wish such a thing?"

"The poor are better. They are not so wicked. They are like you."

"I don't understand."

"My father, my folks, they seem like weak, grabby little fish, ugly and greedy."

I think of the folks gathered round his father at the camp; I think of Jed, standing amongst them.

"Folks are folks. We have weak and grabby poor folks."

"You do?" He raises his head to look at me.

"Of course."

He flops back down onto the bed of leaves and sighs. He doesn't say anything more. Just as I drift off, he throws his arm about me, a movement in his sleep. I rest my hand on his and squeeze it gently.

ELEVEN

As we pack up our bed in the foggy morning, I ask Ethan where he thinks my mother might be right at the moment. "Do you believe we're traveling in the right direction?"

"We must be, we're following their path. Feet made this path, and theirs are the only feet."

"Seems like we've been going forever. On and on, and everything looks the same to me. Trees and trees, streams and rocks. I'm afraid we're lost!"

"I have that feeling too. But let's keep going, Lily."

He hands me the wineskin, and heads down the path. I follow, trying to match his footsteps, though his legs are longer, his feet bigger, carrying him farther than mine. I feel as though I have no memory, no thoughts in my mind, I'm merely moving along, deeper into the New World, farther away from anything I will ever know again.

I don't look up as I walk—I watch for groundroots and stones to trip me, mushrooms to eat—I don't look up, and so I don't see them till I feel them. Quietly as the large animals which often weave round the far trees, they appear, standing about the forest and in our path.

Ethan stops walking, and I stop behind him. I have never seen anything like the man in front of us. He is not like any of my imaginings. He stands like a pale and hairless statue, his head bald but for a short, blond queue tied in a bunch on top. The skin round one of his eyes is colored in a black square. A yellow stripe runs down his nose, and brown stripes along his cheeks. He stands very straight. He does not threaten us; he does not move. A bow is slung over his shoulder. Fur robes cover him.

All about us, I feel eyes watching this man and us. Ethan crouches slightly. I move closer to him.

The man whispers something I cannot hear. I move as close to Ethan as I can, holding on to the blanket that is tied to him. Turning my head slightly, I can see men in the forest who look like this one, bald and colored, covered with animal furs, holding sticks and dead animals. I wish to close my eyes and not be where I am, to disappear into the air—

The man whispers again and it sounds like the wind in the trees, like a bird's wings as it flies.

I look from behind Ethan at the man and see he is no longer standing, but kneeling, his hands resting on his thigh. There is something about his body that I know.

He whispers again, and it sounds like Lily. He is staring at me.

I look at his bald head, at the shape of it, and his eyes, blue as glass beads.

"Lily," he says. I hear his voice clearly now—it strikes me like a drink of hot liquid deep inside. I step from behind Ethan and look closer at the man. I cannot believe it is him. He does not look like him.

"Lily, my big girl. Lilykin," he says.

But his voice can be only one person's voice.

"Father?"

He nods.

"Is it you, father?"

He nods.

I do not believe him. I must see first, see if he's not the Devil in disguise of my father, tricking me. "Why . . . why is your face colored like that? And your hair . . . Why are you wearing those furs?"

"My Lily." He opens his mouth, and begins to sing, to sing our words, the words he made for me only:

> *"Once there was a child,*
> *who couldn't sleep.*
> *Her name was Lily,*
> *she never made a peep.*
> *She woke her father,*
> *but didn't complain.*
> *Oh, fellow Sandman,*
> *fill her eyes again."*

As he sings, he opens his arms to me. I can hardly believe he is real. I stare past the colors, the skins, the bald flesh. I stare at his long arms and the fuzz at the nape of his neck, and I see.

This man kneeling before me is truly my father.

I walk slowly to him, looking at his face, at his mouth. It is his singing mouth which he puts to my cheek. Inside, I feel like a pebble running along a riverbed. I put one arm on his neck, then the other, and he pulls me to him. I fit into his hug the way I always did. I smell his scent of sunshine and happiness. I squeeze him as if I could squeeze out every rotting doubt, every fear. His breath puffs against my cheek as he says, "Lily, Lily, Lily—"

"Father, I thought you were dead, father, I thought I would never see you again; I thought I would have to be alone here forever, without you, without mother, they took mother away, when I was in the forest, washing, they took her away from the baron, he was so cruel to her, that's his son over there, but he is not cruel, he is nice, they took mother away, into the forest where we cannot find her, I cannot find her, I could not find you, father, I did not know, I did not know if you were alive or dead, if you lost your hands and feet and head like those other fellows, father—"

He pats me, shushing me with small noises. "Yes, yes, yes, we have much to talk about, Lily," he says. He lifts me as he stands. "You are so light," he says, and I feel like I am flying on fur wings. He says something in a strange language to a man standing behind him in the forest. They talk for a moment, then father speaks to the men who stand round Ethan, and they nod. Father says to Ethan, "They agree to help you with your things, if you allow them." Ethan nods, and the men take the pot and blankets from him and cover him with a fur. "We've got a way to go," father says to Ethan. "Can you walk?"

"Of course."

Father turns, and we set upon the path. I wish to ask him where we're going and to tell him about mother, but he seems to want me to rest. As he appeared, so he walks—silently. Behind us, the footsteps of only one person make a sound, though I know there are several. I rest my head against father's neck as he carries me. He begins to sing gently to me and I feel the thrum in his neck, real and alive. His heart beats underneath me.

TWELVE

He climbs the path easily, and I think about his face. It's so different. Not because of the colors, but the set of it has changed, the firmness. My father's face used to be softer. His whole self seems harder now. Maybe he's hungry like us, but he does not seem hungry. Maybe I do not remember him properly.

"Time to rest, Lily. Drink this," he says, putting me on my feet in high, yellow grass. He's been climbing with me for a long time, up the side of a mountain. As I stand, I feel the blood run to the cankers in my feet, making them throb.

Father gives me a leather bag and pulls out the leaves which are packed tight at the top. The liquid tastes milky and I drink till I am full. He wipes my mouth with his thumb, and lifts my lip. I see him looking at my face, and at the gap where my tooth is missing. He shakes his head, and turns to look down into the forests below.

"A few nights ago, Lily, the vision man saw you in a dream. You and the boy walking in a serpentine, back and forth in the forest alone." Father stares down the slope, and goes on. "Yesterday, we saw you and the boy from up here, and we came to get you. I hope we didn't frighten you."

I shake my head, looking down the mountain. I've never seen a real mountain before, nor been to the top of one. A vision man? I am not sure what father means. Down below, the fiery trees glow like lanterns, smaller and smaller, as far as I can see.

The land is vast and waved and complicated.

"But the vision man did not dream about your mother. Lily, when—when did you last see her?" father asks.

"Days. I don't know exactly."

Ethan is playing in the field with another boy and a long stick. I call to him. He comes to us, and I ask him when we saw mother last.

"It was days and days ago, maybe a week, maybe longer," he says to father. He holds up the long stick. "They gave me this spear. Daw-ika is teaching me to walk like a cat," he says with a grin. He drops into the grass in front of us, laying down the stick and his body, seeming to disappear, though I know he is right before us.

"Do you think we can find mother . . . soon?" I ask father. I stare at his nose, his mouth and eyes, the colors on his face; he pushes my hair from my forehead and nods.

"With help," he says.

I wish to lie down upon this mountainside and sleep for many days, to wake and find mother and father curled in the grass, into each other, together, beside me.

The sun has faded once again, and the clouds hang low and bright gray. "Who will help us find mother?" I ask father.

"I believe, if we ask, the people will help us," he says, waving to the men in the grass. Some are kneeling, opening their packs and taking things out. Others drink from leathery bags. A few have tails tied to their waists, striped and bushy, some wear bird feathers. In the tall grass, they've laid their kill.

We sit to rest, and I tell my father the whole story of how we came to this land, of the baron, the captain, and the ship. I tell him how me and mother took the trip to find him, and how we crashed, and how the captain and the men stole mother away.

"I followed her, and Ethan came after me. We walked till . . . till . . ." I stop and touch father's hand.

He has been watching me as I speak, but he turns away from me now. "You came over the sea to find me?" he asks quietly.

"Yes, me and mother—"

He tears up a weed and pulls at the grainy head. "And the baron was with you, you say? The baron of Myrthyr?" he asks.

"Yes, our baron. That is his son, Ethan." I point to Ethan in the grass, and father looks at him for a long time.

Father shakes his head. "I did not think it would come to that," he says finally.

"What do you mean?" I ask him.

"Lanther getting the baron to come to the New World."

"What are you saying, father? Frere Lanther hates the baron," I say. "The baron—"

"Frere Lanther is not who you think he is, Lily," father interrupts. I look at Ethan, who is sitting up and listening now. I do not know what to say. Father stands abruptly. "But we must find your mother. I want you to look down from this mountain carefully. Over there, far over, is the sea. From there, you must have come."

Past the top of the forest, with its many shades of red and brown, is the beginning of a gray sea. "Yes, yes, I see it," I say slowly.

"So you came upon the shore, and then what happened? Where did you go, do you remember?"

"We went into the forest." I tell him about the bodies we found, the headless bodies of the men. "We camped near there." I do not tell him about trying to find him with my spirit.

"We were near a river," Ethan says as he stands and comes to us.

"Yes, and there were birch trees and pine and fir, and trees with star leaves and nuts, all living together. And I thought . . . I thought they buried you—"

Father pulls me to him and turns my face gently and points down to the forest. "That dark green crescent is the river, do you see?" he asks me. It's almost as far away as the sea, the arc in the land faintly greener than its surroundings.

"We walked a long way," Ethan says.

Father closes his eyes. I wait for him to open them again.

I hear a soft clacking noise, and look round. Most of the men in the grassy field are gone, and the few who are left seem to be making the noise with rocks.

"I don't see her," father says. His eyes are still closed. I look at Ethan, and he shakes his head and shrugs.

"Nor do I," I say. I do not know what else to say. Father opens his eyes and smiles sadly at me. He lifts me once again and begins to walk with me. Ethan picks up his stick and stays beside us.

My hands feel swollen and cold, my feet raw as a skinned animal. My tongue tastes of metal. "Where are we, father? This place, what is it?"

"I'm taking you to the people who saved me. They call this place Turtle Island. We landed in the middle of a battle, those—

those murdered fellows you saw and I. In a storm of snow. More snow than you've ever seen all together in one storm," father says.

"Are they English, the people you are taking us to see?" I ask.

"No," father says. I lay my head on his steady shoulder. "We were lucky they took us in—me and the others," he says softly, almost to himself. "When we arrived in this land, it was covered with snow deep as our waists. We were freezing, dying—and then caught in a battle. We wouldn't have lived without them." As he speaks, I close my eyes and try to imagine so much snow, but I cannot. In Myrthyr, it hardly ever snows. "We landed in the middle of a war between the Nooh people and the bloody Awthas . . . a terrible war," he whispers.

He shakes his head and holds me closer. "Anyway, Lily—and Ethan," he says louder, "I am taking you somewhere warm and safe, with sweet food and good people."

I think about the people who saved him, and wonder if they are the same men who walk with us in the forest, the painted, brown men with furs hanging from their shoulders and about their legs, unlike any people I've ever seen or heard about.

"If they aren't English at all, the people who saved you, how will we understand them?" I ask.

"I'll be with you," father says.

As we round the bend of the mountainside, I smell the wood smoke of a hearth fire and see a billowing grayness pressing into the falling light. I feel sore inside, sore for not having mother with us. I miss her so badly. I drop my head against father, feeling the bone of his shoulder against me, real and living under his furs. I hug him harder about his neck, and he squeezes me closer to himself.

Homes, long homes built with wood slats stand among a sprinkle of trees. They are not like the small, one-room cottages of Myrthyr nor the larger stone manor of the baron. Two sides are long and two sides narrow—homes like stretched boxes with roofs low and flat. They stand three together in a horseshoe with a dome-shaped hut in the center.

The homes appear to form a village. On the outskirts stand shapes like huge cone hats or tents with smoke puffing from their pointed tops. In the coming twilight, a robed man with long, shiny black hair and a woman in a painted dress are bent into each other, talking in a corner by a long home. Two girls with plaits in dresses with tassles play a jumping game near a tent. A muscled old man slowly scrapes at a hide beside a fire. A blond woman walks by, tall and pale as a spirit, wearing furs. She slips between two homes.

I wish to stare at these people from a secret place and not from my father's arms which bring me closer to them. I feel he is carrying me farther away from anything I know, as though I am being pulled against my will in a cart dragged by a stubborn ox, being pulled into fields not my own without hands to rear the ox, to stop him.

"This is where I live," father says. He puts me down just outside one of the tents and stretches his arms.

I wish to hide, to find a blanket to crawl under, or a table, or a pine bough, to bring Ethan and father with me and hide till it passes, till the world passes in a whole circle and comes round to the way it was so long ago in a land that was my home.

Ethan comes from behind us, still holding his spear, fur draped about him. His wide eyes pull in our surroundings. "It's hard to believe this existed all the time we were in the woods, hungry and cold and sure we were alone," he says.

I feel eyes upon us from unseen places, curious eyes piercing. I reach for father's hand. "You were not so far from where we were, from mother and me," I say.

He nods. "I wish I had found you sooner, together."

"We missed you so badly, father, we missed you," I say. "Mother—she was not—"

A flap in the tent suddenly opens, startling me, and two women rush out at us, screeching in high voices and coming directly for me. I do not know what to do. I look for a place to run.

One woman comes after me; I run behind father. The other, the older of the two, goes after Ethan; he holds out his spear. I do not know what these women want with us.

Feeling the younger woman's hands pawing me, I bury my face in father's back and shout. Father pulls her away, and I hear him talking to her, to them, words I cannot understand. And then he speaks to me.

"It's all right, Lily, it's just Kri-ki and Mah-da. They are friends, Lilykins. Come." He reaches for me and hugs me.

"They're not going to hurt me?" I look up at father's face and he smiles, shaking his head. I peer over at Ethan and see the other woman standing by him, stroking his shoulder and weeping softly. He puts down his spear. The woman moves a little closer, murmuring at him. The younger woman cranes her neck to look at me, her eyes thickly circled with black, tears staining black upon her cheeks as she mutters words at me.

Ethan asks father, "Why are they crying?"

"They're happy to see you."

A man comes out of the flap and calls to father and the women.

He does not attack us, but seems to be motioning us inside.

"You're tired," father says. "Come inside now, where you can rest and eat."

A fire at its center warms the tent. Things hang about, wooden sticks with webs on them, long materials with colored patterns sewn through them. Soft furs and skins make the ground.

I watch the younger woman as she hits at a kind of dough, shaping it quickly with her fingers. She has long dark hair folded into braids. Her skin dress swirls with colors, and she wears bird feathers and clear rocks about her, in her ears and on her fingers. She does not look English at all. I wonder where she came from if she did not come from England.

The older woman wears a longer dress. Her black hair is twisted with yellow and blue strings, her forehead is lined and colored delicately with curled patterns, her hands have many scars and rings. Tied round her ankles are long white bird feathers.

The tent smells of smoke and cooking food. My head swims with glimpses of memories of mother cooking before the fire pit and father watching tenderly, the way he is watching the young woman now. I feel as though I'm falling into a dark place that will take me back to a time before, when it was mother cooking and father singing to us and reading the Bible.

The older man wears no hose or vest. I sneak looks at him, not sure if it is allowed. He has no colors on his face. His privy is covered with a leather patch, his bum, legs, and chest revealed. I can see every bump on his body. Thick, gray hair grows uncut upon his head; none on his face or chest or legs. I glance at Ethan. His mouth hangs ajar as he examines the man.

Father removes his fur robe and underneath he wears a similar patch over his front. The rest of him is naked, even his bum—

I feel myself gasping and drowning as I try to look only at father's face. It is not right to look upon one's own father's nakedness. The Bible says to honor thy father and thy mother. Honor thy father. But is this my father before me, without a tunic, with a painted face, living amongst savages, people who are not English?

I am drowning.

Mother says father is the most pious man . . . he is choir-master . . . he is minister in the church of Frere Lanther. Frere Lanther, Frere Lanther, he is not who you think he is, Lily, he is not who you think—

Black dots with eyes in them swim before me, and I feel father's arms catching me, laying me down and covering me with furs, warm, rank furs into which I bury my face before I fall into a watery darkness.

I feel mother inside me thick, heavy, as though she is a wet mushroom growing in the place of my heart and becoming a part of me that I cannot see but can only feel with the weight of my own self. I feel her as though she has come and laid herself upon me, muffling me with her heavy kirtle, scratching me with her woolly shawl, pushing me down with her cold fingers, her strong cold fingers that have pushed away bad men from the door.

I feel father, father, like a found twig whose end is too wet to light, who does not hold the heat of the flame—father, who has become a bird, an illuminated bird wearing feathers and skins upon his back. And his bareness, as though he is without feeling for the cold and the sense of his own nakedness.

I feel mother the way I feel darkness coming, coming even though I try to stop it, though I do not have fire against it, though I know she will embrace me in her cold and hold me frozen as a leaf in a pond, frozen till the winter's end, but by then it will be too late. I must act before it is too late, I must find her, but I am too stiff. Too frightened. I hold myself unmoving as a frightened beast, waiting for the end to come, waiting for the attacker to leave, to sniff and leave, famished still, unsatisfied, my flesh uneaten yet.

Father is just a shadow of a tree on the ground in bright sunlight, not the tree itself, but a shadow without detail. There is an ache inside me where he used to be, like my tooth, a gap held in my mouth, a piece missing. I reach for him and touch him and smell him and talk with him, but I do not feel he is the father who was mine. I do not know where that man is.

They are all there, the Marys and mother, Mistress Grey and Maister Johansen, all the members of father's choir standing in voice order in Mistress Grey's stable. The pigs snort, joining the harmonious notes of the little crowd, mother in front, singing in her high pitch, father directing, keeping time with the stick in his fist, pointing, directing all of us. He wears his brown tunic and has all his hair and he smiles at the music that comes from our mouths. Smiles and hums with us. I cannot help smiling at his smile.

Mistress Knapp has come with her poodle; Maister Johansen has brought the new ale, "just a nip for ye." The dog natters when he is tied to the beam. We sing psalms to Jesus our Lord and Savior, to save our souls which are dying every day that we live, to Jesus our Shepherd to guide us through, to teach us how to live in this land of good and evil. I sing, breathing in the pure melodies of the others. Mother carries the lead, Maister Johansen right behind with his big voice, then us, the girls, light notes for Angels' feet to tread upon, notes to raise us up.

I stand with the Marys upon barrels behind the singers; we are nearest to Heaven. The Marys' lips form O's, their eyes reach skyward, searching for the miracle of God. I see only backs of heads before me—Mistress Grey's bun pushing against her keercheef, Mistress Knapp in her three-pointed hat, mother, her hair loose about her shoulders.

It is when I am looking at mother that I see the room filling with smoke, putrid black smoke that stings my eyes. Smoke lifts through mother's shoulders, her hair, a smoldering flame underneath her, winding about her like a long cloth, tying itself tighter. Mother! I try to call out, but no word comes from me, only smoke in my lungs, black smoke filling my lungs as my mother burns before me.

My chest convulses.

What is before my eyes changes. I am unsure where I am. Smoke in a room; it is not the stable. I am not in Myrthyr with mother, the Marys, father.

Smoke from a fire, from a man's mouth, a man I do not know.

I get up and stumble. I am in the tent; I stumble to the flap and outside, into the cold air. I hear drums; my eyes tear from the smoke. My head floats in exact pain, held by the air's crispness. The drums, they are real; I follow the sound of them into the night.

"Father," I cry. "Father, where are you?" but the beat drowns my voice. Father, father, his name flies in my head like arrows, landing with shooting pricks behind my eyes, in my temples. I stumble on my sore, bare feet toward the drumming, and turn to see a hut ablaze before a horseshoe of homes, a man inside it, howling out in a bizarre melody, moving in a violent rhythm against the smoking walls.

I stop.

A circle of men and women surround the hut. They dance with bells upon their feet, dance and sing with feathers and waving arms.

My eyes catch father in the dancing circle.

Dancing in nakedness with the woman from the tent, holding her close to him, close to his sweating body, dancing with her so their bodies touch. They touch as though they love each other the way mother and father love each other. It is father, it is not mother, but they touch that way. They dance about the circle together in their bare skins, while mother is burning, burning from the smoke that rises from her hair.

"Father!" I shout, but he does not hear. My head swims with their movement, with the bells, the drums, and the smoke, with the howls of the trapped man.

I shout again and run to him. They must stop the fire, stop the flames and the dancing and the swirling bleeding. I throw myself at the moving bodies, trying to grab father's swaying arm.

I see Ethan's face before mine, pulling me away.

Father turns from the woman toward me, his lips shining in the firelight, the look behind his eyes troubled as a dark sea.

I dream of hands. They clean my feet, my face, my eyes which will not open; they give me food. I dream of feet which walk past me. I dream of knees, bending down to bring a body closer.

I dream of God. I dream that I am an insect in His hand and He is poking at me from different sides, making me walk this way and that with a great smile upon His face. God has long, stringy muscles. He puts me down in a village of dignified rich people, all well dressed in their finery, with well-combed, furry dog's heads. One of the dog's-head people leans all the way to the ground where I crawl and says to me, "We are not who you think we are," and laughs, showing all his dog teeth. His breath smells like the blood of the dead.

God picks me up again and lets me down in a village of whales who live upon the land. They swim with grand smiles through the air and bump into me, throwing me about with their weight, biting me up into their mouths and belching me out when my hundreds of insect legs tickle their tongues. They fly by me, whispering into my ears, "We are not who you think we are." The lady whales are wrapped in velvet covers, and the men whales wear hose upon their tails.

I crawl into the hand of God, an insect upon the Earth, amongst the stars, and He drops me in a land that tumbles with pale people who live in homes so close together, they can hear one another cry. They have no shoes, though they must walk in heaps of snow as high as their chests. In huts made of leaves, they ret and scutch flax with their frozen fingers, their children hackling and spinning it quickly, to make flaxen cloaks to cover their icy limbs. Mother directs these poor people with a stick, orders them in a worried voice to spin faster, before the end comes for them all. I know it is mother, though I cannot see her face.

I crawl upside down upon the wall, then right side up; I crawl round and round, knowing I will not be taken up into God's hand again.

THIRTEEN

They've given me some medicine for sleeping, I think, nether-wort or the heavy mugroot that mother took sometimes. My bones feel hollow. All I can do is rest upon the furs.

Fingers gently rub a salve on my temples that prickles like mint. The smell stirs me to wake. I force my eyes open. They meet the young stranger's eyes whose black-painted roundness is familiar. Her dark eye-skin is painted all the way to the eyebrows, and down, the black touching the hill at the top of her nose.

Her eyes brighten when they meet mine. Seeing her reminds me of her shameful dancing with father. I close my lids. She talks to me in her language, rubbing on the salve and talking. She smells of the skins I sleep in, and of food, ointment, breath. She does not belong to me; I do not wish to have her so near. She leans over me, looking under my clothing, touching my feet, returning to my head, push-ing the hair from my face, tucking the furs up under my chin.

They are her fingers, her knees, her feet that I have felt cleansing, bending, moving past me. I open my eyes once again, trying to look about the tent for father, but I only see the other, older woman, sitting by the fire, her head bent into her work. I do not know the day, nor whether it is night.

"Okri," the young woman says to me, and I shake my head. She points at herself and says, "Kri-ki." I look at her.

"Okri," she says, pointing at me. "Kri-ki." She points at herself.

I close my eyes.

She calls out to the older woman, and I hear the whoosh of the tent flap as the older woman leaves. I am afraid to stay alone with the black-eyed one; I try to rise, but can barely move my arms to push up my body. Without helping or stopping me, she watches as I struggle then lie back down again. I look at her and frown, trying to push anger through my eyes at her, to push her away with my eyes.

She leans over me and speaks with her arms folded into herself, her eyes lit up inside their blackened circles. When she is quiet again, I speak.

"I don't know what father told you, but you cannot touch him anymore," I tell her. "He belongs to my mother. He is my father and she is my mother and we are going to look for her. She is alive somewhere in this forest of yours, and we will find her and leave you and go back to Myrthyr." I speak loudly and slowly, so she will understand.

She says something back; I do not know what.

"My mother has brown hair and green eyes. She is tall and she wears a gray cloth kirtle with shawls. The kirtle is not fancy like your dress, but in it she looks very pretty. My mother does not wear black round her eyes," I say, making a circle with my finger round my eye. She nods her head. "No, my mother does not powder herself nor wear black about her eyes."

The woman says something. She gets up and goes to the fire and comes back with a blackened piece of coal and rubs it on her finger. The coal comes off, black like the circles about her eyes. With two fingers, she holds the coal up to me. I think she wishes me to use it. I shake my head.

As she is speaking, the tent opens, and father rushes in with the cold, outside air and the older woman directly behind him. He comes and sits at my side, taking up my hand. "Lily, you've been so sick. It is good to see you awake." He turns and speaks to the younger woman.

"Father, who is this woman?" I interrupt. Behind my lids, my eyes ache. I feel as though I will never move from the ground. I ask again, nodding toward her.

"She's Kri-ki. She's been taking care of you."

"That is not what I am asking," I say. "Who is she to you, father?" He stares at me, deciding, it seems, what to tell me. "I wish to know," I say. I cannot bear to bring up what I saw, him dancing with her. It is the last time I remember seeing him.

Father's face is not painted now. It is as it was, smooth, broad, and clear.

"Father?" It's as though he cannot answer. He opens my hand which lies unmoving on his frigid palm. With a finger, he follows a crease in my hand, till the tip drops into his own hand.

"I nearly lost my hands to the frost," he says slowly, looking into our palms. "They did not ask anything of me. She took me in here and saved my hands and feet. She talked to me, kept me alive, kept me in the light of the world when all was black."

In that time, did he remember us, did he think of his family back home? In his eyes, I can see only the reflection of the black-eyed woman.

"Did . . . did you miss us, father? All this time away, did you miss me and mother?"

He looks at me sharply, breathes in. "Lily, I missed you and your mother so badly, I was not sure what I would die of first, cold or heartache. Kri-ki—Kri-ki helped me." He looks over at the woman, who is watching us closely. "Lily, I thought I'd never see you again. That is the truth." He looks down at his palms, at my palm cradled there.

His words feel too grand and empty, like a giant cloudless sky, birdless, motionless, hopeless.

FOURTEEN

Ethan asks father about Frere Lanther that night, over the first supper I attend sitting up. Ethan has rid himself of his highborn clothes and is wearing a skin like father and the other man in our tent. I have seen his nakedness before. Beside the men, he seems as pale and helpless as a plucked chicken.

The women pull meat from small cooked birds.

"What made you believe in Frere Lanther in the first place?" Ethan asks father. "Why did you turn from Father Leeman? My mother and father granted Father Leeman so much gold and goods. We had him in our chapel for private mass."

"I did not turn from Father Leeman; I turned to Lanther," father says. I look at the wrinkle in his forehead as he sorts out his words, his fingers picking at the food before him, white, breadish triangles, green mush on an impress of bark. How much, I wonder, has he thought about Myrthyr, Father Leeman, Frere Lanther?

Father continues. "Father Leeman was ordered by the Deacon of Rudrick, who answered to Cardinal Dennish, who followed the laws

of the Archbishop, who, of course, was commanded by the Pope."
Father glances at Ethan, who nods. I see they have spoken of mat-
ters before this, that they have passed words between them that
make them know each other.

"These churchmen told people that they could get into Heaven
when they sinned if they paid—"

"Indulgences," Ethan says, nodding.

"Yes, Indulgences and other payments. The list of sins was long.
At every turn, human error was considered a sin. I looked at the
hungry men and women in the choir, their clothes coming apart
because they'd traded all their flax, their shoes worn through. And
our sick children . . . I found I was grieved at the church, asking for
Indulgences on top of what we had to give the baron. Half our
goods, and half from the field."

Ethan moans and shakes his head. "Bloodsucking fiend."

"We were all suffering from this. We lost our boys before Lily. We
lost them to this . . . poverty."

Mother and father had had three boys before me. I knew nothing
of them. Their graves were just grassy mounds mother and father
would visit. We did not speak of them. We had lost few compared
to other families in Myrthyr.

"One day, I was gathering haybales at our neighbor's, Maister
Johansen—"

"The fellow with the public house, yes, I know him," Ethan says.

"He'd picked up this pamphlet in Merceyville when he went there
for his ale barrels and told me to look at it. Lanther's pamphlet shed
light on everything for me. Explained how we could have God in
our lives with faith, and not have to pay Him money for our every
human foible. How we could attend church and worship our Lord

without this burden of guilt that weighted us heavy. How our belief in God was about faith, pure faith."

He glances from Ethan to the bread in his hand, its edges torn by his nervous thumb. "I was thunderstruck," he says.

Father's words remind me of the clean joy that came when Frere Lanther arrived. Even though there was always danger about, fear that he would be caught, and us too, that we'd all be hanged for having him—still, the calm that he brought to my father and mother, the righteous strength, made us willing to do anything for him.

I long to see Frere Lanther again, to hear his sure voice and feel his caress upon my head.

Father goes on. "With a Rhinelander merchant at the market, I sent a letter to the abode printed upon the pamphlet, but Lanther never wrote back. I started to feel that the man was not real, that he didn't exist. But one evening, as I was returning from the field, a man in brother's robe called to me as he came toward me—called out my name—and I knew it was Lanther.

"As soon as it was safe, I took him into my home. He corrected all my wrong thinking. He explained how he'd been a brother in the Rhineland, and had come near death many times through fasting and whipping himself till he drew blood, just to rid himself of his sins—small sins, of omission, of thought. The cardinal heard about him, and sent him to Rome for church business to help him rise in status for his piety. There, Lanther met the Pope and saw the opulence and extravagance that the Indulgences of the poor had bought. He saw that no one in the Holy Roman Empire experienced guilt over their sins as he did. It was as merry as Harry's royal court. Not holy. When he returned to the Rhineland, he was a changed man."

I have never heard Frere Lanther's story this way. All round me fly the languages Frere Lanther knows, the people he's touched, the places he's been. I wonder how he behaved with the Pope in Rome, how he would be with these people of the New World. Before I can find the right words to ask, Ethan speaks.

"But something happened, didn't it? Between Lanther and my father?"

Father looks up at him, surprised. They stare at each other for a moment.

"I hate my father, you know that," Ethan says. "Please tell me the truth about him. Tell me what you meant when you said that you didn't think it would come to this, between him and Frere Lanther."

Father sighs, rubs his fingers together, thinking. "I cannot say I know how it started. I gather that I never knew Lanther as well as I thought. He was a brilliant writer, he convinced me—"

Father stops and holds his forehead. I can see the blue lines in his arm, the strain in his mouth.

"Ethan, your father and Frere Lanther have interests in common. On the ship over, I found out it was your father's men who took me and the others away from our families and brought us here. But worse than that, I discovered that Frere Lanther was working with him, and with others—princes, dukes, earls, and barons in England, France, and the Low Countries—to organize this trip to the New World. It was Frere Lanther who sought to settle here and start his own land, with his religion and beliefs and people."

Father hits his fist into his palm with a cry, frightening me.

"He used me!"

I feel soul-sickened at father's words. Frere Lanther, I cannot imagine . . .

Father speaks on. "Lanther told these . . . these nobles of the riches that others had encountered in the New World. He made an exchange—passage to the New World for his believers. Any riches found would belong to his benefactors. Do you understand?" father asks Ethan. He does not look at me. Ethan nods slowly.

Father continues. "The baron was the first to believe him, to help him gather the finances from these other nobles, which is why Lanther came to Myrthyr. He did not come for me, as I had thought, although he trained me with the purpose. As a minister for Lanther, I was chosen, unbeknownst to me, to lead the party to settle this land as a Lantherite, a protester—my God, against my will! Is it a holy man who would tear a man from his family like an animal to do his bidding?"

I feel I am slipping as I listen to these words, slipping into the murky pit I have existed in for days, the pit of bad dreams and unsolid ground.

Father talks quickly on, as though he cannot stop himself. "My wife tried to warn me, the day before they came for me. She said that she'd heard the baron was coming for me, to send me away on this trip. She said it was because of the baron. She did not know about Lanther. I . . . I heard, on the ship, that the only way she could have known was through the baron—oh, this is too much to tell you!" he exclaims, but Ethan urges him to go on. Father shakes his head and looks down. I feel as if a great force is holding its hands about my neck, my arms to my sides. Father is about to tell us something even more awful and I wish to close up my ears but I cannot move.

"Ethan, you know enough now. That is all I am going to tell you."

"My father," Ethan starts, his face reddening, his fists clenching, "my father was in love with your wife. With your mother, Lily, you saw it, on the ship."

No, no, I don't want to think about it; I don't want to think about what happened with mother and the baron on the ship. He is gone. I wish to look forward, to finding mother.

Father glances at me, looks away. "He was—he was—I—I discovered too that your mother found out about the baron taking me, not through gossip, as she said, but through the baron—the baron himself," father stutters.

"Mother hated the baron," I protest, but I know that father's words are true. She bed down with him on the ship. He forced her because of Frere Lanther, he said, but now I see the baron was lying, that he knew the frere all along. Pieces of sense fly about me, but none of them come together. I cannot grasp any of it long enough to truly understand.

"But the baron did not hate her. He was using her against her will, and she did not tell me. She could not stop him. She was afraid, Lily, that he would kill you or me, so she did not stop him."

I hear the fire crackling, the women and man eating, voices passing our tent outside. I look at my own feet, bare, covered with healing sores. I do not know how my mother could have held such a thing inside of her, away from us, for so long.

Mother did it to protect us, and that makes me feel like dying.

Beside me, father sits, his head so bowed, it almost touches his chest. I hear his sobbing groans, deep and hard within his chest.

Ethan mutters through his teeth. "Even while my own mother was sick and dying, my father—ugh!"

Father covers his face and gets up from the fire and leaves the tent.

Ethan follows him out.

I crawl back to the skins where I've been sleeping, and close my eyes.

I look through the smoky hole in the tent top, up to the sky, where the blue morning wavers like a faraway star. I wish I could turn to smoke, to float like a hot, gray cloud up into the sky and drift till I find mother, drift on the wind as I come apart slowly, till I become the air she breathes. Mother—her name is so raw in my mouth. I feel sick with knowledge.

She had not wanted to come to the New World.

I moan at the thought, and of me telling her I wished to go, to find father. Frere Lanther, he convinced me. All along he lied to us. He took our food and our care and pretended he was someone he was not. All along, the baron knew about Frere Lanther and tricked mother for his own purposes. Those days I stayed with Mistress Grey or the Marys, those afternoons she disappeared and I had to wait for her. The baron forced her onto the ship; she could not escape him. He used her, they used her and father. She hadn't wanted to come to the New World.

I moan, my insides like a black knife I cannot pull out. Mother. Forgive me. I did not know.

FIFTEEN

I am alone when the woman Kri-ki and three others like her come into the tent and surround me. They grab at my arms and legs. Screaming, I try to strike out at them. I don't know what they want from me.

They get hold of me and lift me from the rugs.

As I kick and struggle, they carry my body out of the tent. I do not know where they are going with me nor what they will do. Kill me? The woman does not want me between her and father. She is getting rid of me! I scream into the sky, into the cold sunshine for father, for Ethan, for anyone to help. My screams meet no ears. I can see no people. It is just me with these madwomen, these witches who carry me by the arms and legs.

My throat aches, my wrists and ankles rubbed sore. I tire of screaming. I cannot see their faces as they walk, only their parted hair, their backs. Their strong hands grip my bones. Where are they taking me?

Upside down, I look at the blue sky pass. Furiously, I kick and twist, but their hold on me only tightens. An old woman shuffles along from behind and looks over into my face as the women walk with me. "Help me, help me!" I shout at her. She smiles and nods and shuffles away. Some children run by and look down at me, laughing. There is no sign of father.

I twist my head this way and that to see where we are going. The women bring me through the village and out of it. I'm in a blackened field, burnt. If I do not escape, they will kill me for sure as they kill the animals they carry this way. They will kill me and skin me and use me for meat. Father, help me! The women haul me into the beyond forest where bare branches stick out above me and they call to each other in words I don't understand.

I scream again, echoing screams into those branches.

Surefooted, they carry me down a hill on loose rocks which tumble ahead of them. I hear water running swiftly like a river, the sound becoming louder as we near. They stand me up. A narrow river flows as sharp and cold as dreams of drowning.

I try to run; it is my only chance to escape the death before me. But two of the fatter women grab me and hold me in their grip while the others remove my kirtle and bloomers, leaving me naked and shivering, miserable and frightened to my very bones as though they'd stripped me of my skin. I turn away as best I can. I cannot stand their eyes on my bare body.

Kri-ki and the fourth woman remove their own dresses and boots and stand in front of me naked as insects, naked as me.

I freeze into horrified silence.

They hold me, and the two fat women take off their dresses, till they too stand naked. The four women lift me again and begin to walk into the river. I struggle and mutter prayers to God in Heaven. To mother, wherever she may be, to father, hiding away from me as he has been.

I begin to thrash as the women lower me toward the water, lower and lower till I can feel the cold wetness just below me. Like a rabid dog, like a wild animal, I thrash to avoid the freezing water that flows swiftly by. They dip me down till my head is covered and I can hear nothing but the water filling my ears, water so cold I think my blood may forget to run, my breath may stop—

They raise me up and rub upon me a greasy liquid. A sweet smell fills the air, of flowers, grasses. They rub this liquid upon themselves also, which makes them laugh. Their laughter seems evil and foreign and faraway. It does not touch me.

They rinse me off and take me out of the water. I've become exhausted and can only stand and shiver and shiver. They dry me and dress me in one of their dresses, animal-smelling, decorated with embroidery. They fit my feet into tall boots.

They dress themselves. One of the women wraps a fur about me and ties my hair into braids like those upon her own shoulders. I'm madder than a swollen cow, but I do not make a sound nor a move. One fat woman slides my arm up easily under her arm and leads me back up the hill, with Kri-ki and the other women silently following.

At the top of the hill, the other fat woman holds my other arm. We walk. As we pass through the blackened field, I see stirrings ahead, as though the village has come alive. People pour into a home, one of the long homes round which other homes are built. I feel the women pushing me there, and I wish to run, to be away from so many strangers.

They bring me into the home, which is low and long and filled with sitting people, a dull light, smoke. A fire burns in the center. In the hot air, more people push in, talk, whisper, pick amongst each other for a sitting place. I do not see father or Ethan. The women remove my fur and place it on the ground for me to sit upon. The woman Kri-ki takes a place beside me and clutches my arm. The others sit on either side of us.

A man with father's light skin and hair passes. I look more closely; it is not father. I see others: a blond woman who sits near me, a tall white-skinned man who lurks against the far wall. No one that I recognize; no one that I know. In the crowd, I feel small and invisible, trapped by the tyrannical women who beset me.

A rhythmic shaking sound fills the room and the people fall quiet. A procession of boys passes through the door. They throw off their furs into a pile; underneath, they are dressed with skins, bird feathers, sticks, face and body colors. Ethan walks among them, colored with brown upon his cheeks, his yellow chin thrust out, red streaks upon his chest. The look in his eyes frightens me. He is changed—so distant and untouchable, as though he walks high upon clouds. The boys make a circle round the fire and sit. Ethan sits in front of me, his back to me, but I do not feel I can reach him.

The shaking sound begins again, and men come in throwing off their skins. A huge man leads, made bigger by a hat of white feathers which stands straight up on his head and runs all the way down his back. His face is painted bright yellow, with blue lines running down his chin like animal fangs. At the sight of him, I wish to crawl under one of the skins, but the women's hands hold me tight.

Behind him walks father, looking ahead.

My father. Without hair, in animal skins draped about his waist, with red earth smeared upon his forehead in lines, mud painted into his chest, lines and circles drawn with the brown of God's earth. God. Is He watching this pagan gathering?

Father wears a white bird feather in his queue.

Nothing is the way it seems. Father is not the way I remembered him to be. Lanther is not what he had seemed to be. I feel as I did when the women carried me upside down, as if everything were moving backwards, sidewards, utterly wrongwards, and I wonder: Is anything what it seems?

Father is taking a place between Ethan and me in another circle forming. I look down at my palms, at my square hands. Like mother's hands, I see her hands in mine. The room is silent but for the shaking instruments. I hope they will not dance the way they did the other night, naked, father and this woman beside me. The shaking stops; the room falls completely silent. Father sits in front of me, his bare back to me like a cold stone wall.

Father's back covers Ethan in front of him. I can see Ethan's head to the right of father's shoulder. We are all lambs in a burning manger. I hear a voice and look up; standing by the fire is the man with the huge feather hat. He is speaking, pointing in my direction and speaking. Beside me and the fat woman, I hear a whisper, words I understand; I turn to see who it is. The blond woman, the one I saw, is whispering in English. She meets my eyes. Ethan turns and looks at her. She nods at us both, then looks up at the speaker.

I understand that she is translating what he is saying into English. I look at the man and try to fit her words to him. Ethan leans back to listen, his spine stiff.

". . . has called this council, he holds the talking stick today. He wishes to tell us his concern. We will deliberate on his need and give him our answers. As we share the talking stick, we must keep to our own truth, without offering false advice."

The man gives the stick he holds to father, who takes it without rising. The man goes to the front of the home and sits alone upon a bench there. Father holds the stick for a long time, his head down. I cannot see his face. Faces from across the room look at his, waiting for him to speak. I smell fire, bodies, breath. I wish to push these things away, to grab father's hand and run with him and Ethan far, far away.

Finally, father lifts his head and clears his throat and begins in a low voice to speak in the strange tongue. The woman whispers his words in English. "I've been with the bear clan of the Nooh tribe for near twelve moons. When I first came amongst the Nooh people, I could not say anything, and so I did not speak of who I was or where I came from. As I learned Nooh words and about the bear clan, I began to forget those things of my old land. I think we all did, those of us who came from there." He stops and clears his throat again. He turns slightly toward me, and I look away.

"I learned to speak Nooh, I learned your ways and traditions, about Grandfather Sun, about the four winds, about Mother Earth. I was taken by Little Worrier and her family to replace her husband who was lost at the same battle in which I was found. After a time, and as a new member of the bear clan, I replaced my God with your Great Mystery, my beliefs with your tradition, my wife with your woman."

I curl into myself like a garden snail into its shell as I listen to his words.

"I did all this because without you, I would not have survived."

He forgot us. He forgot us. When I see mother again, I will ask her if she ever forgot him.

"But now something has occurred that has brought me back to that other land, the old land; something I did not dare to dream would happen. You all know: I have found my daughter." He turns and touches my leg, then turns away. The touch burns into me; I stare at the spot as I listen to the woman's whisper, to father's words. "She has brought a young man with her, and they tell me that somewhere in our forest, my—my wife roams." Even in the strange tongue, I can hear father's voice falter. "The mother of my daughter, Lily." He stops. The people in the room turn to each other, looking with questions on their faces. The grip of Kri-ki tightens upon me. No one speaks.

"I wish to find her. I know that I am husband to Little Worrier, and I love her, but I cannot leave Sar—Sarah in the forest to freeze and to be used by mad sailors." Father bursts out into a cry which frightens me. "The truth is, I wish to see her." His voice tears the air in two.

He clears his throat, wipes his face with his palm, and breathes in. "Today, my daughter Lily and her friend Ethan have begun their initiation into the bear clan. I do not wish to leave the tribe. I only wish to go in search of Sarah, to bring her back. For this, I need help. From what my daughter says, we will need to enter the Awthas' territory to hunt for her mother. According to our last treaty with them, this is not allowed. I need permission and help. This is why I called the council today."

Father holds on to the stick with two hands and brings it over his head, then slowly lowers it down. He turns to the man beside him and hands him the stick.

The man has a long profile, a thick neck, unpainted skin the color of cured leather. "Singing Bird speaks of another wife," the man starts. "When he took his place with Little Worrier, he did not tell us of this wife. We did not ask. He replaced Fish's Ghost. That was all we wanted of him. He made Little Worrier happy, he became a hunter, a warrior. A bear.

"When he came back from the hunt bringing the girl and boy, Little Worrier thought he'd brought her a son and daughter for her own. The girl, Leelee, has been very sick, and Little Worrier has given her health. The girl can be claimed her daughter, as Little Worrier wishes, and the boy, Ehan, can be her son. If Singing Bird wants to leave her, he must settle this with her." The man stops speaking, and hands the stick to the man next to him.

"It seems Singing Bird wishes to have two wives," this man starts. The people in the room laugh softly. "For that, he must live with the Awthas of the wolf clan, for here we have only one," he says, and passes the stick to the next man. Father's head is bent into his chest. He is not looking at anybody.

The next man has all his hair, graying and long. It is the man who lives in our tent. "Little Worrier is my daughter and Singing Bird is my son." He closes his eyes and touches the stick, the feathers and stones that hang from it. Kri-ki leans into me to look at her father. I shift away from her, forward, till my forehead is nearly touching my own father's back.

"I have lived with Singing Bird for his time with us. I know him. He says he replaced his God, beliefs, and wife for ours only because we saved him, but I know otherwise. He believes in Great Mystery as fully as I do. He loves Little Worrier as much as I. He has learned his traditions as a bear with more attention than the young boys in the inner circle," he says, pointing to the circle Ethan sits in. "But this does not mean that he cannot have feeling for this woman he seeks. She is a two-legged who is in trouble, and he wishes to help her. He says he will not leave the bear clan. I know he will return to me and Little Worrier. I hold him to his word and offer my help to him." He holds up the stick. The room fills with murmurings, both agreement and dissent. I hear Kri-ki fussing with the other women in whispers.

The gray-haired man passes the stick behind himself, to a woman sitting there. It is the older woman who lives in our tent. She stands the stick on the floor and looks at it as she speaks.

"We do not own our people. We do not force them to stay with us if they do not want. Even captured Awthas or Madriakes are not forced to stay once they are adopted. We love Singing Bird. That is enough for us." She touches her lips and nods. "He asks us for help in finding this woman. Help, Singing Bird, what kind of help do you seek from us?" She points the stick at him.

Father speaks. "I wish to send a runner to the Awthas' chief with enough wampum to assure our passage through the forest. I wish to take at least two men with me, the vision man to guide us and another. I wish to take Lily and Ethan, as I do not believe they will stay here without me."

The woman turns to me and fixes me with her eyes. She points the stick at me. "And what do the children say? Leelee?"

I did not think I would have to speak. I shake my head.

"Do you wish to go with your father?" she asks.

I nod. "Yes," I whisper.

She points the stick at Ethan. "Ehan?"

He nods. "Yes, of course."

"The children will go. For the shaman and a warrior, they must offer their service to you." She lowers the stick and hands it to her husband, who passes it to a boy's outstretched hand. Sweat sparkles on the boy's brow. He takes the stick.

"Singing Bird has already asked me to accompany him," he says. "We've hunted and fought together. I would be honored to help his search." He passes the stick on.

The stick travels around the room, the people giving out opinions on father's problem. They seem to believe we will return. I do not know that father really means to come back once we have found mother. I know I do not wish to. The stick reaches Kri-ki next to me, Little Worrier, who holds it with a trembling hand. With her other hand, she grips my arm. She speaks to father's back. He does not turn to look at her, but leans his forehead into his palms.

"It was not long ago that you brought me two children to care for, a gift beyond equal as I—I cannot birth my own. It is not right that you should give this gift and take it away." I glance at her face, at her tears welling up. I've not understood her words before; it's strange to understand her now. "I can see that the girl is not happy with me, and since you returned with her, something has changed in you. I feel that you must go. The woman may die if you do not, I feel that. But I have a question for you, Singing Bird. What will you do with this woman when you return?"

She touches his shoulder with the stick, but he does not answer. I feel that he is falling into a hole in himself, that his answer is important, and yet he is falling and cannot give it.

I force myself to look directly at her. She turns and looks back at me, chin raised high, eyes like watery dark holes that lead to a mysterious place below ground. I push words out of my mouth.

"I will take mother," I say. "I will keep her. You can put me and her in a tent at the end of the village; we won't need much. You don't have to worry, we'll return, and I can be your child and hers, you can share me. You can. I will be yours."

I say these words quickly to convince her to let us go, though I do not care what I am saying, as long as we go, soon, to mother. Time's sand is running out—I feel it, that we must go, we must go now, or it will be too late. I do not even know how much time I have spent here, lingering, sick. But I feel the surge inside of me, like a fed fire waving up to the sky.

"We must go to her or she will die. She will die! When we return, I promise I will come to you, when we return!" I cry, listening to my words being changed into her language, watching them soak into her. I feel nothing, no shame for my lie, just the desire to stand and run from the room.

She looks at me warily, then slowly nods, smiling at me. She reaches out and pulls me to her in a great hug and sob.

"Okri," she cries, "Okri."

"Daughter," I hear the blond woman interpret behind me, "Daughter."

I hug Kri-ki back, thinking of mother. She brushes the hair from my face and kisses me, then lets me go.

She turns to the man with the big feathered hat who sits on the bench. "I will give Singing Bird the wampum he needs," she cries to him in her teary voice. "Send a runner to the Awthas, to Chief Long Fingers of the wolf clan."

PART THREE

SIXTEEN

We travel by moonlight and sleep in the day between great rocks, under covers of skins pierced with twigs to disguise us. The dead winter forest twitches with movements and sounds—claws skittering up a tree, bird cries, hooves in leaves.

Upon the trail, we do not talk. We move through this land without permission. Father fears we could be killed at any moment by the angry wolf clan, since the Awthas did not accept the strings of wampum shells Kri-ki sent in exchange for our peaceful passage through their forest. We walk crouched, each footstep considered, quietly placed upon the path. As we walk, I picture the heads back home which sat upon lances in front of the baron's woodland—heads of those desperate men who dared enter his forbidden woods to catch a coney or pigeon without approval.

We do not cross the same land we came by, but descend another side of the mountain. Father says it is much quicker this way to the place of our first arrival. Leafless, with branches bold, the unwelcoming forest seems to turn its back on our advance. Winter has fallen hard; it reveals itself in the bitter air and beneath our feet in the crackling leaves and in the white frost which collects upon rough bark. Snow begins to drift down from the sky in search of a place to land, as we search, for any sign of mother.

The vision man touches tree trunks as we walk, and bark and snow-dusted stones. Father says he is looking for traces of mother the way a cur tracks a fox, or an owl a mouse, only differently. These hints of mother give the vision man dreams of the future, of where she may be. He saw me and Ethan lost in the forest this way. I don't quite know how his powers work, but each time we stop, I wait for the vision man to turn, eyes shining with knowledge of her, but he does not. He touches leaf or rock delicately as we wait to hear his pronouncement, then shakes his head, turns away, walks on.

It is not easy to look for mother. We cannot cry out her name, nor do we know where it is that she huddles to keep warm. Where is her fire? Who cares for her? Is she with the fellows and the sailors from the ship? I wonder about her beet-smelling hands—the reddened tips that I used to hold, that stroked my forehead on a cold night such as this—are they frozen now, or does she stretch them out toward friendly flames?

I pray for her as I have never prayed before. I pray with all the hope I can gather, with all the strength I have gained from my time-eating rest. I pray with all the faith I have left in God, though I cannot feel the goodness of Him in this place. I wish I could see like the vision man; I wish I could call upon a true vision of mother at the touch of a branch or rock. But this forest seems to have failed the man now. My memory of mother is fading, my own vision shrinking. I can just smell her, see her hands, feel the thin presence of her as she was. I work to bring her back, to see her instead of the bottoms of father's wet leather boots in front of me.

I walk behind father, with Ethan behind me on the path. I feel as though I walk between two strangers. When we were alone in the little village waiting for the runner to return, father stroked my hair gently and sang to me, but he would not speak of important things. Ethan ran about with Daw-ika shooting arrows into trees with their special cry, as if he were a Nooh person himself. At night, Ethan would lay beside me and stare into my face as I spoke to him. I wished to know how he felt about seeking mother, about our way through the forest, and our plans after we found her. He'd smile at me oddly, as father did when I began to speak this way, and would simply say he did not know the future. I know that he and father met for private conversations, but they would not tell me what they talked about together.

Father follows the vision man; behind me, Ethan is trailed by Daw-ika, who came along to teach him the way of the woods, Ethan says. Another man who arrived in the same sailing ship as father walks behind us. Philip is very tall and doesn't speak much; he is intent upon helping us to find mother, knowing as he did, he said, of hunger and cold—and of the pain of missing another.

In the Nooh village, as we prepared for our journey, Kri-ki had moaned and lamented our leaving as though we would die or had already died right before her. I watched her, but could not feel her sorrow. She did not wish us to go through enemy wood. When she saw we were going despite this, she packed for me a small bow with arrows which I do not know how to use. They hang loosely upon my back, along with the heavy bag of victuals she arranged.

As we progress farther and farther in, the forest becomes strangely quiet, as if the last of the birds and animals have gone into their winter nests. The only sound is our own footsteps carrying us over the snowy ground.

We take care to cover our tracks to remain hidden from the Awthas. Philip trails behind us with a long stick, pushing the snow back over our marks. He does it so expertly, one would never know we had journeyed through.

We rest beside dead logs covered with our twigged skins and eat the cold food we have brought. One night the moon guides us, but another night the clouds come. The air is so black we cannot see even our own hands before us, and must hold on to each other to walk. We move slowly, like the blind, carefully through this dangerous forest.

This evening, as we are readying for our night's travel, the vision man places some stones in a small circle. He takes a stick and scratches out something on the ground in the snow inside the circle. I see he is drawing pictures of animals, a dog and a bird, and other lines which seem meaningless beside them. He steps inside the stones and sits and chants in a low voice. He has not done this before and seems to be in a transfixion. I ask father what the man is doing, and he whispers that he is trying to contact his eagle spirit so he can fly above us and see below, to hunt for mother.

"He has been looking for scent of her for the past three days, a drop of her essence, some leavings of her skin or hair, but he has not found anything. His second step is to fly ahead of us, through the great bird, the eagle."

I look at father's wrinkled brow as he intently watches the vision man, and I see my father, father, behind the peculiar mask of dull colors and odd beliefs. Mother will cure him. Being with mother again will bring him back.

The vision man sits hunched into himself in the snow-covering, a pricking cold wind passing round him and us. He does not move. We wait for long minutes, listening to his chant, but he neither becomes an eagle nor does one suddenly appear, so I don't understand how he contacts this spirit. I did not know eagles had a spirit. I have never seen one before, and have only heard about them through father. As we watch, the vision man begins to move within the circle, waving his arms slowly up and down, raising his body as if he could fly. He does not step out of the circle, though he seems to be looking down, at the earth, speaking in his foreign tongue.

"Father, what's he saying?"

"He can see—he sees a fire. The Awthas."

We have not had a fire since we left.

Father listens. "The wolf clan sits by the fire," he says, shaking his head, watching the vision man, "with a woman behind them, moon-face." He draws his fingers over his face. "Pale, he means, pale like you, my girl. This is what he says."

A woman—like me. "Is it mother?"

The vision man is standing tall now, arms straight out like a soaring bird's, speaking excitedly.

"It is a woman from our land, he says. He does not sense whether it is Sarah or not; he does not know what she looks like—" Father stops, listens. "He says there is some longing in her, for a man, children—could this be her?"

I feel Ethan's hand upon my shoulder. In the blue light of the moon, I can see the question in his dark eyes, the hope. I feel, seeing father and Ethan eager this way, as if the weight of worry which has been pressing down upon my head has begun to lift.

"She is not ill," father continues. "She lives . . . with the Awthas . . . and sits by the fire, comfortable but unhappy."

My heart sings.

"Maybe that is why the Awthas did not want us to search for her in their forest," Ethan says. "They have her and want to keep her."

"This way, he says. We must go this way to get to her." Father points in the same direction as our vision man, who shakes himself out of his transfixion. I grab Ethan's hand and squeeze it for joy, and he smiles at me. Father hugs me hard to him with a great grin. We gather our things and catch up to the vision man, who has already started to lead us on the path to mother.

SEVENTEEN

We walk more quickly through the forest, no longer having to stop at stones and trees. I see what the vision man saw: mother leaning into the warmth of a fire, thin and hungry, waiting for us to come, as if she knows that we'll soon be with her. I wish to call out to her, "We're coming, mother, just wait—wait!" but I hold the words within me, and they build till I can barely stand to hold them anymore. "We're coming," I whisper to her, colors of happiness blooming within me like the flowers of a fresh May morning.

Once we get mother, we will go back to the sea and make ourselves a ship and leave this place. We'll go back to Myrthyr and we'll all live together, me and mother and father and Ethan, in our cottage. We will reveal Frere Lanther for the cruel trick he played upon us and chase him from our village. We'll celebrate saint's days again and feast with the others and tell our stories and earn victuals through our telling like the scraggling minstrels and troupes that come to Myrthyr. I will see the Marys again, and Mistress Grey. We'll be together, together, like peas in a pod, like ants in a hill, and nothing will disturb us again till the end of our days.

Ethan cups my shoulder with his hand and I turn to see him smiling at me. Father has reached out for me several times with smiles upon his face. We are as full of hope as can be—so soon we have found her, after so few days of searching. Father's way was quicker after all.

The vision man stops upon the path, halted by markings in the snow that pass in front of him, across one side of the forest to the other. The footsteps have been scratched out by a stick or a lance— the way Philip disguises ours. Daw-ika crouches to the marks and examines them.

"Awthas."

They are in the woods with us.

He points out the heel of a foot, indicating the direction in which its owner continued. He speaks, and father repeats what he says.

"Daw-ika suggests we make a plan. We cannot keep going this way, or we may walk right into them."

The footsteps cross the path before us, coming from the forest and going into the forest. We do not know when they passed, or how many they are, or what kinds of weapons they carry. We do not know if they are far away or nearby.

"Why don't we follow the footsteps?" Ethan says. "That way, we'll always be behind them, and we won't lose them. Since she is with them, they'll lead us right to her!"

Father tells this plan to the others. The vision man speaks rapidly, and father translates: "He says it is a dangerous plan, but it will save us time. We must be very careful not to get caught. Use the trees to shield you, and move in a circle like the squirrel, always protected by the tree trunks."

Anxious to move on, we start cautiously into the forest, off the path, following the footsteps of our enemy.

We walk the cold night vigilant and wary, expecting at any moment to come upon the men whom we are following. Walk and wait and listen, circling the trees, walk and listen, making sure there is no one close.

Then, as if their owners have vanished, the scratched-out footsteps end. We look up into the bald trees, but they have not climbed there.

Father talks in a hushed voice with the vision man and Daw-ika and Philip. Ethan stands close to me; I don't know if he's as frightened as I am, but if he is, he doesn't show it. As the men talk, we look at the empty branches of the trees above us and at the ground, at the unbroken white powdering of snow. I feel them all round us like spirits, jeering. Ethan hooks his arm into mine, holding me to him.

"Don't worry, Lily," he whispers, his breath warming my cheek. He is like a shield, protecting me. I wish I could understand what father is saying. I feel as though I am falling. I lean against Ethan, and he holds me.

Father turns to us. "Shaman can feel them near, but he does not know where they are." Father's eyes shift left and right, as if looking beyond us into the night to where the Awthas may be. "He thinks we should continue on, though we do not know where the Awthas' camp is from here."

We are lost.

"To go back would be to lose too much time, he thinks. He believes there is a hill in front of us that we must climb before we begin to see our way clearly."

I look ahead, and see we are about to go into a small stand of pines. Pines, my hidey place of long ago . . .

We begin to walk toward the pines when a bloodcurdling howl fills the forest. My heart stops, my feet freeze, Ethan walks into me. Howls puncture the night. Many men come running at us from behind. Men with dog's heads.

The men with dog's heads, as I had so feared—

Father grabs me and runs with me into the pines. Ethan runs— crazy howling men chasing this way and that after us. I want to scream, but I am too frightened. We are surely going to die. I think of my bow—to shoot them, kill them—but it slips off and falls away as father carries me in his arms. He runs with me till we are thrown to the ground by several men. I look up at their awful dog's heads with long dripping teeth and dead eyes, dog's heads which I have imagined and feared since we left Myrthyr. "Away dogs! A plague on you!" I cry, right before they tie belts round my eyes and mouth, wrists and ankles.

I've been captured by a possessed demon. He slings me over his shoulder and runs with me, baying deep into the crazed night. The forest is filled with screeches and howls and footsteps running, sounds that cleave me with blinded dread. The demon cur runs for a long time as my forehead pounds against his thick back, his shoulder digging into my stomach. The belt stifles my breath far down in my throat.

My last hope is that I get a glimpse of mother before I die.

He stops finally and throws me down against other bodies; I hear their grunts. He tears the blinds from my eyes and the belt from my mouth, and I see he has thrown me in a pile with father, Ethan,

Philip, Daw-ika, and the vision man. When I look up, I see that we are surrounded by men with dog's heads who stamp and yip at us like vicious barbarians.

Daw-ika and the vision man attempt to rise and speak to them, but are knocked in their jaws, onto the ground. We are all tied hand and foot and cannot see where we are for the wall of dog's heads surrounding us. I can feel their teeth on my skin, and wish more than anything to escape these torturous beasts. But I cannot move, cannot see beyond them.

The dog's-head men glare at us. One of them sticks his fingers under his own furred neck and pulls. His face moves strangely. I squirm nearer to father.

The man removes his head. As I watch, I feel the world open beneath me, the Devil below, gyrating about the hot fire of Hell. I am in Hell with them.

The others remove their dog heads, showing sweaty, sneering man heads. These men look like the Nooh people, their black hair long, their skins dark, but their eyes and manners are too cruel. They shout at us, and spit on us through their teeth. Their words make father and Daw-ika yell back at them, father struggling to his bound feet.

One of the men grabs my father by his hair and stands him up and slits open the belt that binds his hands. He forces father to kneel on the ground by twisting his arm behind him. Another man holds down father's other arm with his foot and takes an enormous rock and throws it upon father's hand. I hear a terrible crunch, then father's anguished, surprised cry. It happens so fast, before we can scream or speak or stop them. They let father loose, and he writhes on the earth in the muddy snow, his bloody fingers hanging oddly, surely broken. My poor father. Tears blind me as I squirm toward him. The men push me back. All I can do is listen to father's moans which stab inside me with their pain.

It's as if it is my own hand they've crushed.

They grab the rest of us by our tied wrists and drag us through the snow. My arms feel as if they will break off from my shoulders at any moment. Our bones, to come so far only to have our bones broken by these ungodly, immoral barbarians. They dump us into a round hut that is open to the elements, snow falling through the bent sticks that make up this cage.

One of the men is left to pace like a hungry rat outside, to watch us. Other men drag father by his feet into the cage and cast him down. I slide over to him. He breathes but is not awake. The demons quickly bind his hands again and kick him before they leave. Poor, sweet father—I touch the blood of his fingers with my bound hands, my own fingers frozen and numb. I pull his heavy head into my lap and feel the wetness of the blood upon it, battered against the ground as he was dragged. My tears drip onto his forehead. Ethan crawls over; so do the others. We watch over father in the dim night's light and shiver and huddle together for warmth.

The gray morning shows faces—rough, pocked brown faces with wide features, young faces with black, angry eyes. Raging men and women shake handfuls of hair at us and poke their fingers through the cage which holds us—as if we were bears to be baited.

"The wolf clan," father mumbles as he wakens. His head is still upon my lap. I am leaning against Ethan, who is curled beside Daw-ika. We have slept this way.

"Father is waking!"

"It is only the wolf clan who would do such a thing," father goes on.

I look at his hands which lie upon his stomach, one swollen berry-colored, like a plague hand, bloating round the leather tie.

"They are too fierce and do not listen to reason—"

The guard outside our cage watches us. He sticks a branch through the bars and hits the air before us, yelling. His face is a fearsome twist of evil.

Philip whispers, "He says we done wrong by coming here. He don't want us to talk. We better listen to him."

We sit in the cage waiting for someone to come or something to happen, looking at the wicked faces which taunt us. Hunger and fright eat away at me. I do not know what these creatures will do with us. Cut off our hands and feet? The thought makes me boil with nausea. I feel Ethan's arms near me, puffs of his breath hot and quick upon my neck.

We sit the day long, imagining escape, father's head on my lap, Ethan or Philip or Daw-ika behind me, the vision man apart, squatting with his tied hands tucked between his calves. We return the stares of the gawking, spitting people. We make water and dung in the cage, in front of them.

The tall Philip has wriggled to a place next to me and sits in a brave stare, watching the Awthas as they bring their pointy teeth close to the wood and lick their lips at us. He mutters to us over and over, "We are in an awful fix, it's true, we are in an awful fix." Philip says they might kill us and feed us to their dogs. My stomach aches at the thought. He tells us about the hanks of hair they hold in their hands and wear about their necks, human hair, "locks of the Nooh people they won from our heads." I think of the headless folk I saw in the forest, the men who came to the New World with father. To imagine any one of us, or mother, that way brings me to tears.

I must think hopeful thoughts, or I will wither off in despair. I think of mother, here, as the vision man said he saw her. I whisper to Philip, "Can you ask the vision man if he still sees mother?" Maybe she is here, maybe we could still find her and save her somehow. Philip nods and asks the vision man.

"He says the woman he saw is still here," Philip says quietly, craning his long neck to look round.

My insides leap for joy. But looking at the sharpened branches held before our faces by these beasts, I hardly dare to wish we'll see her.

"Can he see where she is in this place?"

They exchange whispers again. Philip turns to me with sad eyes and shakes his head slowly. "She is too frightened to show herself."

The ashen sky begins to deepen with night when a man in stiff furs with a glaring white dog's head comes to us, followed by a gathering of men with lances. The white-dog man holds up his hands when he reaches our cage; upon them sit two long paws whose nails look sharp and crooked as scythes. He wears teeth and hair about his neck. The people crowd round the cage, crouch at his feet and look up at him.

"Long Fingers," father says through his dry lips.

An opening in the dog's head shows the man's mouth, speaking. No one speaks back. I think father or Philip will tell me what the Long Fingers says, but their wide eyes only stare at the man. Father struggles to sit up. He still cannot.

The Long Fingers says something that seems to alarm father and the others. Daw-ika yells streams of words at him. The Long Fingers screams back, his words climbing over Daw-ika's, silencing him. The Long Fingers turns to the guard and waves his paws and bellows. The guard comes into the cage and drags Daw-ika out by his feet and throws him in front of the chief. With all his force, the evil chief kicks Daw-ika in the side with a sickening thud. An airless shout escapes the boy, and Ethan cries out. I pray and pray and pray to God in Heaven to see this, to stop this evil!

With his long claws, the chief grabs Daw-ika by his queue and pulls up his head and shakes it by that small hank of hair, yelling and spitting into Daw-ika's face as he does. He pulls a knife from his belt and quickly cuts off Daw-ika's head-skin, taking his hair with it. He has cut the skin from Daw-ika's head! I cover my face and scream, seeing behind my lids the never-ending river of red blood flowing down Daw-ika's forehead, into his tormented eyes.

EIGHTEEN

It is very late, and the Awthas are asleep, all except the guard. Daw-ika leans against the vision man's chest. Ethan presses his hands upon the muddy leaves the wolf people slapped onto Daw-ika's torn head to stop the gushing blood. The boy breathes shallow, fitful breaths. The vision man holds the boy with his tied hands, whispering Nooh words which sound like prayers. Philip is holding father's hands aloft, to drain his swelled fingers of the blood that pools within them.

"They want to keep us here, they do, to make us one of them," Philip mutters. "That's why they're keeping us alive. Too much, that's too much retribution for what we have done. We have merely trespassed."

The guard, a man with glittering teeth, grimaces and takes out his privy in front of us and pisses into our cage. I would cut him if I had my hands free. I would scream in his ear and tear off his head-skin hair by hair, to make him die as slowly as a man can.

Mercy. There is none here.

Hatred poisons my blood to my very core. To smell this crude man's vulgar stink above our own—he is Lucifer himself! Oh, I long to sing, to raise my voice over his filth and overcome, but I do not believe that would help.

The guard spits upon my father as he passes. I have never felt such rage before, sending its flaming arrows up through me. I feel I could scream and scream and would never empty myself for the dreadful, bloody screams which build inside me.

In the shadows of the thick trees beyond the guard, I see her— her kirtle. Startled, I shake my head and move my eyes. The bit of her kirtle glows egg white behind that tree, just beyond—

I whisper, "Father? Ethan, Philip? Do you see? The kirtle? Look into the trees, where they stand thick."

None of them move their heads, but I can feel them straining to look. In the distance, the bottom slip of kirtle, and now, a hand from beneath a shawl of furs, a glowing hand which moves slowly back and forth. Waving.

I wish to jump up, to shout out, to wave both my hands like an anxious voyager, but I just wait till I see the guard turn away, and then stretch my bound arms up, and move them side to side, nodding my head.

I dare not even breathe the thought that it is truly her.

She does not come for a long time. We wait till finally the guard tires himself with his pacings and taunts and sits against the tree opposite us. He sucks at his teeth and flicks his long nails, muttering words to us angrily and laughing to himself. He is thin and strong, and I do not think I could kill him all alone. I would try, if I could. I think of the many ways I would like to kill him—chop off his head and watch it roll; poison him and watch him writhe and choke; stick a dagger in his heart.

She runs up to the tree behind him, and my heart tightens like a clenched fist. I fear he will turn and notice her. Closer, I see there is something about the shape of her, her hair, the look of her face that is familiar but not right. I want it to be mother, but as she creeps round the tree, doubt clouds my vision. In her hands, she holds a heavy branch. She raises the stick and with forceful, fleshy thumps, knocks the guard once, twice, thrice in the head till he sprawls upon the ground. When she turns to us, we all see, those of us who know her, that it is not mother.

For a moment, I cannot contain my disappointment. My eyes burn with tears.

I know the woman who throws down the heavy stick and comes before us, but I cannot place her.

Not till Philip cries her name—"Margaret!"—in a hoarse whisper.

It is Margaret, from our ship, our Margaret. But not my mother. Not mother.

"Philip. I wasn't sure 'twas you! But it is!" She kneels to the cage and looks in. Her hands tremble. "I never killed a man . . . ," she says, glancing at the slain guard.

"You saved us, Margaret," I say.

"Bless you, brave woman," Philip says.

"Lily! Oh, Philip!"

She opens the cage and cuts us loose from our bindings. Our hands and feet are so numb, none of us can stand. We rub and shake ourselves, trying to return the vital air to our limbs.

"We must hurry, we must go," Margaret whispers frantically.

The vision man lifts the bloodstained Daw-ika into his arms; Ethan and I carry father beneath his arms as we move out of this camp. Philip and Margaret are behind us. We have no food, no weapons. No mother.

We have only our lives.

We move as fast as our sore limbs will allow through the black forest whose heaviness is suddenly rife with animal howls, bird cries, nut rat chatter. The vision man leads us into a maze of soft firs which brush gloom through our hands and hair. He follows by smell and by feel the way to the trading sea, to the place from which we came—where the sailors may be with mother.

Father stops often, drooping his weight against us, so laden with pain he cannot go on. His head, he says, aches so badly, he can barely see.

Daw-ika lies in the vision man's arms like loose hay, without life or spirit. I think his soul may already have left him.

Philip and Margaret walk behind us, covering our footsteps with scratchings over the muddy snow, whispering.

"The miracle!"

"It's a miracle!"

"Oh, Philip, I came for you. I came all the way here to find you, and one minute I'm looking for you in the trees, and the next minute they come, the heathens—took me right into the forest, right here."

"Did they hurt you, love?"

"No, no. They did nothing."

Father falters on the path; he slips from our grasp and falls to his knees. Philip and Margaret rush to his side to help him along. Ahead of us, the vision man's outline in the dense shadows moves faster. We hurry to catch up, feeling that the Awthas may be upon us at any moment.

The vision man snakes us through a brambly slope to an opening; I walk behind him to the small, jagged mouth set in the hill—a cave. He steps inside with Daw-ika. There, the blackness is pitch. I can hear his breath, but I do not know where it comes from exactly. Water drips; the cave smells of loam and rot and chill air. Beneath my feet, the earth slips like sandy silt.

In search of light, I return to the opening, though the moon doesn't shine brightly. Philip and Margaret carry father in, careful to avoid the man and boy. Ethan hangs back beside me for a moment, then slips into the cave. Its darkness seems to devour everyone with a covetous hunger. I do not wish to go back in.

I wait at the mouth, listening to animals snuffling in the brambles nearby. Are they animals, or are they men, creeping up the hill closer to us?

Early in the morning, a luminous sun heaves itself up and lights the cave, making snow drip in its heat. During the night, my stomach bent back upon itself with hunger, leaving me flat as the ground. I stand from where I was curled next to father, and my head wobbles upon my neck, the humors of a food desire flowing through me. I touch father's wound and he moans. His hand has billowed to the size of a melon.

In the vision man's arms, the boy, Daw-ika, has not woken, but still he breathes. Next to them, Ethan sleeps. The vision man places Daw-ika on his fur cloak upon the ground. Silently, he moves farther into the cave where he plucks a handful of moss from between long, cracked rocks that are wet with seeping water. He holds open his hand and looks and picks at the moss. With low, muttered words, he delicately lays the damp greens upon Daw-ika's open wounds. When he is finished, he crouches before the boy, his hands moving above the shallow breaths that come from the struggling mouth. It's as if he is pushing in and pulling out the injured boy's air.

I go to where father is sleeping, his head resting upon his furs, and sit as close to him as I can without touching him. The vision man clicks his tongue at me. He holds up his hand and puts a nearby stick in it and waves it at me. I shake my head. He tears a string of leather from those that encircle his waist and places the stick in his hand and wraps the string about it. This he points at father.

He wants me to bind father's broken hand.

I nod and go to the vision man, who breaks a piece of the stick and shows me on my hand how to gently bind father's. I take the string and stick to father, but as soon as I place the stick in his raw, swelled palm and try to straighten his fingers, he wakes and cries out.

"Father, it's only me. I'm trying to bind your hand, your broken hand—"

"Leave me be. Leave it alone," he growls, his face reddening with pain.

"But your fingers, they will not grow in properly—"

"I don't care!"

The vision man calls to father. The others wake, and Philip comes over to help, his breath smelling of swamp rot.

"He's right, Eric. You see, those fingers are already becoming twisted. Let's us do it, there's a good chap," he says to father, his voice quiet and soothing. Father growls again, but allows me to bind his hand straight against the smooth stick. When I am finished, I hold his head, stroke his face, and pray for him to get better.

None of us wish to leave any of the others to hunt and be seen by roaming Awthas, but someone must find food. Ethan and Philip offer to go. As they climb out of the cave's mouth, Margaret jumps up and goes after them. I am left with father and the two Nooh men. The vision man prays fervently to his strange gods over Dawika. I watch him and wonder about my own God, whose presence I feel as slightly as a dying old man's. I close my eyes and try to pray for father, my faith flickering listlessly over him.

NINETEEN

The boy's eyes open in the dim cave and he cries out. My heart jumps like a frog. He will live! The vision man cleans the boy's wound with melted snow, examining him as I tend to father's hand. Ethan stands, paces about the cave, to the mouth and back, sitting at the boy's side to stare and stare at him, only to rise and pace once again.

The small fire Philip and Margaret have made reflects in Daw-ika's eyes. The whites burn dark red, the skin about his wound has become blue, and the huge, weeping sore upon his crown festers with yellow pus. His face shows his agony, his voice too, as he begins to moan pitifully. The vision man talks constantly to him, trying to quiet him, but the boy keens like a young injured lamb. Ethan sits at the boy's side, leaning into him as if he is trying to take in his friend's suffering.

A black skin has formed at the back of father's head, and his sight, he says, has cleared; it's his hand now which gives him much pain. He speaks to the vision man about Daw-ika, about mother, and when we can begin to search again. Father says the vision man tells him that the boy floats on the cusp between this world and the spirit world, and it won't be long before we find out his destination.

Philip and Margaret clean and roast the two nut rats and the fat dove they've caught. The vision man tries to feed Daw-ika, but the boy is too delirious. He keens, the sound wrapping about our hearts like vines. Sweat shimmers on his agonized forehead; the vision man presses handfuls of melting snow upon his cheeks. Ethan cannot take his eyes off his friend. I have never seen him so agitated.

We eat without much appetite and hope for the boy to heal.

The water drips and trickles, and I wait to hear howls, running footsteps, an attack. Wait to see the dog's heads that threaten our lives; wait and wonder where mother may be in this land, where in this bedeviled New World her soul may linger. I press my mouth to the cave wall where the water drips and cup my hands together and gather water for father, to wet his dry lips. None of us dare leave this shelter the vision man has found for us.

He holds Daw-ika in his arms. The boy fitfully sleeps. The vision man cools his forehead and keeps him near. In the night, I wake to see the vision man looking down at the boy, answering his moans with low, comforting sounds. Before I fall back asleep, I see Ethan beside them in the flicker of the firelight, muttering. I drift off to the words of his prayer, though I am not sure what curing power it will have. "Our Father, if you reside in this world, please hear me now. Please bring round to me my friend and guide, Daw-ika. I have never had such a friend before, and don't wish to lose him now. He has never harmed another. Please, oh Lord, bring him round. . . ."

Daylight comes again strong, the sun shining into the mouth of the cave, the air cold. Ethan sits alone in the sunlight, looking out, his furs drawn tightly about himself.

I poke at the ashes of the fire, but there is no hot tinder with which to rekindle it. Ethan hugs his knees, looking down into the wild brambles that skirt the cave. He has not slept near me, nor spoken to me in the time we've been here. I go to the opening, into the sunshine for warmth, and to be near him. I know that sometimes it is better not to talk when the air between people is filled with moody spirits. But I miss him, and cannot help myself.

"Sleep well?" I ask him. He shrugs, staring into the forest whose bare limbs stick out like so many lances. His chin rests in his clenched fist. I wish to press my cheek to his, to feel his warm breath upon me—but he seems as cold as the New World itself.

"What are you thinking, Ethan?"

He does not answer. He squints at me, his eyelids half closed in anger, and looks away.

"Ethan! What is it? Why do you look at me like that?"

He pounds his forehead on his fist. "It's—it's mad, Lily."

"What is mad?"

"What we're doing here!" He scrambles to his feet suddenly, to get away from me, it seems. "We've almost lost two lives—"

He seems like another boy, one who does not know me, one who has not been with me since the beginning of our journey.

"What are you questioning, Ethan? I don't understand."

"It's madness, Lily, like we're exchanging lives." He paces before me, waving his arms as he speaks. "That's what it seems we are doing. I don't know what we're doing, by God, I don't know what we're doing here at all." He stops, turns, looks down at me, shaking with fury, "Must Daw-ika die—is that what you wish? Must Daw-ika die for another to live?"

I'm stunned. I don't understand this attack; I expected no one to

die for another. Our search for mother in this place, this world—
how, even for a moment, can I doubt the value of looking for her?
"Do you . . . do you believe that this search is . . . is useless, Ethan?
That we should give up?" My head, my heart shakes—

He throws his hands out. "I don't know!" he shouts. My heart
falls; tears hurry to my eyes. He goes on, "Who else has to get hurt?"

"Ethan! I can't believe—"

"It's mad, Lily, mad!" He moves away from me, outside. "I can't
bear it!" he cries out, his cry echoing into the woods.

I thought, I thought that everyone who'd joined the search came
because they wished to help. I should say that, tell him, but I cannot find the words. I stand up. "Go back then. Go back," I say. "I
will go on myself." I cannot imagine giving up the search, never
knowing if mother could have been saved or not. "I'll go alone. I
don't need you to come with me," I cry.

Ethan turns and runs down the hill, hollering into the bare trees.
"You're not going anywhere alone!" he shouts.

I turn back to the cave.

"What's all the noise about, Lily?" father asks.

"Did you hear?" I ask. His puffed, sleepy eyes reflect the light of
the sun. I feel as if all the air has been drawn from me. "What Ethan
says, is it true?" I turn to the others, to Philip, Margaret. "Do you
all think this way?"

"What does he say, Lily?" father asks.

I try to gather my breath into me. I feel as if Ethan himself took
it from me with the surprise of his secret accusation. An exchange,
a life for a life.

Was he right?

"He says it's mad, this search, that we have nearly lost two lives."

"But we have gained one," Philip says, glancing at Margaret. "The poor lamb's not thinking right." He's at the fire, rubbing together two black stones over dried grass, then hitting the stones quickly. "He better be careful, bawling out like that."

Father does not speak, but stares at the flicks leaping from the black stones.

"Should we stop, father, what do you think? Should we go back? I don't know. I have not doubted before, but now, now I wonder. Why must we go this way? Why must we go through the Awthas' territory? Couldn't we go the way me and Ethan came in the first place, where there were no Awthas? Perhaps Ethan is right, we are being mad—"

"Calm down, just calm down, Lily. Listen to me. Inland from the Nooh camp is Nooh territory. But from Cracked Moon Mountain to the sea grass is Awthas. We know the sailors who have your mother are probably near the sea. We went this way because it's shorter, but it's through the same territory you passed. You were very lucky you didn't encounter Awthas. I believe they felt you children were harmless, and simply left you in peace."

I wish I could speak to the vision man, to learn what he feels about our journey. He rocks with the moaning boy whose head will not heal. Poor boy; I go to him and look into his face. I cannot imagine his injury, the skin of his head torn asunder, his skull left to the open air, the agony which shows in his eyes. I think of him teaching and playing with Ethan, his generosity and kindness, to offer to join our search, to join with us, strangers, to find a stranger. . . .

Why had he begun to yell at the Awthas chief the way he had? What had the chief said that made the boy so angry he would yell at such a fearsome person? All their faces, father's and Philip's, their outcries—what had the Long Fingers said to make them all so alarmed?

"Father, what—what caused Daw-ika to make the Long Fingers so angry? Why did he do this to him?"

Father looks over at Philip, who pokes at the smoldering fire. Philip glances back at father and clears his throat. "Long Fingers felt that the trespass was another breach of our territory agreement. The offense was made the worse since we asked and he refused our request to pass through their hunting grounds. He said we well knew that Awthas territory would open up and be shared with the Nooh in growing time, but the fact that we didn't wait until then meant—"

"Meant death," father says.

"Death for one of us, not all," Philip says.

They wanted to exchange one of our lives for the rest.

"And, well . . . Long Fingers, well . . . Long Fingers wanted you, Lily," Philip says.

I let out a cry.

"And we protested. Daw-ika protested. We all protested, my girl."

I cannot imagine. I cannot speak, for I would not know what to say. For my sake the boy dared go against the Awthas' king? I cannot think what to do—to replace his life, to cure him, to heal him, to fix him, to help him, help him, Lord, for I cannot imagine.

I am mad. Ethan's right. This is mad.

"The search will continue, Lily, as soon as Daw-ika can move. I have Shaman's word on it," father says. "Ethan just needs some air. He'll come to his senses, you'll see."

"We'll be with you, lassie, don't you worry," Philip reassures me.

I don't want to put their lives in danger anymore. I wish I could go alone, or with father, and send the rest to the Nooh camp where they'll be safe. But I couldn't go alone, I don't have the strength.

I get up from the fire and sit at the mouth of the cave, looking down the slope, into the forest, to see where Ethan may be. He's right, right to be angry with me. We should all go back.

Yet I sit in the warmth of the sunlight, listening to the birds hoot, to the nut rats chitter, and I think of her wandering in this forest helpless. I think of her lost and hungry and tired the way I was when father found me. Will we ever find her? Will we all end up dying? Beneath the many questions I have, beneath the hissing doubts and confusions, a fierce voice urges, *mother.*

TWENTY

According to the Bible, between Heaven and Hell is a place called Purgatory where God puts those who are destined to wander till their Fate can be decided, if it ever is. This is where we are. In God's nowhere. In an endless forest by an enormous sea in a world that people call New, but which is as old as any of God's creations. I am angry at God for putting us here. He seems a weak old man who cannot fight evil.

I walk to the mouth of the cave and back to the injured boy, to the mouth to look for Ethan, and back to the boy, stopping to check on father, to ask him what we'll do next. He says our direction will become clear in a short time, that we must just wait. Wait, Lily.

Philip and Margaret talk of their children and of the rolling meadows of their village. Philip softly answers Margaret's questions about his hair and dress, about the Nooh people, the baron.

I cannot listen.

"Father," I say, rising to go out, to look for Ethan who has not come back. "It's been a long time. I must go and look for him."

He nods. "I'm thinking the same myself," he says, starting to get up when Philip stops him with a hand on his arm.

"No, let me go with her, Eric. You stay and rest. I'll fetch us all some food, as well as the boy." He turns to Margaret. "Stay with Eric, take care of him. We will be back shortly."

A frown passes her lips. "But, Philip, I want to go with you. To be near you."

"We'll be back in a moment, promise, love."

I'm outside already, in the sunshine, edging down the hill after Ethan, following footsteps faintly impressed in the mud. I don't hear Philip behind me till he touches my shoulder and whispers my name. We wind through the forest silently, listening for Awthas, for Ethan. I look up into the bare trees and down under the brambles, still following the glimpses of his footsteps which lead the way.

From a short distance, I see the shine of water glittering in the sun. We circle round trees till we are standing in front of a great body of water, like a pond, only much bigger than a pond. A deep blue body of clear water surrounded by tall grass and sharp trees.

"Lake of Eight Clans," Philip breathes behind me.

Ethan's steps end where the shore begins, as if he jumped from its stony edge and disappeared under the clear depths.

Philip begins to track round the shore, looking closely at the snow and grass and earth. "The boy went in; he must have come out."

I don't know how Ethan could've swum in this freezing air, this icy water. Then I remember the river, how he cleaned me in the river.

"But his clothes, Philip. If he went into the lake, would he not remove his furs?"

Philip stops walking and turns to look at the water, then at the shore. "Nowhere about, eh?"

I shake my head, feeling the fog of fear like a bitter cloud taking over my chest, spreading ice to my stomach. "Ethan!" I cry out in a panic. I clap my hand over my mouth. Philip grabs my arm and pulls me down into the tall grass. He points to the far end of the lake. In the late-afternoon light, I can see only purple and black shadows there. I shake my head; he keeps pointing till I see it. A long moving thing like a smile gliding in the water. Is it an animal, a bird, a fish?

"A boat. We must leave here at once," Philip says softly. "They've got him."

He pulls me to my feet and drags me back toward the cave. The whole way, I resist. I want to cry out and run and stop them from taking my Ethan, but Philip keeps a hand over my mouth, nearly carrying me. Thoughts jab at me like thorns. Another one of us swallowed by this Godforsaken forest. Why did I not look for him sooner? Why did I quarrel with him? What if they kill him instead of me? It was me they wanted, it was me who thought of searching for mother. I talked him into it. They should have taken me.

"Father," I cry once we are back and Philip releases me. "Father, they took him! We must—we must stop them! Oh, this is dreadful, awful, I cannot—cannot—" I cannot bear it as Ethan could not bear it. The last thing he said to me—he could not bear—he said I wouldn't have to go alone, and now he's left me. I'm frantic, in a murk.

I throw myself at father's feet, sobbing.

"What happened exactly?" I hear father ask Philip.

"They've got him," Philip says. "We seen their boat at Lake of Eight Clans, where we followed his steps, his marks that ended at the shore." He sits heavily at the fire, staring at it. "'Twas a bark of the Awthas that took him, I feel it certain."

"Did you see the Awthas? Did you actually see them take the boy?"

"Nay, 'twas too far. But his footsteps ended at the near shore, and the boat at the far shore . . ." Philip shakes his head. "'Tis certain they took him."

I just want to go home, to go where it's safe and quiet and there are no animal men with hair and teeth hanging from their necks who eat people. Home, where there's a bed and a hot meal on the fire pit and friends to laugh with. Why did I not listen to Ethan? The thought makes me cry harder—Ethan, whom I wanted to return with me to Myrthyr to live in our cottage. Sobs break through my chest. I feel a hand on me, father's hand, and then another, Margaret's thin fingers.

"Where's Daw-ika and Shaman?" Philip asks, making me look up through my tears at the cave.

"They've gone back," Margaret answers. "The boy, his head was burning up, and the man, he took him back, back to where you came from." She looks at father. "What did he say when he left?"

Father shivers. "He was afraid the boy would die here . . . or on the path during our search. He felt they would slow us down, and that if the Awthas did come again, the boy and he would not be able to fight. He has returned to Nooh territory with Daw-ika to get the proper plants to heal him, or to aid him on his journey to the spirit world."

They're gone. I look round the fire at the few faces left: Margaret, Philip, father. We'll get lost. We're not enough to go to the Awthas to fetch Ethan, to demand him. I feel an emptiness in the world I have never felt before, a true faithlessness that leaves a terrible blackness inside me.

"That poor child," Margaret says. "Will they be safe?"

"He's willing to take the chance for the boy," father says. "We must go on without them."

"Shouldn't we stay and wait and make sure Ethan is—is taken? We're not sure, are we? We're not truly sure he won't return." I think of the vision man and the torn Daw-ika, and of poor Ethan, alone with the horrid wolf people, their claws on him. Ethan, who came from riches, tables laden with goose and clothes sparkling with gold, who lost his mother and father and everything he knew, till he was left only with me, me and my mad search. I feel exhausted and empty. It was he who kept me alive in the forest, and now I am without him.

"No, Lily, we must go on."

"I don't want—"

Father turns to Philip—"You said we're at Lake of Eight Clans?" Philip nods.

"We're not far from the sea, then. It's just as Shaman said."

"Two lakes off," Philip says, "Lake of Eight Clans is two lakes from the sea. There we'll be safe."

"Shaman said we must go on. I wasn't sure what to do, and he said we would find a way, that I should heed my . . . my feelings." Father shakes his head. "I feel we must go on to the sea. We can't stay here—"

"But what about Ethan?" I cry, but they are already moving.

"I can speed us to the sea, I know the way," Philip says, standing from the fire. "I'll make us weapons—lances, daggers—we'll push on."

"I don't want to leave Ethan."

"We aren't leaving him, but we can't stay here like ducks to be clubbed in our sleep," Philip says, turning to me. "We'll find your mother, lambie," he says, dipping down to pat my teary face. "It'll be a blessed day when we find her."

Margaret squeezes my shoulders as she stands.

"And when we do," Philip continues, "we'll come for Ethan. We'll come back with the whole clan of warriors and get him, won't we, Eric?"

"That we will," father says. "Lily, we must move on now. It's the only thing we can do."

Through my misery, I pray Ethan will live till we come for him.

TWENTY-ONE

I do not think I will ever get used to losing people. I cannot imagine how father and mother had so many children before me and lost them without suffering a madness. People lose people to plague, sweating sickness, lung pox, belly rot. Before everyone's eyes, a child or grandmother, husband or sister drops their strength and dies. Is that more terrible, to lose someone with no hope of ever seeing them again? Or is it worse to be on the edge of a silence?

No one there.

A silence of possibility unanswered and unfulfilled.

Without Ethan, I feel as if I'm missing a leg. I limp along behind Philip, holding the stick he has sharpened for me. It is longer than my entire body and gets caught in roots and rocks when I forget I'm clutching it. Margaret, who walks behind me, trades her shorter club for my stick out of fear she will lose an eye from my lance.

As I walk, I imagine that I am queen, that today is my grand coronation and as I glide down the track, folks throw rose petals up in the air and their fragrance fills me. My king is Ethan and he walks by my side teaching me grace and dignity, whispering words of love to me, saying how he will never leave me, never allow them to take him away.

I must stick to the path. The rank animal smell of Philip's furs and body comes to me through the cold air.

Ethan in all his glorious riches lies upon one of those elegant mats of rushes I've heard tell, eating those figs that the merchants bring from the big city of Rome. I've never seen a city. Ethan feeds the figs to me and touches my cheeks and lips with his lips, as Philip and Margaret do, as father and mother did. We laugh together, we laugh.

I stare up at the place where Philip's hair is growing back, his unshaven head round the queue.

Mother calls to me from a room in the manor where we live all together with Ethan: "Lily, will you bring a fagot of wood for the fire?" Wait—no, we shall have servants to bring the wood. Father will never have to chop another piece with his broken hand again.

Hidden in the tall grasses, we pass round the lake and cross a marshy bog that has begun to freeze over.

I'll go back to when my faith in our strong, ever-present God ran hot in my blood. Pictures will hang about our walls of Mary holding the baby Jesus. Frere Lanther and the baron and all their bad ways will be gone. Myrthyr will have only the religion of home, God in every home, prayer among friends, without a treacherous priest to pay. Every morning, I'll wake in bed with Ethan beside me, his hair all ajumble.

We pass another lake, smaller than the last. Like a dart of lightning, Philip catches a fish with his hands and slams it with his club. We clean it and eat it without cooking it.

We'll take over the baron's abandoned manor and we'll have cows which I will milk and fresh water from the well and cool lettuce from the croft garden. Every Sunday, we'll open the manor to all the poor folks for supper and we'll sit and pray together our very own prayers which we will think of ourselves. Father will lead us in song. I have not heard father sing a hymn since I found him.

We pass the final lake, and then the smell comes to us.

A wave of salty air fills my breast with the memory of my sad mother which I've tried to plant beneath my ribs and shroud with the skin of me.

"The sea," Margaret says. I look behind me at Margaret's and father's white faces. We stop, though the water is not yet visible. My mind teems with thoughts of the horrible, dirty ship which brought us to this forsaken land, our long, starved journey, mother's afflicted face when the baron came for her.

Father and Philip exchange nervous glances.

I would give anything to have that ship back, without the sailors and the baron, just a ship to take us home again.

"Almost there," father says.

"We got to keep going," Philip says. "This place, 'tis a bad place to stop."

I follow him, the others behind us, nearly trotting as we push to reach the end of the Awthas' land, through the stiff, dying grasses which grow far over my head. The rush of waves hitting each other sounds like the wind in the dry grass. Waves landing their weight upon the shore.

We arrive at the open water.

Its unknowable depths give my heart pause; its grandness thrills through me like the day I first saw it. As far as I can see, the gray and rippled sea goes on, endlessly being swallowed by the craggy land. Water as powerful and destructive as the Awthas, yet a way, our way to find mother and return.

The wind blows hard and cold through my furs. We stand, shivering on the shore, staring out over the frothy white and green sea that is filled with animals and fish, whales and shells, demons and ghosts that can't be seen. Father draws me close to him, pulling me under his furs; Philip and Margaret come near.

The sea is loud and alive—a vast, scaly monster twisting and writhing in its own depths.

"Which way now?" Margaret shouts, the wind throwing her hair about her head and pushing the words back into her mouth. "He told you to feel it," she shouts to father. "What do you feel now? Which way?"

Father closes his eyes, fighting the wind which buffets him. We wait. He shakes his head and sighs.

"You must, you have to try," Philip urges him.

I hold him closer as we wait and he touches his forehead to my head. We close our eyes, and I picture mother, her edges shimmering faintly, her eyes closed like ours, her face drawn pale. "That way," father says suddenly, lifting his head, opening his eyes. He points left, to the ragged, bouldered shoreline he means us to follow. "I feel we're to walk that way, up the shore. I feel no more than that."

"Good enough," Philip says, giving father the lead as we set out along the edge of the grasses where they meet the uneven rocks.

The shore runs straight, then arches and bends, then runs straight again. Its shape is arduous and difficult as we follow high and low, climbing where we cannot walk, walking where other feet have carved out paths—fishing and trading paths, father says. We break through naked thorny bushes and yellowed goosegrass, traveling on without meeting another soul. We find reprieve in small pockets where the water floats inland but the wind doesn't follow. In these pockets, we make fires and eat and rest, warming ourselves, finding relief from the harsh rocks, the cold wind.

We walk all day without finding a trace of mother.

Father tries to feel mother the way the vision man did, stopping to sense her presence. He touches a rock or bush, closes his eyes, breathes in and holds his breath. The wind pulls the hair from his queue, blowing it about his face.

He pauses by a log of wood that has been washed bone clean by the sea. He kneels to it, holds his good hand to it. I stand over him, wondering if he is looking for her spirit the way I looked for his in the forest before I found him. I wonder if he doesn't see her because she is using her spirit for living. He lets go of his breath and shakes his head.

"I feel, a terrible, darkness—"

"Don't stand over him, Lily, let him work," Philip tells me, but I'm losing patience.

"I—I feel we're going the right way, but I also feel quivery, like something's wrong about it," father says.

"But this is the right way, you do feel this is the right way, eh?" Margaret asks.

"Leave him be, Maggie," Philip tells her, watching father closely. "He's coming to it."

"Yes, yes, we're going the right way," father says. He struggles to his feet, and we start off again.

In the misty evening, after trodding another day along the lonely shore, the rhythmic, never-ending waves bring and take my thoughts as if they were hymnal refrains, the songs of my loved ones, as precious as the songs of Our Heavenly Father once were to me.

Mother, your eyes upon me, warmer than the light of the sun— shush.

Ethan, we'll never fight in all of our lives—shush.

Mother, I will bring you sweets and flowers and sing to you— shush.

Ethan—shush—mother—shush—

TWENTY-TWO

"Look," father cries.

It's been so long since any of us have seen one, we stand for a moment, unsure, staring.

"It's not a whale, eh?" Margaret asks.

"No, it's definitely not a whale," father says.

"Is it moving off?" Margaret asks.

Philip answers, "Nay, looks like she's anchored. See, watch a bit, she isn't moving a tip forward. And her sails are down."

A grand miracle in the distance, a wonder of all things hoped for, all things prayed for. Suddenly, I feel God again as clearly as a burst of fire lighting a dark night.

A ship, swaying ahead in the sea.

A tremor seizes me. A ship! So glorious in the distance, like a floating chariot which carries God in its bottom. A ship, all made, sitting on the water whole and secure, just waiting for us. A ship, a ship! What good people have come to save us?

"Father, whose ship do you think it is?"

He shakes his head.

"Do you think they'd take us back with them?" I look up into his face, his eyes staring hard at the ship. "Do you, father?" He doesn't answer, his cheeks high and red from the cold. Does he believe they will take us back home? Is he thinking about mother, as I am, about leaving without her—we won't, we'll ask the people of the ship to help, people from our world, the Old World, to help us find mother, and Ethan, to find them and bring them back to England and Myrthyr where we'll live all together.

Father is staring.

"We don't know who they are," Philip says. "They anchored off a ways—we don't know if they came to shore, neither. We'll have to get closer, is all," he says.

"Oh, it'd be so nice to get back to the children, the children," Margaret says, sighing.

Father's eyes disturb me. "Say something, father," I start, and he breaks his gaze and looks down at me and flashes a smile that does not touch me. He turns quickly and picks up our trail once again. Margaret passes ahead of me, after father, and I let her. I look to the ship, never letting it out of my sight as I follow them down the shore.

Evening threatens before we finally come close enough. "I can see her banner. Look there, can you see it?" Philip cries out.

"What do you see?"

"The yellow and white of good old Harry. That's the king's pennant!" Philip shouts.

"It's Henry's?" Margaret cries. Henry, our good king.

"What's a ship of Harry's doing here?"

Father stops walking and holds up his hand. "Hush. Listen," he says.

The wind carries to us voices and laughter like eerie phantasms. Whistling through the world, voices flying up and down in the way of the white birds who clutter the shore with their piercing cries. The laughter, raucous and wild. We glance at each other. A chill goes through me.

"Folks!" Margaret whispers.

"But what kind of folks?" Philip frowns, quiet now.

Loud voices, then low, too low to be heard over the waves, the wind. Father takes us forward slowly.

Ahead, the land snakes inward, and in this pocket the voices are kept. We cannot yet see whose they are.

The smell of roasting meat, and the laughter of men—how many men?

We creep along the rocks, scared suddenly to come upon these men, their laughter hard and bawdy. We come round the bend and hide behind boulders on the shore, looking ahead to where we can see them.

Red flames shimmer through the gray eve, showing the outlines of people, a bunch of men, arms waving, one standing, another walking from the fire to a tent and back. And another fire, a handful of men crowded round it, talking and laughing. On the rocks, their shallops lie. Up in the grasses, it appears they've set a camp with sloppy tents. Men wander in and out. Nearby, a group bets with shiny clumps of coin.

"They don't look like the king's men, that's certain," father whispers next to me.

I think he's right, these men are too messy, their laughter too hard, and their words, which float to us, filled with curses and languages I don't know. They don't look dangerous like the Awthas, but they could be dangerous like rich folk.

"Are they traders?" Margaret whispers behind me.

"Don't know," Philip answers. "Don't think so."

"Should we go and ask about Sarah?" Margaret says.

My heart rushes to the surface of me. We should go now, I think wildly, we should go straight to them and ask if they know where mother is. But I don't move. Their laughter frightens me.

"I don't wish to approach till we know who they are," father says.

"You're right, Eric, let's us wait," Philip says. "They can't see us behind these boulders. Let's us stay here and listen a bit."

We're so close to them, I can see the birds they're roasting. A man raises a torn, cooked leg to his mouth.

Bits of words come to us on the wind. "Ya did right good ta snumb off his nose like 'at—" Laughter.

A reply.

"French," father whispers.

"Dutch, I hear," Philip says. "Or German."

One fellow has a trunk open before him. Men sit on rocks beside the trunk, watching as the fellow pulls out a long shimmery cloth.

"That's mine! I'll take that!" a young man cries.

"You wait your turn, you arse," says the fellow holding the cloth. "We've got to lay it all out before we divvy it up."

He pulls out a sack and shakes it and flicks his hips back and forth to the sound of coins. The men laugh.

"Aye, lookit, the cap's divvyin' the store," says an eating man.

The men look up from their bets.

"That hain't right, Cap." The men begin to gather round the trunk, looking in. "We agreed to wait for mornin'."

"Yea, I want my ten percent fair."

Philip whispers, "Looks like a fight brewing."

The captain punches a man's arm away from the trunk. "No touchin' a fukkin' coin," he warns. "I says we're doin' it now. You'll all git what's comin' to ye."

"Maybe we should go," Margaret says. "Our sailors aren't among these, are they, Lily?"

I don't remember hearing so many languages, nor seeing such fine clothing. I shake my head.

"I think we should just go, father, and talk to them. Ask them if they've seen—"

"No, Lily," father says.

"It's too dangerous," Philip adds. "They look like sea dogs, pirates, privateers—using the king's banner."

"But maybe they're not—maybe they're the king's men, like you said, men of our good King Harry who've come for us."

"These don't sound like the king's men, child. Listen, I've a bad feeling. These fellows kill anybody who's not one of them. I've seen it with my own eyes. In Dunbar, they were hiding in the coves there, they took all our boats for themselves—"

"What do ye suppose we have here?"

Startled, I look behind us, and see in the evening shadows what looks like a nobleman standing there.

"Could be some spies, I says, spies," a second voice says.

"Nay, they look like more o' them savage Indians—fukkin' beasts, they should all be killed like the vermin that they are. Stand up there, lads. Ye too, ladies, let's take a look at yer," the other man says. He comes closer, to where we can see him. He is dressed in a fine jacket, doublet, and hose. He has two firearms stuck into a scabbard about his waist.

"We are not savages," father says, standing.

"Ye shut the Hell up, am I talking to yer?"

"He says he's not a savage, George, did ye get that?" The two men laugh. "Ye look like a bloody savage to me, all of ye, except maybe this doll," the second one says, grabbing Margaret round the waist. She cries out; Philip moves to help her. The first man quickly pulls out his firearm and shoots it. The air fills with smoke and Margaret's screams. I cannot speak or move as I watch bright red blood drip from Philip's chest. Men from the camp come running, shouting, tripping and scrambling over the boulders—too fast—there is no way to escape. They are coming to kill us—where are the king's men, the king's men?

"We got us 'nother one," the first man cries out, pulling at Margaret's kirtle. "Take her," he says, throwing her at the men.

"What with these others?"

"She's mine, the little one—"

"Pass that tender roast on here—" I feel arms upon me, pulling at me, at my dress.

"Leave me alone! Father!" I cry as the men pull us over to their camp, to the others round the fires. They are shouting, standing and laughing. The men gather in a circle and push father and Margaret. They yank off father's cloak, showing his half-naked body. Father tries to move, but there are too many, too strong. They pull at me, at Margaret.

"Savages, dirty savages, what do ye deserve?" the men chant. "Savages, dirty savages, what do ye deserve?"

One man grabs me about my neck from behind and drags me outside the circle. I fight and claw at him. He chokes me as he drags me till I feel my breath going black. I'm falling out of the world. The Earth has finally let go.

I tumble down as the man pulls at my dress.

"Aye, ye like that, ye little barbarian—I'll make ye straight, I will." He grabs at his hose with one hand and at me with the other, yanking me from the ground. Another man comes running over and clutches at my free arm while pulling a fistful of my hair. Pain sears through my arms, a hot pain at the back of my head. I feel my arms cracking, my skin ripping, bones breaking. They are going to kill me, to tear me in two.

The one man twists my arm as he tries to snatch me back. The other won't let go. They shout over me. I am the frayed rope in a tug-o'-war, a breaking rope.

"She's mine! I hain't ev'n started with her yet."

"Give 'er back!"

One paws at his hose and my clothing and the other punches at him and clubs me in the cheek with his fist. I fall to the cold, hard ground, my arms freed suddenly. They've let me go, I must get to my feet, to run. The ground feels so cold beneath me, my arms wrenched broken; I will never move them again. I taste the sharpness of blood in my mouth, hear the men arguing, hear their fists upon each other's flesh.

I stand and stumble, blind from pain, away from the shouts and jeers that fill the sky, waiting to feel hands upon me, arms dragging me back, fists knocked into my cheeks. I spit blood as I blunder along the sand and rock in the dull dusk light. I cannot see for the pain from the blows which echo in my cheek and head and arms. I must keep on, away from the men, to save, to help, they will kill us all, I must get away, to keep on though I can hardly move.

I step and miss the ground and fall and fall down to a place that goes below the earth. I try to catch myself, to stop myself from falling. I turn and twist to find something to hold, but I find nothing. I land on my back upon a slippery, dark shifting mass, the red sky above me, the shouts of the men in my ears. I have no strength in my aching arms to pull myself up to the edge where the light dully glows. I try to lift myself off my back, to stand on this unsteady mass below the earth. I look to either side of me, and in the fading evening, I begin to see what surrounds me. Hair, hands, legs, cheeks, mouths open wide in silent screams.

God help me, I have landed in a pit of corpses.

I scramble onto my knees to get away, to retch, to flee this pit of Hell when I see that the body beneath me is mother.

Beneath me is mother.

The body beneath me is mother.

The wind escapes me, a groan as I lift my broken arm to touch her cold lips. "Mother," I whisper into her closed eyes, "look at me." I trace her nose with my swollen hand. I try to feel her breath on my cheek, to hear her say my name, my name, but she makes no sound. I push the hair from her face. I move her lips with my shaking fingers. "Oh, mother, talk," I sob from the ache that is me. "Please say something," but she does not answer.

Dead faces all round grimace at me. Even in the cold, I can smell them. I must get away, to rouse her and take her with me, far from these corpses. I shake her, calling into her pale and empty face. "I need you, mother, tell me you're alive."

I crawl from her, heaves throwing up my belly. She looks just like the others.

I know it's no use.

If ever Hell, ever I wondered about Hell, there is no wonder. The corpses reek of a fleshy decay. Dizzy with the stink, I retch a stream of emptiness. She is so cold, her flesh so chilled, her closed eyes so unmoving.

I fall on my back beside her and begin to go black—but I can never go black enough. I stare at the darkening sky, the red dark sky, like blood, a violent apocalypse sky at the end of the world, it is the end of the world, this world, the Dead World. I hear the echo of the men's jeers and taunts outside the pit and I know I am in the Dead World now, spinning down into its darkness, into unlit corners where evil hides in cold, dank pits of the dead.

Through the vicious insults of the men comes a sound that sends jolts of a violent fear through me. Howl.

More howls, wolf cries from the shore, barks and howling down the shore, as if they'd been following us, they had been, the Awthas, following, and now they've come upon us.

From the pit, I can hear the sea dogs shouting and fighting and insulting.

Till the howls penetrate.

"What the pissin' Hell is that?"

"Who the fukk—"

The screams of attack come to me, the sound of flesh upon flesh, fighting and stabbing and tearing. I want to shout, to stop the Awthas from hurting father, but the words stick like knives in my throat. I move close to mother's cold body and nestle my face in her neck, hoping that wherever she is, she will come and take me to her soon.

Men fly by the pit then. From the corner of my eye, I see a different people, other beings joining, scooting round the pit from behind me, from the forest, moving down to the shore. In the rising moon's light, I see the painted faces of the Nooh people.

Warriors.

There will be a massacre.

Such screams as I've never heard, horrible, bloody bellows, man screams, the cracks of wood or necks, one pistol firing and the weakening curses of the dying pirates.

I bury my face in mother's side, but still hear the sounds of war.

I don't have enough left inside me for hope. I wait, blank of mind, with my fear and pain for company.

"Can you hear me, Lily? Where are you? Answer me."

My name comes from a place too far away to answer.

"Leelee?"

The stench of dirty bodies and rotting blood comes to me. I open my eyes to a blue moonlight and lift my head to see mother's face. I cannot hold myself up; I lie back and close my eyes.

I feel a bright light at the edge of the pit, people there, looking in, but I do not wish them to see me, so I keep my eyes shut.

"Lily, is that you?" At the sound of his voice, I open my eyes. Ethan stands looking in with others, all cut and bloody, with flames that light up the night. "Good Lord, Lily, are you all right?" I am dreaming. The Awthas took him, they took him like the sea dogs took mother. I look into his bloodied face, his wide eyes which examine the dead all round me. He lowers himself into the pit and shines his torch into my face. "Thank God you are safe!" I cannot raise my arms to touch him; I do not know if he's real. He leans down and breathes my name into my ear, and I smell his breath, his sweet breath. He helps me to sit; I cry out, faint with pain.

"Come, I will help you. We must go now, we're going back. They're all gone, and we're going back home, Lily."

"Mother!" I cry. I turn to look at her.

Ethan sees her, he touches her cheek. "For God's sake!" He covers his mouth with his hand and shines his light on the other bodies, clothes torn from them, men, women. "I'm so sorry. We must get away from this—this nightmare. We'll take her with us, Lily. And Philip, Margaret, your father."

"Where's father?"

"He's—he's down there. He's been injured."

"I want to see."

"He's alive, Lily, just injured. You will see him." Ethan looks at me; I look down at my ripped dress and limp arms. He wipes a line of bloodied spit from my mouth. "Lily, let us carry you, let one of the men carry you." Behind him the vision man and the warriors crouch to look over the pit at me. The vision man climbs down and covers me with a fur. I close my eyes and feel his strong arms picking me up into the air.

Night sounds of Nooh people flying through the woods. I fly like a bird in the vision man's arms, a dead bird, carried on another's wings.

I try to feel for the edge of my mind, the place where my thoughts begin, but it's like slipping over a ball, trying to feel for a start to roundness. Thoughts come, but I can't hold them for long.

Tonight, God was not with me.

As the vision man flies through the wood, parts of me take to the air—my heart, my bones, my muscles—till only my skin faces the outside world and I'm hollow inside. I am nothing in the vision man's arms.

TWENTY-THREE

Corpses dangle from dark trees whose hard branches pierce the soft night like lances in stomachs. Laughing corpses wave the king's banner and grab at me with their long-nailed claws. They climb the trees and howl like wolves and fly like birds, white wings against the black and stormy sky. Their voices fill the night, calling to each other, calling out mother's name, and father's, calling in my voice. They speak in foreign tongues and scramble up ship's ropes and cut each other's throats. Into a dark pit, they throw me, bodies falling on top of me, heavy with death. I cry out, but I can't breathe, I can't see, I can't breathe, I'm being crushed flatter, down beneath so many bodies that I'll never climb out again.

Voices like dreams call me. In my sleep, I hear my name. But they are not calling, only moving closer, talking and moving closer and closer. The voices crowd inside my head, in the air, in my head, talking. The darkness inside me opens, and I hear people whispering in a language I don't understand. My body aches, and I cannot move my arms.

I open my eyes and see smoke floating up through a hole in a pointed ceiling. Faces move beside me, talking red mouths, laughing teeth, black eyes. Where is mother? She was carried slack in a man's arms. Father, carried between two warriors, his eyes shut.

I am on the ground, in furs, all round me furs, buried in furs near a warm fire. I can't get warm enough, I shiver.

With a hot damp cloth, she touches my face, looks at me with black-circled eyes, with dark, dark eyes that are not mother's.

Not mother.

"Let her help you."

Touching my arms, my broken arms. "Stop," I cry because the pain is enormous. They are going to tear my limbs from me. "Father!" I shout. A man grabs me about the shoulders, and I try to shake him off. "Mother!" He holds my shoulders. He is stronger than me; I will not let them be stronger than me. Kick, kick him, use your legs, use your legs to kick—

There are more of them now, holding me down, but I'm a vicious boar, a roaring, wild boar—this time I will fight with everything inside me. I will not let them hurt us, I will not let them kill her, I don't care if I live or die.

"Lily, Lily—it's us, it's me, Ethan. Stop it, Lily, stop," he shouts at me, his face before mine. Ethan? Where did he come from?

"I can't see, they are hurting me, stop them, Ethan."

"You're safe now, nobody here is trying to hurt you, understand?"

"Please, my arms." The hands on me stop.

"Everyone wants to help you, Lily. Your arms are broken and they need to be set. That is all. They're helping you," he insists.

His voice calms me. I do not want them to touch me.

I feel them holding my broken arms straight, binding them gently with cloth. The old woman presses wet leaves to my lips and cheek, nodding with worried brown eyes. I see other forms beside me, lumps under furs. One of them is father. I watch his breath slowly move his chest. Up. Down. He is alive.

On my back, with furs covering me, I am warm next to father and Margaret who sleep motionless, the smoke of the fire drifting over them, making me think they are moving, but neither of them do, not even when I whisper, "Father, are you there?" and stare at his stone face. I put my cheek to his nose, to feel his breath which blows light as a breeze. He is wrapped in blankets and buried under furs. I curl next to him, tiredness pulling me with strong fingers into the swell of his chest.

I wonder where mother is.

She cleans father's face and body and whispers to him, but he doesn't answer. She watches him with her black eyes and lights fragrant herbs over him. She rubs sweet-smelling salve into my cheek where I've been cut. With the old woman's help, she washes Margaret, who cries out in pain before she falls back into the darkness of her agony.

When the corpses come to me in my sleep and wake me with the screams which turn out to be my own, she sits beside me and looks into my face and mutters words to me in a singsong rhythm. Somehow, her foreign words seem familiar; they soothe me and send me back to sleep.

The days pass, and she lifts food to my mouth. In the morning, she holds a bowl out and helps me to make water and dung. When

I cry in pain, her eyes fill with tears which drip through her eye circles in streaks down her cheeks. Though her smell and voice are strange to me, her arms round me comfort me.

I feel legs pushing into mine, hear a yawn. I wake and turn as father wakes. He opens his eyes, and we stare at each other. His face is bruised the color of fallen pears. He blinks. A crust has grown about his mouth. He looks at my bound arms. "Forgive me, my child," he says, his voice cracked and broken. He reaches over to me and pulls me close. I feel his tears in my hair, running down my face.

"Father, do you know where mother is?" I whisper to him.

"They have found her?"

"Yes."

He wipes his tears away and searches my face. He doesn't know. I cannot bear to tell him, but I feel he can see the corpses behind my eyes.

"Oh, Lily, I am so very, very sorry."

In a pained flash, I feel angry and hurt and I don't understand. I don't know why all this happened. Whose fault is it? Father's? Should I be angry at him for not waiting for us, for not believing that he would see me and mother again? That does not feel right to me. My anger turns to the men who sent us to this New World, for they are the ones who destroyed our family. I picture father landing in a snowstorm, sent here by Frere Lanther, the frere whom I once loved almost as much as father himself, and the baron with his cruel words and acts against mother. A bitter hatred for those two men knots my heart.

"It is not your fault, father. You did not bring us here."

"If I had fought, somehow."

I shake my head. The evil men were strong. God did not help us. I feel there are some things a person cannot fight alone.

Father lies back on the furs and covers his eyes with his badly healing hand. I close my own eyes and listen to the sounds of his mourning.

The worst of the swelling has gone down from my arms and my cheek has healed over when Ethan comes to us with words from the vision man. He says the man suggests it's time for the farewell ceremony for mother and Philip. He says that since me and father and Margaret can now rise from our beds and walk, he would like to perform the ceremony this evening.

All afternoon, young children toddle into our tent holding carvings of bears and wolves to remind us of the joining of Nooh and Awthas that saved us. They fought together that night, Ethan tells me, both against the sea dogs who had also stolen some Awthas women. Father says that the bear carvings the children bring promise new beginnings, and that the wolf represents age and wisdom for the Nooh. I shake my head at their beliefs, trying to find a place for them inside me. Women come to our tent with embroidered slippers and dresses for Margaret; two tall men with braided queues bring meat for us all. Ethan and father sit and talk with them, the brothers and sisters of Kri-ki, children of brothers, cousins, friends. Ethan says their gifts are for our healing, both in our bodies and our spirits. Margaret watches them curiously, her eyes sad.

All the guests leave to prepare for the ceremony, and I follow Ethan out into the deep snow. He brings me to a house by the field.

Her body and Philip's lie high up on a wooden loft. I cannot climb up to see them. The freezing room smells of bee honey and a sour spoilage. I feel faint. Ethan holds me up, his arm round my waist.

"Shaman watches over them," he whispers, "so their spirits will pass safely."

We go closer to the loft where the vision man sits with his legs dangling over the side. I see feet. Her bare feet.

Spirits and God, where has mother gone? Heaven, Hell, God's arms, I don't feel them here. I feel as if I've been in a dream all my life, the dream of God and Jesus and Heaven, and someone has been trying to wake me since I arrived here. I feel as if everything written in the Bible has been a grand story, a widows' tale, rumors which simply never happened.

Looking at mother's body, I feel as if I know what is true: that mother has gone cold, gone black like a doused fire and I can press down upon that wishing place in my soul till I ache all over, but I will never see her again.

The knowledge hits me like a river's current, and I feel as if I am going to be carried off by it. So many others gone, killed. Philip, Daw-ika.

"Ethan, tell me about the boy," I say quickly. "Daw-ika?"

"His injury is healing very slowly. He's in and out of the fever."

"But he's alive?"

Ethan nods.

The vision man saved the boy's life. I look at him whispering words beside mother.

"And how long has it been since . . . since we got back, Ethan?"

"The moon has become nearly full. It's been several weeks since we returned."

Father pushes aside the skin door and steps into the room with us. Beneath his eyes are streaks of a deep orange color. He is followed by other Nooh folks, and Margaret, who's bent with crying. Others crowd round, gently pushing against me to get into the room. Their hands upon me, their breath, so many people all together consoles me. I stand close to Ethan, who touches my back and holds me near. Father comes to me, trailed by Kri-ki and her parents, their faces wrinkled with worry lines.

Father climbs the ladder to the loft alone and talks to the vision man. Two men come with long boards in the shape of fish and pass them up to father. Between the men, they lower the bodies of my mother and Philip. When I see her ashen face in the light, I cannot hold myself in. It's as though I come apart in all directions. I cannot see her this way, without life or spirit. I have to go, to run from this stinking room. I shoulder past the people, out into the cold, where I breathe the frosted air deeply. Ethan comes after me and pulls me to him. Father and the Nooh people walk by bearing the wrapped bodies.

Four piles of wood are set in a square marked in the snow. Young boys stand by each pile, their faces painted dark yellow like autumn hay. The vision man signals the men carrying mother and Philip to put them down inside the square. The boys say some words, then start fires in the woodpiles. They will burn the bodies!

I cry out to stop them. They cannot be burnt like martyrs or saints or witches.

"Aren't we going to bury them?" I lurch away from Ethan toward father. "Won't we give them a proper burial?" A proper burial, proper with God? But He has left me alone to be harmed, He has taken mother away, He has sent us here for a reason I cannot comprehend and forced upon us evils which even father is unable to fight. I look at father's face, his calm eyes which take in the body of mother. He changed long ago, away from God in Heaven.

What, then, is a proper burial?

Where will her spirit go?

"Tell me, father!" I shout.

He holds his arms out to me, hugs my head, and shushes me. "Lily, we are warming the earth so we can bury them the way the Nooh do."

The Nooh people stand in the snow all round us. They are dressed in furs, painted in brown and orange, holding clothes and food and wooden animal figures in their hands. Several of the women look at me and shake their heads sadly when I look back. Kri-ki stands near.

Father bends to me and whispers, "If you want to go and lie down again, you can, Lily. But now we must give your mother and Philip back to the earth."

I nod and breathe in. I look at the bodies, then turn toward the people who will help us to bury mother. The serious eyes of the Nooh watch as the ground softens beneath the flames. These people have come to bury Philip, but they did not know mother. They brought gifts to our tent, gifts for me as well as Margaret. In their hands, two women hold beautiful dresses and a cloak of fur. Others hold carvings, necklaces, dried meat.

"Father, why—what is everybody doing here?"

"They have come to witness, and to bring gifts for your mother and Philip."

"But why?"

"Because they are family. They have taken us in, given us clothes and food and care, and we are all family now."

The Nooh people's faces are warm, their hands filled with generous offerings, their eyes sharing my sorrow, and I know that without them, we would never have survived.

I turn to father and look into his eyes deep blue as the sea I will never cross again.

EPILOGUE

I feel the weather changing, the snow melting, birds and animals beginning to emerge from their winter nests. I ache for the spring-time show of flowers and fruits.

Father and Kri-ki and others of the village try to teach me the Nooh tongue. The words are long and hard, with funny sounds that buzz in my mouth like flies. When I get a word or sentence right, I feel very happy. I ask for my dinner in Nooh, and Kri-ki gives me an extra sweet. I watch her and wonder about her ways. She doesn't touch father when I am near, but they sleep under the same cover. She teaches me Nooh by saying a word when she hands me a thing; others teach by taking me outside and pointing to the sky or to the houses, talking all the while. Ethan tells me what he's learned, challenging me to catch up.

In the day, Kri-ki shows me how to weave cloth or string wampum shells into belts. I can't understand all of her words yet, but with my eyes, I learn from her.

The family in the long house where Philip lived came to our tent to adopt Margaret. They brought her skin dresses and boots and sang to her. She had become so thin from her sadness, two of the young men in the family had to help her to walk.

As we settle for sleep at night father takes a place on the furs next to Kri-ki. I can see the air between them is filled with messages. Even though I know Kri-ki and her family care for us, it is strange to watch her and father together. I don't know if I will ever overcome that feeling.

I hear a wolf howling one night, long, chilling howls. The sound wakes me and a fear sweat covers my skin. Sometimes, I hear wolves howling in groups far away, but this howl is lone, and nearby. I sit up. Only the dying embers of the fire light the tent; no one else seems to have been awakened by the cry.

I lie back down and listen carefully to the world outside the tent. Father and the others say that the wolf spirit contains wisdom and is nothing to fear unless it is an angry Awthas in disguise, but still, my heart beats like a drum. For a few moments, I hear nothing, and then light, fast footsteps splashing through the mud. The howl comes again. I sit up and look over at father and Kri-ki, but no one has moved. Before I can wake them, the tent flap opens, and in the doorway stands a brown wolf.

I scramble to my feet and try to scream, but no sound comes from my mouth. The wolf stares at me with green, sparkling eyes, half in, half out of the tent. I can't understand it, but there is something familiar about its long-nosed face, a disturbed look in its eyes, a beautiful sadness that I feel somehow I know. I don't think the wolf came to harm me. Before I can think or move, the wolf turns and disappears into the night.

Ethan comes for me in the morning. He does not sleep in the tent with me and father and Kri-ki's family, but in a long house with Daw-ika's family. He comes to take me to see Daw-ika, his brother, as he calls him. Ethan doesn't wish to be my brother, and so lives with them.

"He's begun to speak, and has asked for you," Ethan says. "Leelee," he smiles.

"Are you used to living with his family? Is it not strange?"

He grins, holding a mystery behind his lips. Daw-ika has not been ready for visitors, and so I have never visited Ethan's house to see for myself how they live.

"They are very kind to me," he says. "Father takes care of us all."

I look at him blankly.

"His father, my father—oh, come, you'll see." He laughs, hurrying me along.

The long house is covered with branches and leaves. Smoke floats from a hole in its top. Before we go in, Ethan stops and clears his throat. He looks at the skin-covered doorway and says, "You know, I miss you very much, Lily."

I am surprised by his statement. He has come to visit me many times, and to help the vision man heal my arms.

"I wish one day we could have a house like this one. A place where we could live together, you and me," he says.

His words strike my heart with an unusual heat. He raises his eyes to meet mine. In them, I feel a hope and a longing that I have forgotten. My cheeks flush with a burning shyness.

He turns and pulls aside the door and calls out a greeting in the Nooh tongue. A woman working with thread on the floor calls me daughter, and I smile at her.

"My mother says you are now welcome in our home anytime," Ethan tells me. I'm not sure how he can call her his mother, but maybe it is some Nooh custom with which I am yet unfamiliar. I look over and thank her for her invitation.

At the back of the house, I see the vision man kneeling by a pile of furs that make a bed. Ethan takes me to Daw-ika, who sits up under a warm bearskin. I want to thank him for saving my life, but I don't know how to tell him of my gratitude. When he sees me, he grins and looks at the vision man, who smiles too. I kneel to him and thank him, trying not to stare at his healing sore. His head-skin is covered with brown and broken scabs and reddened flesh. Round the scabs, hair has grown.

"Your mother's spirit has taken a new life. She has become powerful. I see her," Daw-ika says.

At the mention of my mother, my heart flits as if with wings. I look at his eyes.

He goes on, "If you ever meet a wolf face-to-face again, you must treat her with respect."

I feel myself staring at the boy. How is it possible that he knows what I saw in the tent? I shake my head at him, and a big, toothy smile covers his face, like when a person is sharing a secret.

I smile back slowly. "A wolf," I say. "Of course, I will always be respectful." I turn to Ethan. "Daw-ika sees a lot, it seems."

"Like many Nooh people, and none so clearly as his father. Our father," Ethan says.

"Who is his father?" I ask, but then, turning to the vision man, I know.

She visits me at night in the shape of a wolf, soft green eyes in a pointed brown face, a wolf circling the tent till I let her in. She stands by father and Kri-ki and whimpers quietly, her whimpers never waking them. After, she comes to my bed. I open the skin and she crawls inside and settles down next to me, the warmth of her fur against me, the weight of her body sagging real and heavy on my belly. She passes her thoughts to me without words, and I understand.

With her nightly visits, I feel myself strengthening as though inside me flows wolf blood.

I am learning more and more words, learning how to be Nooh like my father and Ethan and Margaret. All this learning is like a skin that I must wet and stretch, cut and sew to fit.

Mother is not the only animal who visits me at night. A big, serious brown bear comes out of his winter hiding and holds open the flap of the tent for her. Both mother and the bear come to me and nose out a place under my covers. They steal most of them. Mother's fur keeps me warm. A young skunk wanders in out of the cold and nestles at the foot of father's blanket. I go to him and pet his fur gently, knowing to be careful of his stinker. He lets me know that he only uses it when he's scared, and that he's not scared of me.

Some nights, when the light remains long in the sky, I go to the budding forest by the river to sit and think about all that the Nooh have taught me. I think of the animal spirits which visit me, and other spirits contained in every element—rocks and trees, fire and humans, cool water and the burning sun.

As I sit, a feeling builds in me, the most enormous feeling I've ever felt.

I feel the whole Earth, with all its plants and trees and animals and people, inside me. I feel the Earth's blood and vapors running through me. I feel the sky, the clouds, the soil—as though they all speak to me in a language I don't have to struggle to understand.

* * *

Everyone is named according to their behavior. Father is called Singing Bird. Kri-ki is Little Worrier. Ethan has been named Arrows Slipping Through Fingers, and I am Sad Wolf.

Under the ground in clay jars, beans and corn are wintered, and tubers and grain in baskets, and dried fruit, hidden in the cold depths of the earth. Every morning, before eating, Kri-ki sends me to the cache for scoops enough to feed us. The food was planted and harvested by her and the other women, to be used by us all.

In Nooh this morning, Kri-ki says to me, "Now that you are a woman of the bear clan, Sad Wolf, you will help us in the planting season which comes soon."

"I've planted before. With father."

"Here, women fertilize the earth. Men hunt, fight."

"How do we plant without . . . without—" But I don't know the word for horse. There are no horses, nor pigs, nor cows, nor hens, nor sheep, and only a few dogs. "Without an animal to help us?"

"Animal to help? What do you mean?" she asks.

"To pull the—" ploughshares? I shake my head at the useless talk. I will see, as with everything Nooh. I turn and fetch the morning cache.

At night, after we eat, we go to the long house to listen to stories and talk with the others of the village. Tonight, She Speaks Tongues is telling the story of Sky Woman, which father and Kri-ki and grandfather and grandmother have all told me in bits. I've never before heard the whole as I do now.

She Speaks Tongues says, "The Grand Chief in the Sky Nation

got sick, and he had a vision about it, about how to cure himself. He sent his daughter Sky Woman down through a hole in the sky to pull up the roots of the ever-blooming tree which he knew grew there. He told his daughter to look for this tree, saying that's how he was going to get cured.

"So she crawled down, but the world was all blackness then, all covered with water and dark muck, filled with water animals. All the water animals saw this sudden light, and this woman falling down, and they tried to catch her, to help her. They dove into the water looking for dry earth to make her some land, and in doing so, some of them drowned. Finally, old Muskrat was able to pile some earth on Turtle's back, to make a place for Sky Woman to live."

"Turtle Island," I whisper to myself, remembering this part of the story.

"Then, on Turtle Island, Sky Woman had a daughter who gave birth to twins, a good twin and a bad twin. The good twin was born through her loins the regular way, but the bad twin pushed his way out of her armpit and killed her. The good twin, when he was mourning, made the sun out of her face, and the bad twin drove it west. The good twin made the stars and moon out of her breast, and mountains and rivers out of her body, and the bad twin made the rivers crooked and hurled storms at the mountains. The good twin set forests and nut trees on the land, and the bad twin gnarled all the trees. Finally, the good twin made fire, which started to burn up the bad twin's legs. That drove him to an underground cave, where he still lives, sending out his bad spirits into the world to show us there's good and bad in all things."

She folds her arms against herself. "That's how it was," she says.

* * *

Mother comes laughing into bed tonight, raising her long nose to look at me, then tucking its wet tip under my arm and blowing out air in wolf laughter.

What is it, mother? You're tickling me. Why are you laughing like that?

But she shakes her head and won't tell me. She falls asleep first.

We've been feeling the warm waves of wind, the hint of newness, the sight of leaf nubs on the trees. The real end to winter, the end of the sleeping time for the bear clan.

Me and Kri-ki, and grandmother, and the other Nooh women set to the task of cooking a great feast for the Awthas visitors whom they say will come to our camp tonight for a council. We set out food along the path from the forest for our guests, and wait for their arrival.

At sundown, the warriors come into camp wearing their wolf clan masks which still send a fright through me. Our chief greets them ceremoniously, offering them a place in the house where we gather. Long Fingers is there, smiling, and our whole village joins the Awthas in the long house, some of us spilling out and looking in through cracks, through the doorway.

The two chiefs begin to speak then. I understand many of their words, a mix of Nooh and another language, Awthas.

Long Fingers starts. "Snow is melted, time is coming to open our land to Nooh in planting time. We had bad blood," he says.

"We've evened out our bad blood," Sachem, our chief, says. He's a tall man, with long, black bird feathers arranged down his back and a great skin cloak.

"The time of fighting has ended, now we are entering the time of growing. We wish to open our whole territory to you for planting," Long Fingers says.

"And we will open the mountain to you for hunting."

Sachem offers a small sack to Long Fingers, who takes it and hands it to one of his wolves. The men remove their masks, and all sit on the skin-covered ground, near the fire. The men smoke from a bowl which they pass to each other, and laugh and talk about their families like old friends.

Mother, were you laughing at the friendship between wolves and bears?

She shakes her head.

Why were you laughing, then? Will I ever guess?

She smiles, her long, fine teeth showing white, which means I will have to wait and see.

Daw-ika, his father and mother, and Ethan come to us one evening for dinner. They are in very good spirits, teasing and playing with words. After we eat, we sit round the fire and Daw-ika takes out a bowl and hands it to my father, though I don't know why. The bowl is smoked when people want to agree upon a serious matter, but nothing was mentioned. All we have done tonight is joke and laugh.

Daw-ika speaks then, saying, "Singing Bird, Little Worrier, parents, grandparents, and Sad Wolf, I want to announce to you that Arrows Slipping Through Fingers wishes to say something very important."

Everyone looks at Ethan, who looks with surprise at Daw-ika. "Just like that? Don't you have more to say?"

"No, that's your job. You have to ask her and her family," Dawika says.

Ethan's forehead glimmers in the firelight with droplets of sweat. "Well, ah, I don't know who to ask first," he says.

The vision man says, "She has to consent first, before her parents."

Ethan looks at me and smiles, "Lily." He breathes deeply and says quickly, letting out all his breath, "Lily, I want to marry you. Will you marry me?"

"I knew it!" father shouts.

Kri-ki laughs and claps her hands.

"Lily," Ethan says, "tell me your answer!"

My face feels hot as the flames before me. Marriage! I've always dreamt of marriage with Ethan. My eyes fill with stinging tears. I turn to father and hold my flushed cheeks. "May I, father?"

He smiles. "You must wait four seasons, to give time to the Nooh women to prepare you in the ways of marriage. One year."

"Oh, Ethan, I will marry you," I say.

"You will?" he asks, getting up from the fire and coming round to me.

"I've always wanted to marry you. Known I would marry you. Always, always," I say, laughter and tears all mixing in one burst of my heart.

He lifts me to my feet and thumbs away my tears. He holds me in his arms.

"Now it's come true, Lily. In a year, we'll be together," he says. He puts his lips to mine in front of all the family. I breathe in the warm breath coming from his nose and mouth like a throatful of hot liquid.

Through the joining of our lips, I feel suddenly that I know why we are here.

I see Father Sky reaching down with strong rays of sun and sheets of cool rain to join Mother Earth, who blossoms under his attention. Together, they create delicious plants and beautiful flowers; they make vines and trees and grasses.

I see children, and hear their laughter. The village is filled with red-cheeked children who run and play and laugh, who will grow and make children of their own.

These are my children, the children I will make with Ethan.

I feel that is why I've been brought to this place, to be with this boy whom I could never have married in any other way, in any other place on the Earth.

I hear, as I press my lips to Ethan's, wolf laughter somewhere outside.

HISTORICAL NOTE

Colonization of North America by the English would not occur for nearly one hundred years after Lily's story, when the Jamestown Colony was formed in Virginia in 1607. After that time, European Americans who were captured through conflicts with the Native Americans continued to be adopted by the natives. When given the chance to return to their English brethren, many refused the opportunity.

> "No Arguments, no Intreaties, nor Tears of their Friends and Relations, could persuade many of them to leave their new Indian Friends and Acquaintance; several of them that were by the Caressings of their Relations persuaded to come Home, in a little Time grew tired of our Manner of living, and run away again to the Indians, and ended their Days with them."
>
> —Cadwallader Colden, *History of the Five Indian Nations of Canada,* 1747

AUTHOR'S NOTE

For years I tried to look beyond the basic American history dates we all memorized in school, such as 1492 and 1776, to dig deeper and ascertain what really went into the formation of America. Obsessed with questions like "What were the Indians like before the Europeans arrived, and what reaction did they have to foreigners?" and "Were there Europeans in North America before the colonists settled?" and "Who was brave enough to cross the uncharted expanse of the Atlantic, and what was that crossing like?" I wanted to feel and understand America from its inception, through characters who might have been there.

Throughout the sixteenth century, I discovered, during the first stages of the exploration of America, wealthy merchants and nobles would send adventure ships to the New World (and other lands) to see what riches they could gather, pirate, or otherwise acquire. The masters of these forays often left no intentionally recorded texts, only a history that is mercurial—based on guesses, old ledgers, badly kept account books, and the unreliable, boasting journals of nobles.

In my research I chanced on the story of a group of nobles who had an idea to colonize a part of America, to claim it for England. They sent a ship of about one hundred people to the Northeast (my guess was somewhere around Maine) and left them there with a promise to return in a year with supplies. War detained them for several years, and when they came back, they found only the bones of the unfortunate colonists. They left another boatload of hopefuls and promised again to return in a year. This time they did. They found no trace of the colonists at all and returned to Europe. Almost a hundred years later, when Jamestown and other colonies were being settled, the new colonists encountered in the Virginia mountains a group of white-skinned Indians, whom they called White Indians (though it was never confirmed that they were descended from lost colonists adopted by Indians). My curiosity about these White Indians was set aflame. I began to create a story around them, to place myself in their skin and imagine who they were, where they came from, and how their fate could have occurred.

I found that the people who made the early trips across the Atlantic, besides adventurers, fishermen, and pirates, were most likely to be religious outcasts and their families looking to start anew. Shortly after Columbus's arrival in America (within fifty years' time), Europe began to undergo its metamorphosis from Renaissance to Reformation, sparked by the revolutionary thinker Martin Luther (who inspired Protestantism and, much later, the Puritanism of the Pilgrims). I modeled the main religious character of *Redemption*, Frere Lanther, and his followers, the protesters (and the protagonist family: Eric, Sarah, and Lily Applegate), after Martin Luther and his adherents, using their revolutionary fervor, and Luther's later break with the common people, as my guide.

Working with myths, art, and written memories and oral histories, I began to see the picture of the many different tribes of Indians which proliferated in America both pre- and, for a short time, post–Columbus. The Nooh and Awthas of *Redemption* are loosely based on the relationships between the numerous clans of the Iroquois and Algonquin, northeast woodlands Indians. Their behavior with whites is based on myriad documented cases of Indians adopting whites, and their methods of initiating, teaching, and training them in their practices and beliefs.

The majority of these Indians were decimated by war and European diseases.

FURTHER READING

A number of these books contain outdated information, but I found them helpful in my efforts to understand the visions and prejudices of their time.

Axtell, James. *The European and the Indian: Essays in the Ethnohistory of Colonial North America.* Oxford: Oxford University Press, 1981.

Bagley, J. J. *Life in Medieval England.* London: BT Batsford Ltd, 1960.

Burrage, Henry, ed. *Early English and French Voyages 1534–1608, Chiefly from Hakluyt.* New York: Scribner, 1906.

Cartier, Jacques (1491–1557). *The Voyages of Jacques Cartier.* Published from the originals with translations, notes and appendices by H. P. Biggar. Ottawa: F. A. Acland, 1924.

Cowie, Leonard. *The Reformation of the Sixteenth Century.* London: Wayland Publishers, 1970.

Erickson, Carolly. *Great Harry, The Extravagant Life of Henry VIII.* New York: Summit Books, 1980.

Hale, Horatio. *The Iroquois Book of Rites.* Toronto: University of Toronto Press, 1963.

Royal, Robert. *1492 and All That: Political Manipulations of History.* Washington, D.C.: Ethics and Public Policy Center, 1992.

Sherry, Frank. *Raiders and Rebels, the Golden Age of Piracy.* William Morrow, Hearst Marine Books, 1986.

Wilson, James. *The Earth Shall Weep, A History of Native America.* New York: Atlantic Monthly Press, 1998.

Young, Alexander. *Chronicles of the Pilgrim Fathers of the Colony of Plymouth, 1602—1625.* New York: Da Capo Press, 1971.